Voice In Th ......

Published by

Librario Publishing Ltd

ISBN: 978-1-904440-83-3

Copies can be ordered via the Internet
www.librario.com

or from:

Brough House, Milton Brodie, Kinloss
Moray IV36 2UA
Tel /Fax No 00 44 (0)1343 850 178

Printed by Biddles Ltd., Kings Lynn, Norfolk

Voice In The Mist

By

Nigel Cubbage

Librario

ABOUT THE AUTHOR

Nigel Cubbage was born in 1960 in Solihull. He went to school in Coventry and graduated from Wolverhampton Poly in 1982. He has worked in television all his life, joining Central TV and ITN before moving to BBC Scotland and into the independent sector.

"Voice in the Mist" is his first book and introduces the teenage detective heroine Rebecca McOwan, who first entered the author's thoughts on an island in the Outer Hebrides one sleepy summer's evening.

Nigel lives in Surrey with his wife and three young children.

DEDICATION

To Kitty, Aliya, Stanley and Betty

ACKNOWLEDGEMENTS

To all those who have helped me to write this book, I owe a huge debt of thanks.

To those friends and family who have read, suggested and encouraged.

To Mum, for not minding about the name.

To the late, great Sorley McLean, Gaelic poet.

To Knoydart, Skye and the western highlands, for being there.

And finally, and most of all to Kitty, for her wisdom and intuition, for putting up with this ambition for so long and to whom I owe so much for so many things.

PROLOGUE

On the rugged coast of Knoydart in the wilderness of the Scottish Highlands, a fierce storm was raging. A beautiful young woman in a long crimson dress was stumbling along a high, jagged cliff-top, her face stricken with fear. Slipping and sliding on the uneven, soaking ground, she kept turning to look over her shoulder, scanning the path behind with wild eyes. Above the raging of the wind she heard hounds barking. The woman clasped her hand to her chest, gasping for breath. Black hair was streaked across her pale, rain-soaked face. A small golden locket around her neck was suddenly whipped across her cheeks by the wind. She clutched at it, numbed fingers fumbling it back into her collar.

A short distance behind, a group of kilted men with dogs on long leashes were in pursuit, led by a tall man in a long military coat. The men were armed with swords and muskets. While the others slipped and struggled to keep their footing on the treacherous rocks, the tall man strode on relentlessly, setting a pace his companions could barely match.

The young woman staggered on, searching desperately for a place to hide. In panic, she found she had come to the end of the ridge. The sea was crashing onto the rocks at the foot of the cliffs. Out of land she now had no option but to turn and face her pursuers. As this realisation dawned, she seemed paralysed, her whole body shaking with fear. With her back to the sea, she clasped her hands together in prayer.

Seconds later, the leading hound leaped over a rocky

outcrop just a few yards away, snarling savagely, quickly followed by more dogs and the men. As the woman screamed in terror, two men were upon her. They grabbed her arms and dragged her forward to the edge of the cliff where she slumped to the ground.

"On your feet!" cried a black-bearded man, holding the leashes of two mighty hounds, which were slavering and fighting to get free, their jaws snapping close to the woman's face. She shrank backwards, certain she would be torn apart if they were loosed.

The tall man, who had been standing a few yards off, staring at the crashing seas, now strode forward. He grabbed her roughly by the hair, pulling her to her feet. As she sobbed, shaking and pleading for mercy, he stared at her for what seemed like ages with dead eyes. He touched his finger to a long scar on his neck.

Suddenly and with no warning, he snatched the locket from around her neck, seized her shoulders with both hands and shoved her with all his might. The woman staggered, a look of terror and disbelief on her face, before she lost her balance and fell backwards over the edge and down, down. Her scream hung in the air.

The tall man stepped forward to the edge of the cliff and peered over, his face impassive. The crumpled form of the young woman now lay lifeless on the rocks below. The man opened the locket and stared at a small portrait inside. A faint smile flickered about the corners of his mouth and was gone in an instant. He snapped the locket shut, turned on his heel and strode back past his men without a glance.

CHAPTER 1 – Rabsaig Castle

Gathering mist hides a clear silver pool
Where the taunt of bold Hakon doth play ye the fool
Whispering waters, Phoebus in cloud
Where time has stood still in yesterday's shroud

A girl with tangled, black hair, clad in a denim jacket, stared sullenly at a chiselled inscription above a stone fireplace, sighed, inclined her head quizzically for a moment and shrugged her shoulders. It did not make any sense.

On the wall above was a large oil painting of a tall Viking warrior, standing proud and impassive, a heavy sword grasped firmly in his hands. Where the sword touched the ground lay a huge grey wolf. It had a silvery coat and piercing white eyes.

The girl was drawn into their glare. For a few seconds, she was spooked, unable to break away, as if gripped by an unseen power. She felt a sudden chill of icy air around her and shrank back, her breath momentarily visible in front of her.

Behind her, a metal latch creaked and a heavy oak door swung slowly open. A draught rushed into the room, the distraction enabling her to break her gaze and look away.

For a split second, she saw the back of a woman passing the room, wearing a long crimson dress.

"I see you have found Hakon then, Rebecca." She had been joined in the high stone hall by a tall man dressed in a long coat. His eyes followed her gaze to the picture.

"Uncle Henry." Rebecca stared at the inscription, shrugged her shoulders and made a face. He smiled, noting her apparent disinterest.

"He has a chilling look, the wolf, huh?"

Rebecca was still disconcerted by the white eyes.

"What does the inscription mean? And who is Hakon, Uncle Henry?"

"That's Hakon. Impressive, isn't he?" He had a soft Scottish accent.

"Legend says he guards the grave of a Princess, who drowned in the loch on her wedding day. They say that the wolf can be heard in a raging storm, howling for his lost mistress. There is an unmarked grave on the island just here, which is said to be hers."

"Can you go to the island?" Rebecca stared at the picture, unblinking.

"Why? It's just an old grey stone on a cold windy island."

"I didn't say I wanted to, I just asked if it is possible. Although, I've got to do something in this place, as I'm stuck here for the summer. What's the wolf's name, anyway?" Rebecca stared petulantly at the powerful neck of the animal, around which was a leather collar, with red and green stones set into it.

"No – Hakon is the wolf. I don't know the name of the warrior. The inscription is part of the legend but I don't know what it means. Father would have known. Don't be thinking on it too hard, you'll be getting nightmares."

He smiled at the sudden look of indignation that spread over Rebecca's face.

"I'm not a child, Uncle Henry! I'm fourteen. No stupid painting is going to give me nightmares."

"Old beyond your years, according to your father." The smile had not faded.

"The sassie young lassie, they would say in these parts!"

Rebecca's dark brown eyes flashed him a withering look. She turned back to the painting.

"Who painted it?" she asked.

"One of our ancestors, Donald McOwan, Donald the Wise. See the inscription? 1740."

"The time of the Jacobite Rebellion," Rebecca added in a self-satisfied tone.

"Indeed!" Henry looked at his niece, momentarily surprised. "Donald and some of his sons were killed at Drumossie Muir, the Battle of ..."

"... Culloden," interjected Rebecca, with a forced yawn. "We studied it last term. April 16, 1746, my birthday actually. The English army of King George, commanded by the Duke of Cumberland, routed the clans and the Bonnie Prince fled to France. He was disguised as a woman by Flora McDonald and escaped in a boat to the Isle of Skye. It was the end of the Jacobite Rebellion and the Scottish uprisings forever."

She looked smugly at her uncle.

"I'm impressed!" smiled Henry. "Although I'd not be thinking the Scots are quelled forever. And the English army was as cruel and barbarous as ever in its history to the Highlanders after the battle. Not much honour in what they did. But Flora McDonald is a great legend. Makes a fortune out of the tourists. Loch nan Uamh, where the Bonnie Prince came ashore, is just along the coast. I expect you'll want to go there too."

Rebecca stole a quick look at her uncle, checking she wasn't being teased again. He was studying the picture. She found herself drawn back like a magnet to the white-eyed wolf.

"Is Hakon a Scottish name?" she asked.

"Nordic. Much of the Highlands were once held by the Vikings. A castle has stood at Rahsaig since that time. Legend has it the Princess was from Norway, here to marry a clan chieftain – one of our ancestors." He paused and went over to the window, peering across the loch, above which dark grey clouds were massing.

"We could be in for some weather. I'd best check the animals. You ring your folks to let them know you arrived safely. Miss McHarg will have dinner ready soon."

The heavy front door closed behind him, leaving Rebecca alone. She looked at the picture, turning over in her mind what her uncle had told her about the wolf and the warrior, the Princess, her ancestors, the Bonnie Prince, and the inscription. The white eyes stared down at her from the wall.

Despite her gloomy feelings on arrival at this remote, draughty castle in the wilds of Scotland, Rebecca was now curious about her strange surroundings and the secrets which might be concealed. Her lively, inquisitive nature often got her into trouble. Anything with an air of mystery drew her like a magnet. Not that she would be admitting interest to anyone just yet. The weather was atrocious and she had still to meet anyone within twenty years of her own age. With a determined effort, she forced her gaze from the picture, heading for the staircase. She found herself repeating the words over and again –

"… time has stood still in yesterday's shroud…"

***

Rahsaig Castle was eerie. Tall forbidding turrets, crumbling battlements, hooded Highland crows squawking raucously. The ravages of the centuries had turned the ramparts black. Ghostly shadows flitted across dark leaded windows under the gloomy sky. The castle rang with strange noises, wind whistling in hidden nooks and crannies.

Narrow twisting stairways descended through a warren of passages to the dungeons. Moisture seeped through mossy walls, dripping onto floors worn by the feet of ages. Low ceilings, narrow doorways and solid doors added to the eerie gloom. Parts of the castle had not been inhabited for many years. In short, spooky summed it up.

Rebecca's room was at the top of a turret, recommended by her Uncle as having the best views. From a cushioned seat in the large bay window, a spectacular panorama of Loch Nevis and the mountains of the Highlands stretched into the distance.

Turning the corner at the top of the stairs, Rebecca saw again a woman in a vivid crimson dress come out of a door on the passageway and disappear into another room further along. As she came closer, she realised the woman had been coming out of her room.

As she passed the doorway to the room into which the woman had gone, she looked inside. It was empty.

Odd, she thought but assumed there must be another exit from the room. She did not bother to investigate and dismissed it as unimportant.

Henry McOwan was wise enough to know that a teenager would be less than thrilled about spending her entire summer holiday in a remote, cold castle, with not much to do and little lively company. He wanted to make things interesting and had chosen one of the oldest rooms in the place for her. A grand four-poster bed, whose corners held carved heads of savage beasts, was the centrepiece. A huge fireplace opposite the window was flanked with two ancient claymore swords. In the hearth, a crackling fire gave the room a cosy atmosphere. By the window was a telescope, through which Rebecca had earlier spied on a man fishing on the far side of the loch.

Closing the creaky door, Rebecca crossed to the window seat and looked over to the island, where the Princess was supposedly buried. She decided she would definitely go and explore, with or without anyone's help. She pulled her knees up to her chin, imagining what those days must have been like. The loch and hills were probably not very different, covered in craggy rocks and heather. The weather would almost certainly have been the same! Of course, people in olden times did not have modern heating, although, she reflected, the noisy plumbing of the ancient castle did not deserve the word modern. This corner of Scotland seemed little touched by the modern world.

Rebecca yawned. It had been a long day since she had waved goodbye to her brother Alistair at London St Pancras station that morning. He was going to tour Europe with friends but Rebecca was considered too young to go, which annoyed her considerably.

"We'll be thinking of you, stuck in the wilds with just sheep for company!" he had joked as the train pulled out. Rebecca had scowled at him.

As her train had passed York, she realised she was the farthest north she had ever been. It did not occur to her that this might seem odd to people from outside London. To Rebecca, the capital was the centre of the universe.

She viewed this summer holiday as a punishment for being only fourteen and expected little enjoyment from it. Her parents' business had taken them off for several weeks working in the Caribbean. Rebecca had been cross that they had not taken her too, a mood little improved when the alternative of summer with her uncle in the north of Scotland was suggested. She knew little of Scotland or her Uncle Henry and was not inclined to feel excited about either.

And the journey had really dragged. She even considered getting out and going back to London, and might have done, had there been no chance of her parents finding out.

Beyond Glasgow, the train began a long, slow climb into the Highlands. Rebecca was surprised to find herself enjoying the view. She had never seen such countryside. A panorama of rugged mountains, glens and rivers unfolded. They would pass a waterfall, or round a bend to find a beautiful loch. Rebecca's grumpy mood was temporarily lifted.

However, when the train finally pulled into Fort William and she gathered her things to disembark, she looked out into a desolate, grey gloom. Rain was beating down relentlessly from a leaden sky.

So much for summer, she had thought, trying to blank out mental images of her brother up the Eiffel Tower and her parents sipping exotic cocktails under Caribbean palms. To complete her isolation, her mobile phone refused to work in this mountainous region, so she could not even moan to her friends. As she stepped down onto the platform, Rebecca felt thoroughly fed up.

A loud chime from the clock on the landing brought her swiftly out of her reverie. Supper would be ready downstairs. Hastily she went over to her suitcase to get out some different clothes. As she did so, there was a clunk as something fell onto the floor behind her. She looked back and saw a curious black, iron key. She picked it up and examined it. It was double-ended. She looked around the room. There was nothing immediately obvious which it might unlock. Puzzled she shoved it deep into her pocket and went to change her clothes.

The door of her room was suddenly slammed shut.

Rebecca looked up, startled. She had not heard the door opening nor been aware of anyone else in the room with her. She crossed to the door, opened it and looked cautiously outside.

The passageway was empty in both directions.

It must have been a draught or something, she reasoned. Satisfied, she closed the door.

As she did so, she caught sight of a blur of movement along the passageway. She flung the door open again but whatever it was had gone. She frowned.

She was not sure but it had looked like the same crimson-dressed woman.

Mindful of the time, Rebecca changed out of the jeans she had been travelling in all day, and brushed her tangled hair. Then she got dressed and went down to supper.

CHAPTER 2

THE WOMAN IN THE CRIMSON DRESS

Two black birds were swooping and diving over the lawns out onto the black waters, tumbling over one another, their wing tips grazing the mirror-like surface.

"Manxies? No – can't be." Henry took his binoculars from the mantelpiece.

"What are manxies? Oh, uncle, you're not a twitcher?" A smile broke across Rebecca's face. Henry pretended to be oblivious. This made her determined not to let him off.

"Manx Shearwater. Live to be very old – some records of them living 80 years or more... but they're not usually to be found this close to the shore."

He tutted. Rebecca stifled another giggle.

"Ah, they're away down the loch." He lowered the binoculars.

"You see plenty out towards Rum and Eigg."

"Is that a drink?" said Rebecca, in amusement.

"Close. Rum and Eigg, two of the so-called cocktail islands, part of the Inner Hebrides off the coast here. We'll go to the headland later to see them – if it's clear, of course."

Rebecca seriously doubted it was ever clear or sunny.

"Weird names," she said, gazing out over the loch. She tapped him on the chest.

"And you *are* a twitcher!"

"Aye, well I doubt if many of your London friends will have heard of them," said Henry, pointedly ignoring her attempt to make fun of him. Rebecca smiled to herself.

"Some of my friends didn't know where Fort William was," she said.

"Laura thought it was probably somewhere out of a cowboy film."

"Aye, that's the English for you." Henry smiled as her smile changed to a puzzled frown.

"Will you take your places at table?" Miss McHarg stood in the doorway to the passage to the kitchen, passing a slim pale hand across a bony forehead.

It was more an order than a request, Rebecca reflected. She ventured a polite smile. McHarg was not given to smiling very often and did not make this an exception. Her countenance seemed to forbid humour as an unnecessary frivolity. She wore neither make-up nor jewellery. Her hair was pulled back tightly from her face into a painful-looking bun. This gave her a rather severe look, enhanced by her perpetual frown. Her dress was a very old-fashioned grey pinafore, with sleeves buttoned at the wrist. Rebecca doubted whether modern shops would sell such a dress. It was partially covered by a bright, vivid apron that seemed out of place on the colourless McHarg. Lips pursed, she hovered as Rebecca and her uncle sat down. Satisfied, she uttered a barely audible "Hmm" and disappeared back through the door.

"She's a happy soul!" Rebecca kept her voice low, so that only Henry could hear.

"She looks fiercer than she really is," whispered Henry, smirking.

"And you won't be disappointed with dinner – she is a fine cook."

"I saw another woman upstairs just before supper. She came out of my room."

Henry looked puzzled.

"What woman? The only woman here is McHarg. Must have been her."

"It wasn't, I'm sure. She is wearing grey and this woman had a long crimson dress on.

She was behind you when you came into the hall earlier on, too."

"You must have been mistaken – trick of the light or something. Gets pretty gloomy around here sometimes."

He was cut short by the reopening of the door and the entrance of a large trolley, propelled by the now apronless McHarg. Rebecca was not remotely convinced by her uncle's dismissive explanation but said no more. Whom had she seen, then?

"Can we go to this island tomorrow, uncle?" Rebecca looked down as Miss McHarg placed a steaming plate of stew before her.

"Perhaps. I've some business in the morning. But first we must do justice to this lordly feast Miss McHarg has prepared for us." He picked up his fork, smiled at Rebecca and then at McHarg.

"And remember that tomorrow is the Sabbath," said Miss McHarg, resolutely refusing to return the smile, her lips pursing again as she turned the trolley back towards the kitchen.

"It is a day to be reflective of the Lord and give thanks."

Rebecca looked uncertainly at her uncle and said nothing. He suppressed a smile as he watched McHarg retreat through the door, which clicked shut behind her.

"Is she born again, or something?" Rebecca's low tones held just a hint of derision.

"That was aimed at me. Don't pay her much mind. She thinks nobody should be frivolous or work on a Sunday. Miss McHarg is what you might call a good, God-fearing woman, but a little too full of what the locals call the zeal. Her brother Willie once played rugby on the Sabbath as she calls it – she has not spoken to him these twenty years since."

"That's just silly, "whispered Rebecca, leaning forward and

casting a surreptitious glance over her shoulder to check that the door was still closed.

"Not to her. But I'd be inclined to agree with you – particularly as she sees him every day – he works on the boats and drops her off each morning and picks her up at night."

***

Rebecca stood fuming at her mobile phone in the Great Hall.

"No signal," read the display. She had been warned that this might happen in the Highlands but had hoped to keep the lifeline of contact with her friends back home.

"That infernal contraption won't be troubling you up here," smiled McHarg smugly from the doorway of the passage to the kitchen.

"Telephones should have wires, ring properly and live in the hallway. Cellular phones, or whatever, do not plague us, owing to the mountains. God bless the mountains."

She turned on her heel in haughty satisfaction and disappeared.

Rebecca put out her tongue at her back. She crossed to the telephone table at the side of the hall and picked up the receiver. It was an old-fashioned phone with a ring-dial. Rebecca held the phone gingerly to her ear, as if expecting a nasty noise.

"Laura? Oh thank goodness! … Yes, I've arrived… How is it? Cold, wet, boring and my mobile doesn't work…"

***

After supper, Rebecca sat in the library, awaiting Henry to begin their walk. Although most of the castle was cold and draughty, this long, narrow room was warm and cosy. An old desk and a high-backed leather chair sat beneath wooden shelves crammed with musty, leather-bound books that must have sat unopened for many years. There was a large stone hearth, beneath a painting of a boat full of sheep being rowed across a loch. A man stood at the bow in a long red coat and a tricorn hat, looking intently to the hills beyond. Two soldiers worked the oars. At the stern, a man's head peeped out from under a blanket. He had black curly hair and bright blue eyes.

There was a large bay window with a cushioned seat. Rebecca sat down. She could pull up her feet and stretch out, looking across the lawn to the loch beyond. The island was silhouetted against the early evening sunlight which had now replaced the rain. On her lap was an old, leather-bound book her uncle had picked out for her. She opened it.

'The Bonnie Prince in Flight', read the title page. In the top left hand corner, somebody had written 'To Robert, with love from Mother, Christmas 1913'. Over the page was a map of the area surrounding the castle. Overleaf was a picture similar to the painting above the hearth. She looked up as her uncle came back into the room.

"Ready?" he asked.

"Is that painting the flight of Bonnie Prince Charlie?" she asked.

"It's here in the book, too." She held it out.

"It is indeed – I'm very impressed with you and all this history! That's him hiding from the English as he escaped to Skye. Now, let's go out before the rain comes back."

A turreted gatehouse led across the lawn. The air was fresh and clean. Rebecca buttoned up her jacket against a stiff breeze with a surprising bite. Her hands and fingers were already quite cold. She stuffed them into her jacket pockets, where her fingers brushed the key. Rebecca idly fingered the cold metal, wondering what it might open. She opened her mouth to question her uncle about it but stopped, recalling his dismissal of the woman in crimson. She would do some investigations of her own first.

"We'll have to get you some proper clothes," said Henry, noticing her discomfort. Rebecca eyed what she called his dweeb gear, her mouth open in disbelief. Fashion sense was one thing in which she considered herself infinitely superior.

"Sorry? I would not be seen dead in *that* get up. Cagoules and walking boots are not the height of fashion, Uncle! You should wear something trendy – you're not that old!"

"Kind of you to say so! I'm not quite in my pipe and slippers yet. At least I'll get back warm and dry – you'll get pneumonia if you spend the summer dressed like that. And who's to see your London fashions up here, anyway?"

"It's a question of standards!"

Henry laughed.

"Have it your way but I'll lay money you'll be wearing at least some thick socks by the end of the week."

Rebecca snorted scornfully. Henry continued to smile to himself.

They took a path along the shore towards the sea, half a mile away.

This place actually is quite beautiful, she thought, as they climbed over some rocks, beyond which was a sandy beach. She did not voice this out loud, though.

"The country here is pretty … if you are into that sort of thing."

"The Rough Bounds of Knoydart, they call it – a rare spot. To the south, Mull and Ardnamurchan; to the north Skye, Torridon, and eventually John O'Groats. I don't imagine you have heard of many of those. Not everybody's cup of tea, though, it's a wilderness." Henry smiled. "Your Dad's not so keen. He's a city boy. I think the Highlands either get right under your skin, or you can take them or leave them. I know folks in Glasgow who have never been half an hour up the road to Loch Lomond."

"Really? If this was near London, I'm sure lots of sad, nerdy types would come."

"Now that would be a shame. London is a long way south and we should probably be glad for it. Too many people and this would not be so special." Henry's eyes gazed at the hills in the distance. Rebecca studied him.

"Why did you come back here?" she asked.

"Somebody had to take over the estate when your grandfather died and I suppose I'd always known it would be me. Eldest son and all that. Your Dad's too successful in his business. We agreed. I was a bit unsure but now I'm here … Well, it grows on you. There's time to think up here."

"Why aren't you married?" A mischievous glint flashed in Rebecca's eyes. Henry smiled.

"You're direct, young lady. Is that any sort of question to be asking your uncle on your first day here?"

"You won't put me off that easily! Come on – is there a lady somewhere you haven't told the family about? I bet there is. You're not that bad looking… for an older man."

"Why thank you, I'm sure! That sort of information is on a need to know basis. When you need to know, I'll tell you. Come on – not much further."

Rebecca gave a dissatisfied sniff but Henry had resumed walking. She would have to work on him again.

A little further along, at the crest of a rise, the wind was brisker and fresher. It was no longer so peaceful, the roar of waves breaking now much nearer. In a few moments, they stood at the top of a cliff, some hundred feet above rocks where the sea was rushing in. Plumes of spray soared into the air as waves crashed onto a short rocky beach. Gulls rode up and down on the surging waves, or swooped close above. Henry pointed to some islands on the horizon.

"You're in luck," he shouted. "Rum and Eigg. They seem to be one but actually there are a few miles between them. Eigg is closer. That steep hill at the end is called the Sgurr." He rolled the 'r' deliberately.

"The peaks in the background are the Cuillins on Rum. Not to be confused with the famous Cuillins on Skye."

"Funny names you have for places up here! Can we go out there?"

"Maybe, although it's nearly ten kilometres to Rum. Strong tides and current too. There is a ferry from Arisaig. I saw my first whale from that ferry."

"There are whales in Scotland?" Rebecca was disbelieving.

"Aye, plenty. Seals, dolphins – more beasts here than you'll see in a month on the London Underground! And you are standing on the spot where one of your ancestors supposedly fell to her death three hundred years ago."

"What?" Rebecca jumped back involuntarily. "Who?"

"Becca McOwan, daughter of Donald the Wise. Don't worry, her body was never found, so it's only hearsay. Here, get down out of the wind."

Uncle Henry indicated a rock beneath a large grey boulder. They squatted down while Henry launched into tales of their ancestors and the past. He pointed to a lighthouse on a small island guarding the entrance to the loch and described how he and her father had been stranded there as boys in a storm.

"We'd best be getting back," he said, looking up at the sky.

"I've an early start in the morning. It'll be cold soon and we've a walk before us."

"I'm frozen already!" said Rebecca, swinging her arms wildly in an attempt to get warm.

"Anyway, what is your business meeting about tomorrow?"

"I have to go to Fort William to meet Mr Sibley of Holborn Passage, London, an antiques expert who is coming to examine our paintings and furniture, the McOwan collection. Some of the stuff is very old and rare. I think he'll be with us a few days."

"Are you going to sell things, then?"

"Some will have to go, to help pay some of the estate duties. It's not easy running somewhere as big as Rahsaig."

"Aren't you rich, uncle?"

"There you go again – questions! The heating bills alone would make your eyes water."

"Can't say I'd noticed it was that warm. How big is the estate?" Rebecca looked out across the loch. They were still some distance from the castle.

"We're on it now," answered Henry. "It goes right up past the castle, up the glen to Ladhar Bheinn to the north – that's the great mountain way up there and to the end of Loch Nevis in the east. We're quite cut off. You can only reach Rahsaig by boat, unless you fancy a very long walk. The nearest main road is fifteen kilometres inland!"

Rebecca was silent, gauging the size of the area Henry had described. They were high enough to see the ridge of mighty Ladhar Bheinn, slumbering peacefully in the distance.

"You own a mountain?" Rebecca's tone was one of disbelief.

"A strange idea, I know. It's part of the estate, right enough, but I don't think you can say we really own it. We're just looking after it for the next generation."

Henry walked on, leading the way. Rebecca studied his back, impressed by the unassuming way her uncle described his estate. Her brother Alistair jokingly referred to Henry as His Lordship but this did not sit easily with the man she was getting to know.

"So can we go out in the boat to the island?" she asked, at length, as they found themselves back at the West door.

"Aye, if the weather is good." They disappeared back inside the castle.

Down by the loch, hunched up in the trees out of the wind, a woman had been watching them. After a few moments, she turned and headed quickly and quietly away up the glen, alongside the water's edge. She wore a long, crimson dress.

CHAPTER 3

THE VOICE IN THE MIST

When Rebecca came down the wide staircase into the Great Hall next morning, the sun was streaming in through the windows, sending shafts of bright, golden light across the stairwell and passageways. One could almost mistake it for summer, she thought to herself, with a hint of irony, but for the fact that this was Scotland and rain was sure to come – in her experience so far, anyway. As she came through the Great Hall, the grandfather clock which stood in the corner by the West door began to strike eight.

"Eight o'clock, indeed... hm. Your uncle was away across the loch at six this morning."

Miss McHarg frowned as Rebecca sat down in the dining room to breakfast. Rebecca was not altogether sure if this suggested some form of reproof for daring to lounge in bed for so long after his departure. To be showered, dressed and downstairs by eight o'clock in the summer holidays was not something she felt could be deemed lazy, even by Miss McHarg, be it the Sabbath or not.

"The boatman took him back when he dropped me off – he'll be nearly in Fort William by now. Business meetings on the Sabbath, indeed."

"Isn't the boatman your brother?" Rebecca could not look at Miss McHarg as she asked the question, trying to muster as much innocence as she dared.

There was a long pause.

Swallowing nervously, Rebecca looked up and encountered

the full force of an icy stare from McHarg. After a few more seconds, during which Rebecca bravely attempted to smile, the housekeeper spoke.

"He would claim so, I dare say." With that, McHarg pursed her lips into a frosty line and retreated through the door. Rebecca waited until she was sure she had gone before she allowed a smirk to spread across her face.

As it was such a beautiful morning, she decided to go out and explore the estate. In the large stone porch there was a pile of assorted boots, umbrellas and sticks in a long wooden box. She looked down at her lightweight trainers, remembering the boggy, wet ground of the previous evening's walk, and hesitated. Recalling her uncle's teasing, she looked around to check who might be watching. Seeing no one, she shrugged, grabbed a pair of socks and some boots that looked close to her size and pulled them on. They fitted comfortably. She could not lower herself to take a Gore-tex jacket, however.

She slipped quickly out and took the path up the glen into the hills. The going was not easy. The path wound up quite steeply through the wooded estate, with its huge rhododendron bushes and assorted pines. After about twenty-five minutes, she came to a wooden fence that led out onto open moorland, with the green foothills of Ladhar Bheinn and its surrounding purple peaks in the distance. She stopped to catch her breath, as the gradient had become even steeper. The mountains were indeed beautiful, although it would need something more than scenery to keep her occupied for the whole summer.

She left the estate gardens behind her. A breeze rustled the trees as she crawled under the high wooden fence and left the shelter of the woods above the castle. She was hot from the climb and was now into open wilderness.

After a series of gullies and wooded copses, Rebecca crested a rise by some grey, granite boulders and found herself at the edge of a beautiful small loch. It was less than a hundred metres long and not more than fifty metres at its widest. At its far end the land rose through a series of ridges, right up to the jagged summit of Ladhar Bheinn, a huge U-shape dominating the northern skyline. She looked back. Far below, the castle turrets were just visible through the trees. The deep blue waters of the loch sparkled beyond.

Rebecca decided this tranquil place was perfect for a rest, to sit and contemplate the world. She sat down on a flattish, chair-shaped piece of rock by the edge of the water.

She was not used to such strenuous climbing and felt quite tired. She was not unfit and was a strong runner who competed for her school back home. Nevertheless, her thigh muscles already felt tight. She wished she had remembered to bring something to drink. The water in the small loch looked very clear and clean. She took a mouthful. It was cold and surprisingly good. Just like on the shelves in the supermarket back home, she thought – fresh from the mountain streams of Scotland!

Lying back to catch her breath and close her eyes for a few moments, she turned her face up towards the warm sunshine.

It was short while after this that Rebecca became aware of something stirring nearby. Somewhere away down the small loch, vaguely muffled, there was a noise which she had never heard before: a long, mournful howl. At first, unconcerned, she did not open her eyes. She thought she could also make out a gentle splashing. She imagined it was a bird of some sort. After a few moments, she realised it was becoming louder.

"Becca! Becca!" A man's voice.

That was what her brother called her! Rebecca opened her eyes and jumped to her feet. Instantly, she felt a chill and was amazed to see that the loch where she had been sitting in the bright warm sunshine was now completely enshrouded by mist. She could barely see ten metres across the water.

"Becca! Becca!" The voice was calling from somewhere out on the water. It did not sound like Alistair. There was a definite accent too, not Scottish but European.

"Hallo?" She heard her own voice, tentative and strangely unfamiliar. Standing at the edge of the water, she strained her eyes into the mist to try and make out where the voice was coming from. The splashing was much closer now. It sounded like oars.

Rebecca's heart beat quite fast. She felt a surge of fear. The weather had changed so quickly and she had been certain there had been no boat on the loch anywhere when she had first arrived. The sudden cold brought out goosebumps all over her arms. She rubbed herself to try and keep warm, aware she was trembling.

"Becca! Becca!"

Suddenly, she thought she saw a shape in the swirling mist, moving towards her. It was a boat, with a shadowy figure at the bow. She squinted, straining to see more but, just as quickly, the mist swallowed it up and it vanished. Shaking, she waited for the voice to call. No sound came.

A minute or so passed and she realised she could no longer hear the oars. Silence followed before a ghastly howl rent the air. It was the same as before, only this time much closer and far more terrible. It sounded like the howl of a wolf.

Fear gripped her. Unable to move, her heart pounded in her chest.

But the sound did not come again. Everything fell still and silent.

Rebecca's legs were shaky. She turned to steady herself against the rock.

Behind her, the sun was now out again. She lowered herself and sat down. When she turned back towards the water, she saw the small loch shimmering under the blue sky.

Rebecca was baffled. There was no remnant of the mist that had been there just a few seconds ago, nor a boat, a man, a wolf. Not even a disturbance in the surface of the water. Had she dreamt it? She had not fallen asleep, she was certain. Leaping to her feet again, she stared but saw only tufts of grass and heather, rustling gently in the breeze.

You are not going mad, she told herself. There must be a rational explanation for this. Slowly and deliberately, she walked a full circuit of the small loch, seeking any sort of clue to what she had just seen and heard.

Had she imagined the whole thing?

No, it had been too real. And the voice had been calling her name.

CHAPTER 4

THE ATTIC

Several hours had elapsed since the strange episode on the mountain. Rebecca sat in the window seat of the library looking out over the loch, where rain was now falling heavily. Returning from her walk, she had picked at a light lunch, prepared by a monosyllabic McHarg. She was not really hungry. She had not been able to concentrate on anything, her mind still racing after the weird encounter by the small loch.

Rebecca considered herself a down-to-earth, level-headed person. Although she was known among her friends for a mischievous sense of humour and lively imagination, they usually relied upon her to bring a sense of perspective and reality when others were losing theirs. She was not easily spooked.

Alistair, her brother, had commented how she had more courage than most of his friends put together, when she had completed a parachute jump on her fourteenth birthday.

So she was perplexed rather than unnerved by the events high on the mountain.

The rain seemed to have set in. Heavy black clouds were rolling in off the sea. Uncle Henry had not yet returned and, through McHarg, had left a message that he was taking Mr Sibley via Arisaig to Morar Hall, where there were several McOwan artefacts which Sibley wanted to see. They would not return to Rahsaig until supper time.

This left Rebecca to her own devices for the afternoon and, in the light of the adverse weather, restricted her to the castle and its immediate surroundings.

Since she had only moved between her room and the ground floor so far, she decided to explore. She had already noticed many doors, corridors and staircases leading off landings, which she was keen to investigate.

Leaving the library, she went up the main stairway from the Great Hall to the first landing. To one side was the East wing, where she had her room. To the other was the less visited West wing. When she had asked Uncle Henry what was here, he had mentioned more guest rooms and a music room. There was also the gun room, situated in a turret at the corner, although Henry had stressed there were no guns any more. Rebecca decided to start her investigations in the West Wing.

The first few doors revealed little of interest. Simple bedrooms: a bed, chair, wardrobe, fireplace and a dressing table. At the end of the corridor by a large leaded window, was a bathroom dominated by a huge cast iron bath. The sides were unusually high, set up off the ground by large feet shaped like animals' paws. There was a stool beside it, which seemed essential to enable people to climb in. Rebecca knelt on it to peer over the edge at the shiny white enamel and ancient iron taps.

It was so big it might take half the water in the loch to fill it.

Next door was a low opening through to the rear turret. Ducking down, Rebecca passed through into a small, musty antechamber. The floorboards creaked loudly under her feet, before another door took her into the gun room. Uncle Henry had been telling the truth; not a gun in sight.

A few old oil paintings hung on the walls, one of which caught Rebecca's eye because it was disturbing. A young woman in a crimson dress, with wild eyes and a stricken expression, was tearing at her hair. There was no hint as to why. One hand was stretched out beseechingly towards the person looking at the painting.

Rebecca was transfixed. It was as if whatever the woman

was experiencing somehow involved her too. That dress was very like the one she had seen on the woman in the castle. And there was something in the woman's face which seemed familiar.

She could not put her finger on what.

This remarkable exception apart, the room was plain and disappointing.

She did not therefore linger long and turned around.

As she returned through the little antechamber, Rebecca noticed a small door in the corner which she had not seen on the way in. A large iron latch started to give with an alarming screech as she pulled on it. It had obviously not been opened for some time. Applying all her strength, she forced the latch up and pushed the door open.

A rush of colder air hit her face. Through the low doorway, Rebecca emerged into a gloomy stairwell, with a worn stone staircase leading up into the gloom. Grasping a fraying rope handrail, she climbed the steep stairs and stopped in front of a door. It opened without any resistance, into a long, dusty attic, into which shafts of light fell at intervals through narrow windows. Old boxes and suitcases were stacked up, along with discarded possessions. Thick cobwebs hung from the rafters in ghostly veils.

Rebecca progressed slowly, peering closely at everything, lifting the lids of interesting-looking boxes. There were old dolls, pictures, wooden toys and soldiers, tennis rackets, balls of various sizes and even an old skeleton hanging up.

Beneath one window was a bulky shape covered by a coarse grey blanket. Rebecca started to pull it, but stopped abruptly as a great cloud of dust flew up. She shut her eyes, covered her mouth and swiped the blanket away, turning her back to avoid the rest of the dust. After a few moments, the cloud subsided and she could examine what lay beneath.

It was a wooden chest, from the look of it, very, very old.

There were three carved panels along the front. Iron straps were nailed across the lid and down the sides and a large black iron lock hung at the front.

On the lid, two letters were carved. She rubbed them clean of accumulated dust.

'R.M.' Her own initials!

Rebecca searched for a key but could find nothing. Peeved, she sat down on top of the chest and sighed. She looked up and down at the old crates and assorted bric-a-brac piled up everywhere. If the key was here, it might take her a hundred years to find it.

With a sudden start, she remembered the key she had discovered in her room. Might it belong to the chest? It had certainly looked old enough. It was a long shot but, not hesitating, Rebecca flew back downstairs and headed for her room.

She returned with the key and a torch she had found and knelt down in front of the chest, panting from running. Her first attempt to put the key in failed because she was trembling from her excitement. Calm down, she muttered. Breathing slowly, she slipped the key into the lock and turned.

It opened!

In the midst of her excitement, Rebecca paused and studied the key. Strange. How had it come to be in her room? Had somebody put it there deliberately?

The lid was very heavy and required both hands to lift it. Rebecca pushed it back until it rested against the wall and grabbed the torch, eager to see what might be inside.

The contents seemed to be the belongings of a girl. There was an old silk dress, books, a purse with a silver clip fastening, brooches and a hairbrush and mirror. Everything was very old indeed. The books were leather-bound and dusty, with thick parchment pages, browned at the edges. Rebecca sifted through the entire box, pulling everything out onto the floor next to her, determined to miss nothing.

The silk dress was crimson and quite faded but must once have been very grand.

A book caught her eye. It had the same initials, R.M., on a beautiful, embossed leather cover. Intrigued, Rebecca opened it. What she read made her stop in her tracks in astonishment.

'The Personal Journal of Rebecca McOwan', said the words in beautiful flowing, handwritten script. The ink was black, only slightly faded. She turned the page quickly, ever more surprised as she read on. An inscription read

'This is the personal journal of Rebecca McOwan, in the year 1746, my fifteenth year and a time of great pain and sadness.'

Rebecca was spellbound. She had discovered the diary of someone not only from centuries ago, but her namesake, presumably an ancestor, and practically her own age! But why such "pain and sadness"?

It was too dark and gloomy to read in the attic, so she decided to go back to her room. Impatiently, she replaced all the items and closed the heavy lid, locked it and replaced the blanket so that nobody else might discover her secret. Satisfied she had covered her tracks, she hurried downstairs.

***

Rebecca put the mysterious key in her bedside drawer, picked up the book, tucked up her feet and settled down in the window seat to read.

The author had been born and lived all her life in this very castle. She was indeed her ancestor. Her father was Donald McOwan, Laird of Rahsaig – the man who had painted the picture in the Great Hall, said Rebecca to herself – her mother was Mary and she had four brothers, Robert, Davie, Andrew and young Donald. She was the second youngest, known as Becca and the room Rebecca was now occupying had also been hers.

Becca's writing was beautiful, although her expressions seemed occasionally odd. Rebecca knew that common phrases would have changed since 1746, and Becca's language was not so strange as to be incomprehensible. The main theme of the opening was the return of Bonnie Prince Charlie, who had landed in the July of the previous year and raised the clans to join his attempt to regain the throne of Scotland.

Becca's brothers, father and all the men from the estate had rallied to the cause of the young Prince and joined his army, the Jacobites. At first, they had enjoyed success at Edinburgh and the battle of Prestonpans and had even marched on England. However, the Prince was persuaded to return to Scotland by his generals. There was a battle at Falkirk in January 1746, at which Becca's eldest brother Robert was wounded and returned home to be nursed by her and her mother. He had still been too ill to rejoin the army when it moved to Inverness, to meet the Hanoverian English army of King George, which, rumours had been saying for some weeks, was moving north for a showdown. The English were many, and in no mood to suffer further defeats.

In these pages, Becca wrote little of life at Rahsaig, save to lament the cold, miserable winter and incessant rain. This brought a wry smile to Rebecca's face. She seemed to have to work quite hard for a Laird's daughter, thought Rebecca, noting passages about cooking, tending to the animals and looking after her brothers. She had imagined that the life of a Laird's daughter involved comfort and privilege but that was not evident from Becca's account. The women seemed to do all the work.

There was the odd reference to a *"ceilidh"*, which Rebecca took to mean a party of some sort, since it involved music and dancing with either her brothers or a succession of what Becca described as *"Father's whiskery friends, with their mellifluous odour of tobacco and the dram"*. Certainly, Becca did not seem to have a flourishing social life, or much access to people of her own age. Her only real friend seemed to be her maid, Siobhan, with whom she appeared to share thoughts and secrets.

Imagine being stuck so far away from the rest of civilisation, thought Rebecca, with some horror and a growing sense of compassion for her ancestor. And having to dance not only with your brothers but also your father and his friends! It was not being disloyal to suggest that her own father did not cut a completely dashing figure on the dance floor.

When she turned the page to arrive at 16 April, her jaw dropped.

"April 16th – my birthday, dawns bright and clear, yet I am in no mind to celebrate since my heart is heavy with fear for Father, Davie and Andrew, awaiting the English guns at Culloden. Robert paces all day in the grounds like a wild bear; he would be with them too, but for his wounds. Mother keeps to her room and will not come out until we hear word that they are safe."

They shared the same birthday!

Rebecca paused. This was becoming spooky.

Her heart beat suddenly a little faster in her chest. So many odd coincidences in one day, and the strange encounter on the hillside earlier. She wondered when her uncle would be home and briefly considered telling him everything and seeking his opinion. This idea did not last. Rebecca was proud and independent, preferring to believe she could handle most things by herself. Henry seemed a man given rather to practicality than imagination and she felt he would be certain to tell her she had dreamt it, that she should not be so silly. Why shouldn't two people with the same name have the same birthday? What was so strange in that?

"McHarg said I should find you here, though you take some finding, Rebecca McOwan."

Rebecca looked up with a start, shaken out of her thoughts by the arrival of a young lad at her door. He was dressed in a long waterproof jacket of the type she had seen the fishermen wearing on the pier at Mallaig. He was dripping with water, suggesting he had only very recently arrived in the castle. His accent was Scottish, his hair red and curly. He had no boots and stood in woolly grey socks. She guessed his age at about sixteen.

"Who are you?" Rebecca stood up, closing her book and putting it down on the seat behind her as if to conceal it. She was aware her expression was probably one of horror.

"And don't you knock when you come into a room?"

"Sorry, milady! Why, what was youz up to?" The amused expression on his face was something of a surprise to Rebecca and not the effect she had hoped for. She was momentarily flustered by his easy familiarity and light-hearted tone. She half-turned away in an attempt to conceal this.

"That really isn't any of your business. Look, just who are you and how dare you come barging into my room?" She recovered her composure and rediscovered her indignation. To her dismay, his smile did not disappear under her withering glare.

"My, we are the feisty one, aren't we? English too, as I feared. Aye well, I'm your uncle's ranger, Andrew Campbell, at your service, moddom." He made an exaggerated bow, came into the room and promptly sat down on a chair by the other window.

"You're young to be a ranger, aren't you? What does a ranger do, exactly?"

"Looks after the estate and the animals – wild as well as tame. Actually, it's just a summer job helping out. My brother is the real ranger."

"So why are you here in my room, Andrew Campbell?"

Rebecca had not sat down in a vain hope to persuade him not to linger. She soon realised that this wish was hopeless.

"I'm filling in for my brother Dougie – he's away to Barradale, helping the absentee English landlord, Gordon, count his deer. You ask an awful lot of questions, if you don't mind my saying. I thought it was we folks from the sticks who were supposed to be nosy, not you sophisticated London types."

He picked up a clock on Rebecca's bedside table, examined it briefly before replacing it.

"Your uncle asked me to show you around today, while he was off picking up yet another Englishman."

"You don't seem to like the English very much, do you?"

"Nothin' personal, Rebecca McOwan. I'm sure you're fine, Your name is decently Scottish enough, I'll agree. Just hundreds of years of persecution, injustice and toffee-nosed tourists. My father would say we belong to a nation of downtrodden bog-trotters, whose national sport is shifting the blame. Don't mind me any."

Rebecca was rather bemused by this combination of part-insult, part self-deprecation.

"Well I can't say I'm that impressed with your country either," she eventually replied.

"Not a lot to do is there, other than count the raindrops on the lake?"

"Loch," he corrected her. "Lakes are what they have in the rest of the world; in Scotland we have lochs. More phlegm. Lochhhhh! And you should call me Drew, everyone else does, apart from the witch McHarg. I'm 'Young Campbell' to her, with lots of disapproving emphasis on the Campbell bit. She thinks we're shallow and ungodly. I think it goes back to killing all those McDonalds in the Glencoe massacre. She was probably there."

"At least where McHarg is concerned, we can agree," said

Rebecca, stepping into the middle of the room and putting her hands on her hips.

"So, if you're supposed to be looking after me today, you haven't done much of a job of it so far. It's the middle of the afternoon and you've only just found me."

"Well if you will go gallivanting over the hills all morning, what do you expect? I've found you now, though, so what do you want to do?"

"Do? I'm not sure I want to do anything with you. Anyway, it's raining, so just what do you propose we can do that doesn't in some way involve getting soaked to the skin?"

Rebecca hoped her sarcasm would not be lost on him. He paused for a second, looking out of the window thoughtfully. "We could go over to the island in the boat. Henry said you wanted to see the grave."

This was not the response Rebecca had expected. Surprised and her interest kindled, she looked out of the window and across to the island.

She tried to sound nonchalant and unimpressed.

"All a bit bleak, though, isn't it?"

"Beautiful," countered Drew, looking outside and nodding as if in confirmation.

"D'ye want to go or not?"

"Well … okay … as long as you will promise we won't get soaked."

Drew jumped to his feet and headed for the door. Over his shoulder he said

"This is Scotland, Rebecca McOwan. Rain will fall as surely as night follows day."

CHAPTER 5

ON SHADOW ISLAND

Rebecca barely had time to grab a coat and scramble into her boots on the way out of the West Door. Drew was striding down the lawn toward the boathouse at the edge of the loch, without a backward glance. The rain drove against her face as she hurried after him. Rebecca pulled the hood of her jacket down, for once oblivious to who might see her. Inside the boathouse, Drew was already aboard a small motor cruiser, untying ropes. Rebecca was glad to see that a small wooden canopy at the front of the boat did suggest some shelter from the elements.

"Today we travel in style, since the Laird is away," shouted Drew above the noise of the engine, as he jumped down onto the deck and took the wheel. Rebecca climbed aboard. Seconds later, they were emerging onto the calm waters of Loch Nevis.

"Usually, I don't get much further than rowing the dinghy, being your hired help and all that. Love your clothes, by the way. Henry said you were looking to get into some boots and waterproofs."

"Oh, just tug your forelock and shut up, hired helper," said Rebecca, not looking at him and thereby missing the huge grin that broke out all over his face. Henry had warned him about the sarcastic edge of her tongue, a character trait which Drew considered quite admirable when well delivered.

"What is a Laird, anyway?" asked Rebecca. "Is it like the old Lord of the Manor?"

"Aye, pretty much," answered Drew. "Supposedly the Scottish Lairds were a bit more caring about people who lived on their land and worked for them. More of a family approach. They were supposed to look after them if times were hard. Some folks still think like that today. Why else would he keep McHarg on?"

They looked at one another and shared a grin.

The boat chugged slowly across the loch towards the island. From out on the water, the loch seemed to extend much further than when viewed from the shore. Rebecca was able to see along its entire length, which was not possible from the castle or her room.

"Bleak," said Rebecca.

"Beautiful."

As they drew closer, the island loomed larger than Rebecca had expected. It was at least two hundred metres long, and the taller of the two rocky outcrops was high enough to blot out most of the hillside behind.

"Eilean Dubh in the Gaelic... Shadow Island to you and me. It gets its name because the sun never falls on it. They say it's a haunted place." Drew turned to look at Rebecca, who looked back, slightly alarmed. "Not that any ghost would want to try and scare you, Rebecca McOwan. Even a ghoul would respect the lash of your tongue."

Rebecca considered this a deliberately backhanded compliment and favoured him with a contemptuous look.

"So have you heard the wolf, Hakon, howling in the storm, then?" she asked sarcastically, not looking at him.

"Aye... I have." Before a startled Rebecca could respond, he gestured towards the water.

"We must mind the depth round here," he said, slowing the boat to a crawling pace. Keeping one hand on the wheel, Drew leant out over the side of the boat, scanning the water for jagged rocks lurking just below the surface.

Rebecca leaned over to do the same. There were a couple of

gentle bumps as the bottom of the boat brushed something. By now they were practically ashore. Drew killed the engine and leaped out, clutching a rope, landing deftly on a low shelf. He pulled the boat alongside, looped the rope over a large boulder and made it fast with a secure knot.

"Should be safe enough here," he said, cheerfully, leaning forward to grasp Rebecca's hand and help her out.

Once ashore, they climbed a few short yards to the top of the taller hillocks. The rain had stopped at last and the sky had started to clear, the clouds lifting off the top of the hills. Ladhar Bheinn was still covered away to the north but the rest of the glen had brightened.

Rebecca followed Drew down a small gully round to the far side of the island. They climbed along the shoreline and rounded a great, blackened rock. Here, there was a small sandy beach with an area of smooth grass leading off. A small cluster of stones formed a symmetrical cross at the edge of the sand, partially buried in the grass.

"There lies the Viking Princess… reputedly," said Drew.

Rebecca hurried forward to examine the cross but there was very little to see. It did not seem Christian, simply two lines at right angles, crossing in the middle. She had expected something more significant and was a little disappointed.

"It's not much is it?" she said, pulling a face.

"Aye, well it's been here for about thirteen hundred years, so they say, which I think is quite impressive in itself. The weather will have eroded any inscription there might once have been. And the times were pretty godless, so don't expect crosses."

"Do you think she really does lie there?" Rebecca looked sceptically at the grave.

"Who knows? There's any number of small islands she could be buried on. Eilean Dubh is hardly an uncommon name for an island in Scotland. Not terribly imaginative with place names, I'm afraid. There's a mountain over there called Bheinn nan Lochan… sounds lovely but it means hill of the loch."

"You said you had heard the wolf. Did you mean it?" Rebecca looked at him intently. Drew paused and looked out across the water, his eyes suddenly distant.

"Aye, I meant it, right enough. Some round here might say I'm odd but I don't discount the legend. I don't mean I believe in ghosts and fairies and the Easter bunny, but this land hides its secrets. They say it's the spirits of people who have died but are not at rest."

"So what did you hear?" she asked, sitting down on a rocky shelf and tucking her knees up. The gully gave them some shelter from the breeze and with the rain stopped for the moment at least, it was quite warm. Drew pulled absently at a tuft of grass.

"The last time was during a storm, and only a few weeks ago, actually. Dougie and I were on our way home – we probably should never have set out in the boat, but we did. It was swelling up a bit just along the coast, so we decided to try and put in on a little island until the worst of it passed. Well, we ended up swamping the boat's engine and got stuck overnight 'cause we couldn't get it started again. That was when I heard him."

"Wasn't it just the wind?" Rebecca asked.

"No, Rebecca, it was *not* the wind. What I heard came from the mouth of something living – you may say it could have been a dog but I've never heard a dog howl like that. It chilled my bones, I don't mind saying. What convinces me and what I will swear to you is true is this … it was on the island somewhere. Now Dougie and I didn't take a dog with us and unless some clever collie swam across in the storm, it wasn't a dog."

"What did Dougie think?"

Drew threw a small stone into the loch. "He was asleep. Reckons I dreamt it."

Rebecca paused for a few seconds, before taking a deep breath.

"If I tell you some odd things that have been happening to me, will you promise not to make fun of me?"

For once Drew looked almost serious. "Of course. You tell me yours, and I'll show you mine, that sort of thing."

"I'm serious!" glared Rebecca. "Weird things have happened to me and if I don't tell somebody about them, I'll go mad."

Drew's eyes focused on her. He nodded. "Tell me. I won't mock – promise."

Scanning his face cautiously for some reassurance that she could trust him, Rebecca took another deep breath. She related the entire tale of the mist on the hillside, the voice calling, the attic, the chest and the key, the painting, the journal and the coincidences of the lives of Becca McOwan and herself. When she reached the end, Drew was silent.

He did not tell her she must have been imagining or dreaming anything.

"That is some story," he said, at length.

"But do you believe me?" Rebecca asked, not entirely convinced.

"Why shouldn't I? It's not the first time there have been weird stories, you know. People will tell you of strange happenings round here for hundreds of years. Some tell tales of a Ghost Ship, a great Viking Longboat." He paused for a few moments.

"I'd like to see this journal. How much have you read? There are a lot of tales about your ancestors that your grandfather used to tell us. Becca McOwan died young, threw herself off a cliff and drowned in the loch way down by the lighthouse there, in a violent storm. They said the demons had taken over her mind. She had strange dreams and hallucinations.

Of course, at that time, anybody like that was called a witch. Nobody believed her and they locked her away in the old manse, way up the glen near Ladhar Bheinn. She did those weird paintings you'll see all over the castle. People say they are so strange because she was mad."

"How old was she when she threw herself off the cliff?"

"Not that old – eighteen maybe."

Rebecca shivered. She stood up and stood next to Drew, staring across the water.

"Well I hope that's not going to happen to me," she said.

"Don't worry, there's a fence by the cliff and the old manse is a ruin now." The smirk had returned to Drew's face. "And anyway, they'd never put an English lady anywhere she didn't have room service."

Rebecca hit him on the arm. She looked down at the grave again.

"So what were these dreams about?"

"Nobody really knows, other than some mention of a huge beast howling and trying to break down the door of the castle. And you've only had me trying to get into your room so far and the only beasts around here are deer… unless you count McHarg."

"We must find out more," said Rebecca, her eyes bright. "Whatever it is, it seems to involve me, it's all very curious and I have to find out more about Becca and what happened to her."

It was starting to get cold again, so they returned to the boat to make the short return journey across the loch. Just above the boat, Drew's attention was drawn to something out on the water. He narrowed his eyes.

"What is it?" Rebecca tried to follow his gaze but could not see anything.

"Now what do you suppose those guys are up to?" said Drew and pointed. This time, Rebecca could make out some shapes in the water.

"Aren't they seals?" she asked.

"No seal I know of wears an air tank. Or flippers – look!" As he pointed again, Rebecca could just make out the unmistakeable shape of a frogman before he dived below the surface and disappeared from view.

"Aren't they just out diving?" asked Rebecca. "People do, you know."

"Not in Loch Nevis, if they have any sense. It has awful, strong undercurrents and dangerous waters. The water is dark and the visibility very poor. Even an experienced diver can get into trouble. Plus it's so very dark that there's nothing to see. They normally avoid Loch Nevis. There are much better places along this coast."

"Another part of being a ranger?" asked Rebecca. "You do diving as well?"

"No, not me. But you meet a lot of them and when I've worked the boats with Willie McHarg, we often take divers out for the day. Some of them are even English."

As they neared Rahsaig, Drew suddenly whistled to Rebecca. He pointed to the shore. For a second Rebecca was puzzled, and then she grimaced. McHarg was standing on the landing stage, gesticulating at them and calling out something she could not make out. As the boat came closer, Rebecca could make out the familiar pursed lips and cold stare.

"Ah! So, young Campbell. Where there's mischief, I might have expected to find you. The master has just called from Mallaig. He and the gentleman from London are waiting for the boat. And you gallivanting about the loch like some day tripper."

"Oh great – let's go and get them, Drew." Rebecca put down the rope she had been preparing to throw onto the landing stage and pointed back across the loch.

"Not you, Miss Rebecca, please!" McHarg's strident tones rang out from the shore.

"You'll be needing to dress properly for dinner. Young Campbell can go alone. I dare say even he can manage that."

"Oh I can dress when we get back, Miss McHarg, honestly," said Rebecca, grabbing Drew's arms and helping him turn the wheel back around.

"Come on, get going" she hissed at him, under her breath. The boat turned and as they pulled away, they could hear McHarg still calling shrilly from the shore, but could no longer make out what she was saying.

"See?" said Drew. Rebecca looked at him, not understanding his meaning.

"I told you I'd heard the wolf howling on the breeze."

CHAPTER 6

THE FACE AT THE WINDOW

Simon Sibley of Holborn Passage, London was a short, plump man whose sandy hair was receding quite dramatically. As if to compensate for his shiny bald head, he sported a bushy moustache, the ends of which he enjoyed twirling between the first two fingers of his left hand. Rebecca endured just a few seconds of this mannerism before she found it extremely irritating. He ventured his opinion on every subject discussed at dinner, with a conviction that obliged his audience to listen with appropriate gravitas. At one point he had leant towards Rebecca to impart some nugget of wisdom and she had almost passed out in the accompanying blast of foul-smelling, whisky breath. Viewed alongside a tendency to sweat copiously and pick at a bulbous, red-veined nose, it was fair to say that Rebecca took an instant dislike to Simon Sibley.

If Uncle Henry sympathised with Rebecca's reaction to their guest, he did not make this apparent. He appeared to listen attentively to Sibley's views on mobile phone signals in the Highlands and a discourse on the standard of catering in privatised railway companies. Indeed, it was the dessert course before the subject of the McOwan collection was raised. Sibley was in full flow, his conviction reinforced by his own belief in his expertise and his satisfaction in finding an apparently willing and grateful audience.

"... Yes, I have only hitherto concluded my initial and quite superficial examinations of what you possess here, Mr McOwan, but I am greatly excited by the possibilities. The painting of The

Flight of the Bonnie Prince hanging in the library is probably a Mcleish – the great Gordon McLeish of Perth – certainly most interesting and accords, if genuine, of course, with his other oils in the castle on Rum. I shall be visiting there too during my stay in the Highlands, as I told you, along with a few other notable houses and castles. And indeed you may have another genuine McLeish in your gun room."

"You don't have any reason to suspect our paintings may not be genuine?" asked Henry.

Sibley patted his moustache with his napkin and carefully replaced it on his lap.

"A most excellent repast. You must compliment Miss McHarg for me, young lady."

Rebecca found this to be addressed to herself. Infuriated by what she perceived as a patronising presumption by this pompous little man, she was about to respond when Sibley abruptly diverted his attention to her uncle. In her present humour towards Sibley, Rebecca took this as a further slight. Anticipating a reaction, Henry raised his eyebrows pleadingly and Rebecca closed her mouth without saying anything.

"My years of experience in the field of antiquities has convinced me that it always pays to be, at first, suspicious. This has the hidden benefit of ensuring that all surprises may be pleasant ones."

Rebecca did not join in the outbreak of loud laughter with which Sibley followed his joke and was pleased to see that Henry did not either.

The telephone rang. Henry rose and went into the Great Hall to answer it. Rebecca's heart sank, fearing she would now be unable to avoid more unwanted conversation but, after a few seconds, during which, thankfully, Sibley did not look up from devouring a plateful of cheese and biscuits with the thoroughness of an industrial vacuum cleaner, Henry returned.

"It's for you, Mr Sibley. Mr Gordon of Barradale."

Sibley rose, simpering, to his feet and disappeared through the door which clicked shut behind him. Folding her napkin, Rebecca excused herself and quickly left the room, anxious to avoid further contact with Sibley. She decided to try out the bath she had discovered earlier before turning in.

She passed quickly behind Sibley, who was muttering into the receiver. Noticing her, he paused, placed his hand over the mouthpiece, smiled in what he doubtless considered a charming manner, and returned to his conversation once she was safely out of earshot.

Rebecca gave him one last look through narrowed eyes.

***

In the dead of night, Rebecca awoke with a start. She was convinced she had heard a noise. The clock on her bedside table showed just after three. A fox barked suddenly outside, making her jump. Shivering in the chilly darkness, she got out of bed, went over to the window and pulled back the curtain. The loch and grounds were lit up by a full moon, the trees and bushes casting long, dark shadows across the grass. It was eerily beautiful. She could see nothing immediately untoward. She strained her ears for any unfamiliar sound but everywhere seemed quiet. The fox barked again. But she was certain that was not what had disturbed her.

Rebecca was spooked. She was not normally given to imagining things going bump in the night. Drawing her dressing gown over her white nightshirt and stepping into her slippers, she opened her door quietly and peered out. There was no sign of anything odd in the passageway.

All at once, she heard a strange, mournful howling from somewhere high in the castle. What on earth could that be?

Heart thumping, she stepped out, closing the door softly, and stood still. She shivered involuntarily in the unexpectedly chilly air. Moonlight was streaming in through the windows, sending shafts of ghostly, silvery light onto the walls. Black shadows lay in between.

There it came again, a long, melancholy note. It must be the wind, she reasoned, whistling through the old pipework. She looked out of a window. Nothing appeared to be stirring.

Moments later, she most definitely did hear a noise, of an altogether different sort.

A low thud, which seemed to come from somewhere on the same floor, a gap of a few seconds and then a metallic scraping sound ... and nothing more.

The moon passed behind a cloud, throwing the passageway into darkness.

Rebecca swallowed hard, clenched her fists into tight balls and forced herself to inch quietly along, blocking her mind to the potential danger of discovering an intruder.

Just before the junction of two passages, Rebecca stopped and pressed herself against the wall, listening for any sound.

Everything seemed still. She poked her head gingerly round the corner. Nothing unusual. She stepped out, her eyes darting to either side to detect the first sign of movement. Edging carefully along, she passed the bathroom she had used a few hours earlier, finally reaching a large leaded window at the end. She leaned forward to look outside.

Not a soul about. The lawns were soft and velvet in the moonlight, the bushes and trees stilled. Just as she was turning away, Rebecca's eye fell on a boat a little way off shore, directly in front of the castle. She frowned, certain there had been nothing there when she had looked out earlier. It was too dark to make out whether anyone was aboard. She watched but it did not seem to be moving, nor showing discernible signs of life.

Rebecca turned to be confronted by the door to the gun room. Putting her ear to it, she listened hard but could hear nothing. With every muscle taut and holding her breath, she closed her hand about the latch. It clicked easily and silently open. To her great relief, she found nobody lurking in either the antechamber or the gun room. There had been no further noises since she stood outside her own room.

Perhaps it had been the heating system, she thought, starting to doubt herself. In an old, draughty castle there would be any manner of odd, mysterious noises.

Her pulse slowing down again and relaxing, Rebecca began to make her way back along the passageway to her room. She was relieved but slightly disappointed not to have discovered something, although why there was now a boat in the loch near the castle was puzzling. She reached the turn and threw a quick look back over her shoulder.

This time she did see something at the end of the passage. It rooted her to the floor.

A face at the window!

Rebecca stopped dead in her tracks, uttering an involuntary gasp.

She quickly ducked around the corner and crouched down. Slowly, her heart in her mouth and steeling herself, she peered back round again.

The face was still there, pale and wraith-like in the moonlight, sharp, intense with dark, sunken eyes. There was not a wisp of hair on the head.

Rebecca hardly dared breathe.

Spidery fingers fiddled with a latch. If the window opened, Rebecca felt sure her thumping heart would be heard by anyone.

She was torn between a desire to wake the household and a fear that she might be attacked. In the end, events took over. In trying to shift her weight, she overbalanced. Reaching out to steady herself, she sent a tall flower stand crashing across the floor. Equilibrium lost, she followed it, sprawling into the corridor and staring straight up into the face only a few feet away.

The sunken eyes glowered with fury. Rebecca met their gaze. Thin lips parted, as if about to speak to her but no sound came. For the few seconds they stared at one another, the world went into slow motion.

Then, the eyes shot a glance to either side and gave one last burning look of anger down at Rebecca before disappearing below the sill. Rebecca shrank back, shaken by the ferocity of the expression and the suddenness of the incident. She put her hand to her chest and took some deep breaths.

Her wits gradually returned. She scrambled to her feet and hurried to the half-open window. She was just in time to see two shadowy shapes disappearing across the lawn into a bank of rhododendrons by the loch. They were dressed from head to toe in black. Rebecca wondered if they could have been wearing diving suits. She waited, hoping to see some disturbance in the water. The surface of the loch was still and the brightness of the moonlight such that she was sure to see anyone in or on the water.

She pushed the window wide to listen.

Rebecca convinced herself that what she had seen had a rational explanation. The shapes running across the lawn were definitely men. But there had been something really creepy about that face.

She waited ten minutes by the window without seeing anything more. It was now quite cold, the chilly night air in the passageway making her breath visible. She closed the window and returned to her room, uncertain what to do. She crossed to her own window to watch the boat on the loch.

It had disappeared! She scanned both ways but could see only moonlight and shadows.

Footsteps stopped outside her door. Her heart immediately began to thump again, the blood rushing into her temples.

"Rebecca?" Uncle Henry's voice called gently from the passage.

"Oh Uncle Henry, it's you!" Rebecca flew to the door and flung it open. Her uncle stood outside in his dressing gown, clutching a torch. His face registered surprise as his niece suddenly clung to him.

"Are you all right? I heard some noise along here."

"I'm fine, I'm fine but I saw a man trying to break in!" At a rush and realising she was gabbling, Rebecca tried to relate what had happened, pointing to where the boat had been out on the loch. "I bet that's how they got here! It must have been! It wasn't there when I went to bed."

"Slow down, girl, slow down. Are you sure what you saw? If we have to call the police in the morning, we want to be certain. Did you actually see any men on the boat?"

"Well, no, of course, I mean I can't be absolutely certain – but it's a bit of a coincidence, wouldn't you say?"

"Coincidence is one thing. Look, come down to the kitchen and we'll make some tea. You can tell me the whole thing from start to finish."

***

Henry McOwan put the kettle on the stove and listened, not interrupting as Rebecca, now more measured, related everything she had seen and heard in the passageway. When she had finished, he looked thoughtful.

"The boat you saw was actually sent for Mr Sibley by his friend Mr Gordon of Barradale and is to take him and me to the Isle of Rum tomorrow. His phone call was from Mr Gordon, arranging this. It has probably moved just along the loch, out of the current."

Rebecca raised her eyebrows in surprise.

"So you see why we have to be certain about statements we make. If you say that these intruders came from that boat, then you are implying that Mr Sibley and his associate may be somehow involved with them as well and that is rather dramatic, as you will agree? It is also, I am sure, very wrong."

"Oh," said Rebecca, the wind rather taken out of her sails by this unexpected revelation.

"Well I don't like Mr Sibley and I just don't trust him."

"Why? It's no reason to accuse him of being a criminal, is it? I don't trust a lot of people and I like even fewer but that doesn't make them all crooked."

Rebecca sensed her uncle's reproof quite keenly in these last remarks and felt a little ashamed. In the relatively short time she had known him, she had come to hold him in high esteem and did not wish to lose his good opinion. Henry saw her mortified look and put his hand on her shoulder.

"But hey, you've been through quite an ordeal tonight – and you've shown a lot of courage. At your age, heck, I'd have shouted the house down for help. And – you scared them off without their getting in. I'll get the local copper to look into it. Not quite Sherlock Holmes, but the best we can muster here!"

He went over to the window and looked out, then turned, a mischievous smile playing about the corners of his mouth. "It's good to be inquisitive. And if it's any consolation, I do think Sibley is a plonker."

Rebecca looked up quickly, half-shocked. Henry's eyes twinkled.

"But he is our guest …"

CHAPTER 7

THE FLIGHT OF THE BONNIE PRINCE

Henry McOwan and Mr Sibley set off early for the Isle of Rum, to catch the morning tide. Opening her curtains, Rebecca had caught sight of them on the landing stage. A small dinghy was waiting to take them out to a boat in the loch, which had appeared this morning. Rebecca observed that the boatman who helped them on board had a full head of red hair and did not remotely resemble her intruder. She chewed her lip thoughtfully as she watched them depart.

"The laird has left you a *written* note," said Miss McHarg, somewhat curtly, as Rebecca sat down to a cup of tea and some toast in the breakfast room.

"Quite why he should not have imparted to me the content and trusted to me to pass on the message, I do not know. But, that he did not, and I shall not question his intent, since it is not the housekeeper's place to be questioning the laird. It's there, by your cup."

She made a dismissive gesture towards a small envelope and left the room. Rebecca grinned to herself, not altogether certain it would be advisable to be around when McHarg *did* question the laird. She seemed quite put out. Rebecca opened the envelope.

...Morning, Watson! Escorting 'our Guest' to Rum – back for supper. Local copper coming this evening – checked everywhere and nothing obvious missing. Don't think they could have got in.

Drew has clear instructions that you are to enjoy yourself today!
H.

Rebecca smiled, pleased at the conspiratorial, light-hearted tone.

She was nervous about telling her story to the police. She would confine herself to facts, rather than adding her own theories, for fear of leaving herself open to more of her uncle's disapproval.

For now, though, there was much to tell Drew following the drama of last night and it crossed her mind that she was actually looking forward to his arrival. She chose not to pursue this line of thought since she might have to admit a thaw in her attitude to all things Scottish. She decided to wait in the library, where she had left Becca's journal the previous evening. She was soon installed in the window seat and absorbed once again in the extraordinary life of her namesake in the eighteenth century. She resumed the story on the morning of Becca's fourteenth birthday and the Battle of Culloden.

Becca's father and two brothers perished in the fighting on Drumossie Moor.

The English had opened with an attack of awesome ferocity. Her father had been hit by musket fire in these initial skirmishes, while Davie and Andrew had fallen with wounds and died in the field in the hours afterwards. The battle had been so furious that it had been over in all but half an hour. The routed Jacobite army fled the field.

Becca and her mother had been brought word a few days later by clansmen running from the pursuing English soldiers.

The English Commander, the Duke of Cumberland, ordered the Jacobites to be hunted down without mercy. King George wanted to eliminate such uprisings for ever.

Together with their steward, Hector, Becca and her mother walked over a eighty kilometres to Inverness, to bring home the bodies for burial in the family crypt. On the way they met many, many people on similar journeys, weeping for lost sons, husbands, fathers and brothers. Becca described, in heart-rending detail, scenes of unbelievable sadness. She was very angry at how roughly and shamefully these grieving folk were treated by the English soldiers, who were searching high and low for the remnants of the Bonnie Prince's army.

When the family at last arrived in Inverness, exhausted from days of walking and lack of food, they had been refused permission to take the bodies with them and told to return home. At this, Becca's mother Mary had broken down. It had taken several days of constant pleading from Becca, together with the last of their money, to persuade an old Major to allow them to load the bodies onto their cart under the cover of darkness.

The Major had not been able to look Becca in the eye as he took her purse.

On the way home, Becca's mother's condition deteriorated and by the time they arrived at Rahsaig, she was very sick and babbling incoherently.

They buried their men the next morning in the beauty and tranquillity of the hillside overlooking the loch, a bitter contrast from the last place they saw in life.

The strain proved too much for Mary. She too died, a few days later.

Becca was convinced that her mother had simply died of a broken heart.

While Becca grieved, Robert, her eldest brother, burned for revenge. Despite Becca's pleading and the fact that he had still not properly recovered from his wounds, he left to join up with a band of Jacobite rebels. From here, his life became quite extraordinary.

In July 1746, with the English troops closing in on him, the Bonnie Prince was hiding out on a mountain called Sgurr nan Eugallt, just a few miles from Rahsaig.

To protect the man they believed had the rightful claim to the throne of Scotland, the Jacobites hatched a plan to throw the English off his scent. With his dark good looks and sturdy figure, Robert McOwan was of similar appearance to Prince Charles himself. Robert would pose as the Prince and attempt to lead the English astray, thereby clearing the field for Prince Charles to make his escape to France.

And thus it was that for a time, Robert McOwan lived the life of a fugitive in the hills and glens, making himself known as the Bonnie Prince and trying to stay one step ahead of the English. Most Highland folk had never actually seen the Prince and did not imagine, therefore, that they were encountering anyone other than the Young Pretender himself. For some months, the plan succeeded in causing great confusion among the English pursuers and gave heart to the Jacobite sympathisers. Despite her fears for Robert, Becca enjoyed this hugely, particularly the notion of her brother as the real 'Pretender'.

But the adventure surely could not last and so it was that Robert McOwan was finally captured by the English while hiding out in rocky crags on the Paps of Jura, mountains on a remote island some miles off the mainland. He was taken to Edinburgh castle, where the English quickly realised they had an impostor. Robert was hanged for his support of the Jacobite Prince on October 1 1746 and Becca McOwan, at fourteen years old, born into a family of seven, was left orphaned and alone to look after her young brother Donald.

Rebecca's eyes filled with tears. She put down the book and stared out of the window, unable to imagine the anguish and desolation that Becca must have felt. To lose almost your entire family in a few short months was a tragedy, the poignancy of which was almost unbearable. She thought of Alistair and her own parents for a moment, hoping they were safe.

She looked up at the picture of the Prince hiding in the

boat among the sheep and wondered if it was actually Robert. She noticed that the picture was slightly off centre on the wall, so she got up to straighten it. She tilted the frame slightly and stepped back.

"This day, milady, the master instructs me to take you to the forbidding Castle of Stoer, seat of the Lords of Kintail, on the small island of Soay."

Rebecca was brought abruptly back to the present by the arrival of Drew. She quickly took out her hankie and blew her nose to disguise the fact she had been crying.

"Who are the Lords of Kintail?" she asked, keeping her eyes averted.

"Old geezers – died years ago. Landowners who used to fight the McDonalds and McLeods. Great castle, although it's a ruin now. Anyway, your ship awaits, modom, the weather is on our side thus far at least, so let us tarry here no longer – make haste, wench! Gird thy loins and all that stuff."

"I hope you can sail properly," she said sarcastically.

"Aye well the real boatman, Willie, is away to his day job."

"What's his day job?"

"He's a seaweed farmer."

Rebecca laughed. "A what?!"

"It's no joke, your Englishness. We poor downtrodden jocks must earn an honest crust somehow. He harvests kelp, the flat, ribbon-type stuff. It's sold as animal fodder and is a delicacy in some parts of the world. There's weed from Loch Nevis on plates in Japanese restaurants in Tokyo."

"I do not believe a word of it!" Rebecca was still laughing.

"Suit yourself," said Drew, merrily. "Remain ignorant! So, are you ready?"

He stood by the door expectantly.

"Where is Soay? Is it one of the cocktails?" Rebecca smiled when she saw that her knowledge of the nickname of the nearest islands had surprised Drew. He rallied quickly.

"No, actually, it is not. It lies just off Skye and has a magnificent view of the Cuillins, with which I suppose you are also acquainted?"

"Would that be the Rum Cuillins or the Skye Cuillins, as both would probably be visible, I imagine?"

"You win... this time." Drew looked at her with a wry smile on his face.

"Well, are you coming or not?"

"What happened to the Shakespearian verse? I was quite enjoying that."

Rebecca darted out of the room quickly, away from Drew's glare.

***

As the boat chugged steadily down the loch, Rebecca told Drew about the startling events of the previous night. She included her own suspicions about Sibley but qualified these with what Henry had told her about Sibley's associate Gordon and the boat.

"Gordon would be the Honourable Anthony Gordon, I expect, QC, owner of Barradale estate, stinking rich and Member of Parliament for Knoydart and Morar. He is something of an absentee landlord. We call him the Invisible Man. People say the best way to get to see him is to appear in court. His unofficial home address is Miami."

They rounded the point at the end of Loch Nevis and emerged into more open sea.

About a mile away was the shore of the famous, mystic Isle of Skye.

Gulls swooped back and forth, following the boat's progress and occasionally landing on the bow. There was a gentle swell to accompany the steady breeze but bright sunshine kept them warm. Behind them, the mountains of the mainland came into gradual relief, softened by the light into the distance.

As Drew kept a steady hand on the wheel, Rebecca sat back and found she was enjoying herself. The scenery was certainly stunning and the sensation of being in a boat alone on the seas, exploring on their own terms, was something with definite appeal. She imagined travelling at the time of Becca, Robert and the Bonnie Prince. What must it have felt like to be Robert McOwan, on the run with the English army in hot pursuit?

Drew brought her back to the present with a rather more direct question.

"Been painting?" He pointed at her hands.

Rebecca started in surprise and looked down. There was a sticky globule of gold paint on the end of one of her fingers and smears over both her palms. She thought for a moment.

"No – where on earth has that come from? The only gold thing I remember having touched is the picture in the library." Gradual realisation crept into Rebecca's voice.

"I straightened it up. It must have been that. Come to think of it, it did feel sticky. But that's really old, so why on earth would it be wet?"

They stared at one another for a few moments, uncomprehending.

"Would it have something to do with the break-in?"

"Some very strange things are happening around here," said Drew, slowing the boat.

"Why would an old painting be in a frame that was still wet? If it wasn't so old, perhaps. Maybe Sibley was right and it is a forgery. Perhaps even, a very recent forgery – so recent, it's still wet! And strange too, wouldn't you say, that somebody tried to break in to the castle just last night? Madam, there is mischief afoot, as Sherlock Holmes might have said. What do you say we abandon our little trip and go back to do some poking about?"

Rebecca nodded vigorously.

"If for no other reason than to check that frame where I touched it."

***

"So where exactly did you last see those men?" asked Drew, standing by the boathouse at Rahsaig. "Let's try to retrace their steps."

Rebecca pointed to the rhododendrons further down the shore and they set off. After a few minutes of rummaging through the bushes, Rebecca called out.

"Here! See? Footprints, lots of them and recent. Quite a definite imprint from the bottom of the shoe. Well you can say one thing – no spectre made these."

"Difficult to say if it's diver's feet, though. He's hardly going to be wearing his flippers on dry land – I'm not being funny, he isn't, is he?" Drew put up his hands in protest as Rebecca looked threateningly at him.

"Now that is out of the ordinary." Drew was no longer looking at the tracks in the mud but at a small green shed up among the trees. The door was slightly ajar.

"That shed is always kept locked. I locked it myself two days ago and nobody has had any reason to go near it since – I'd know if they had because I keep the only key."

Rebecca followed him over to the shed, cautiously.

"Somebody has broken in – look!" Rebecca pointed to broken wood on the door frame and the lock hanging free. Unhesitatingly, Drew pushed the door open. There were gardening tools, wheelbarrows and mowers. Sacks of compost and ceramic pots were stacked up. Against the end wall, partly concealed under some sacking was a large flat package, wrapped in black plastic, which Drew did not recognise. Carefully, they pulled it out into the middle of the shed.

"Put the light on, will you?" said Drew, starting to pick at the wrapping.

Rebecca clicked a light on and knelt on the floor next to Drew. Careful not to rip it, they pulled and tugged until the wrapping came clear. They stopped and looked at each other, excitement on their faces. Underneath was the painting of the Flight of the Bonnie Prince.

Rebecca checked the frame and wrapping but there was no trace of any wet paint.

"Two pictures? Unless this has been put here while we have been out. Wait here a moment!" Rebecca ran out of the shed and over the lawn to the castle. She peered in through the library window, saw the painting was still on the wall and returned.

"Two pictures! And what's more, there are footmarks in the mud by the window. It looks like somebody tried to get in there too."

"And probably succeeded," said Drew.

"What does it all mean?" Rebecca chewed her lip in thought.

Drew sat on an upturned pot, a frown on his face.

"Somebody has copied the picture. Why?"

"So they could sell the real one without anyone guessing it had been stolen? I've heard about art theft like that. People will pay a lot of money for an original masterpiece. When I disturbed them last night, they maybe had to leave this here in their hurry to get away."

"If that's the case, they did get into the castle. Did they take anything else I wonder – are there any more?"

Together they searched the shed but could find nothing else.

"Nothing here although that doesn't mean they didn't manage to take something else with them. Hang on, there is something up there." Drew pointed up to what appeared to be a black rubber sheet, draped over a beam above their heads. He pulled it down and brought it over to the light. It was a rubber holdall, with a sealable airtight pocket inside.

"I've seen one of these before," said Drew, triumphantly, "and it proves your theory about divers. It's a diver's bag, airtight to keep water out. What if they meant to put the painting in here and swim away?"

Rebecca turned the bag over. Her face wore a frown. "I don't get it though. Why would they go to all the trouble and difficulty of trying to carry this big painting away underwater, when they had a boat they could quite easily have used? It makes no sense. It was the middle of the night and nobody was watching."

"You were watching. They must have been afraid of being spotted, so they decided this was the safest way. Or maybe it wasn't their boat after all."

He paused, before looking up again, his eyes wide. "Wait a minute! There is no way that the boat which took Henry and Sibley this morning was the same one that was waiting out in the loch last night, I've just realised. Gordon chartered Willie McHarg's boat – I saw Willie this morning setting off from Mallaig. He told me he was away to pick up the Laird. Willie would never be involved in anything like that – and anyway, he was moored up in Mallaig last night, having a couple of beers in the King's Head with my brother. So there *was* a different boat here which vanished before it got light."

"So whose was the other one?" Rebecca's question hung in the air.

***

Rebecca and Drew were in the kitchen, raiding the fridge for something to drink.

"So, we know they got in downstairs. Are we sure they did not get in upstairs?"

"Uncle Henry said not. The man I saw was definitely on the outside of the window."

"That doesn't necessarily mean he was on the outside trying to get in. He may have been on his way out – or trying to get *back* in."

They looked at each other for a split second, before rushing out across the Great Hall, up the staircase and along to the rear landing window where Rebecca had seen the face. A quick search of the rooms nearby found no obvious signs of anything missing.

"As they didn't get away with what they wanted, won't they be back?"

Rebecca looked out across the lawns to the bushes where she had seen the figures disappear in the moonlight. "Yes, they will. And we'll be waiting for them."

"Shouldn't we tell the police and your uncle now? We've got both paintings and we know there was a break-in. And the thieves will probably be back. Surely that's enough?"

"Yes, we could but I reckon Sibley is involved in all this and I want to set a little trap for him before we tell anyone anything. You know how funny Uncle Henry was last night when I suggested it might be Sibley. Nobody will believe us without proof."

"So what do you suggest we do?"

"We get Sibley to look at the painting. If he really is an expert, he will have to say it's forged – except if he's in on it, in which case he will say it's genuine. I think we should see what happens. And I don't think the thieves will leave it long to come back, in case somebody finds the broken door. So after he's seen it, we have to swap the real one back and put the forgery in the shed."

Rebecca sat down, looking very thoughtful for a moment.

"Look, you're supposed to go back to Mallaig tonight, yes? Okay, this may sound mad but I think once we've put the painting back, I should wait outside for the thieves and you should wait in the boat."

"Sounds mad so far," said Drew, looking puzzled. "Why?"

"If they come back and find the painting where they left it, they will take it off with them, unsuspecting. We get in the boat, follow them and find out where they go."

Drew sounded sceptical.

"If we lose them, we risk having no proof to convince anybody. What if they go off underwater? How are we supposed to follow?"

"You said nobody in their right mind dives in Loch Nevis because it's so dangerous. So if they do, surely they won't be going far? If there's a boat waiting, we'll see it. And they'll be taking the forgery with them – they'll never expect that. That way, even if we do lose them, Uncle Henry hasn't lost anything. I think they'll wait for darkness and for the house to go to sleep. So, I slip out, come down here, hide and keep watch for them. You have the boat standing by, so we can follow them."

Drew considered this for a moment and sighed.

"Okay – but I think it's risky. And if you drown in the loch, your uncle will blame me."

CHAPTER 8

LYING IN WAIT

Rahsaig Castle received a visit that evening from Constable Alexander Lennie of the West Highland Constabulary. PC Lennie, an unusually tall man, with short, dark hair and a lean, square-jawed face, was the same age as Henry McOwan and the two of them had been schoolboy friends. Fifteen years as the bobby and marriage to a local girl had rooted him firmly and contentedly in the small highland community. Major incidents, other than storms, were practically unknown in this remote corner and, save for the occasional motoring offender or boisterous, drunken fisherman, his encounters with the criminal underworld had been unremarkable. Hence, the opportunity to investigate a burglary at the Laird's residence represented a major professional challenge. In his understated, languorous way, Alexander Lennie was positively excited.

"The Laird is speaking privately with the investigative authorities just now," said McHarg grandly, as Rebecca sat in the Great Hall outside the door to Henry's study. Her tone suggested a degree of inside knowledge that she was not disposed to impart. Whether this was indeed the case, Rebecca sensed, might be open to doubt.

"You will be called presently, to give your evidence." This last statement was accompanied by a look of the utmost severity. McHarg turned swiftly on her heel and disappeared down the passageway to the kitchen. Rebecca managed to retain a serious expression until she heard the kitchen door close, whereupon she could not restrain a broad smirk at the housekeeper's expense.

She did not have to wait long. The study door opened and she was joined in the Hall by her uncle. His face was unusually serious.

"Rebecca, please stick to what you *actually* saw and heard. Constable Lennie's not interested in theories and flights of fancy."

Rebecca felt a keen edge to his tone and reddened under the severity of his gaze.

"Of course, Uncle Henry." She followed him back into the study where the constable was standing by the fireplace. They sat down next to one another on the sofa and Rebecca was struck by how far he still towered over her. Everything about him seemed to extend slightly further than usual, from his size fourteen feet to his long, angular nose. He reminded her of a stick insect Alistair had brought home from school one day.

PC Lennie took out his pen. Rebecca recounted the events of the previous evening, under the watchful eye of her uncle. The experience of being questioned by the police proved ultimately disappointing. Constable Lennie said very little and asked even less and Rebecca left the study feeling a little deflated. There was no doubt that the police viewed the matter in a serious light but she had not gained the impression that she was considered a key witness. She had been about to voice her theory that the paintings were being copied but abandoned this when she realised she could not produce them without compromising their plan.

***

"I am very pleased to be the bearer of good tidings, Mr McOwan. I can confirm my initial impression that this is the original version of the Flight of the Bonnie Prince." Simon Sibley removed the monocle, through which he had been minutely inspecting the painting in the library and turned to Henry, managing to combine an obsequious smile with a look of utter pomposity on his chubby features.

"Are you sure?" Henry looked pleased. Sibley twirled his moustache importantly.

"It is certain, sir. It is the quality of the brush strokes. The great McLeish is very certain, very dramatic in his gesture. There is real flamboyance – to the trained eye, of course."

"Of course," murmured Henry, a long-suffering expression on his face.

Rebecca kicked Drew, who had been mimicking the manner of Simon Sibley out of view of everyone except herself. Drew's acting was not her concern though, as she made an urgent face at him, motioning him outside. Leaving Sibley and Henry talking together, she closed the door behind them.

"See?" she whispered, her face aglow. "Sibley is definitely involved in it too."

"Are we completely sure?"

"It's obvious, idiot! He says that this one is genuine but we know that it's a forgery – the original is outside in the shed. He *must* be in on it."

"Or he's just a crap expert…"

"Shh! They're coming out."

The reappearance of Henry and Sibley brought a halt to their whispering. They went through to the dining room, where the table was set for dinner. Henry turned to Rebecca.

"So, what have you been up to today? Did you go to Soay?"

"Yes, just like you said."

"And what did you think of Stoer Castle?"

"Oh, we didn't go there."

"Oh? Why not?"

"Well, in fact we didn't go to Soay, actually."

"I thought you said you did?"

"Well, we set off to go to Soay and we were going there for a while but we didn't actually go there. We turned round and came back... before we got there."

"Why?"

Rebecca was saved further embarrassment by the sudden intervention of McHarg. For once, she was very glad to be interrupted by the severe pursed lips and icy stare.

"Dinner...sir!" McHarg's tone was clipped and a glacial stare was directed firmly at her Uncle. The gimlet eyes alighted on Drew, the discovery of whose presence seemed to cause further affront.

"Will young Campbell be staying to dine... sir?"

"Aye, yes, Miss McHarg, I'm sorry, I meant to tell you we were one more. He has been so good as to put in extra hours as holiday rep for Rebecca, so it is the least we can do."

"Well, we will have to hope that the potatoes stretch. Come, Campbell, you can collect your own cutlery. I'll not be waiting on the assistant ranger."

Out of sight of McHarg, Rebecca and Drew exchanged smiles. Uncle Henry's attention was back on Sibley, who was holding forth on the subject of the great McLeish's use of canvas. Rebecca sat nervously fiddling with her napkin, hoping dinner would not last too long so she and Drew could put the rest of their plan into action.

***

Rebecca and Drew watched Sibley and Uncle Henry disappear into the drawing room to continue their examination of the McOwan collection.

"Hurry!" whispered Rebecca urgently, propelling Drew towards the North door. They ran across the lawn to the shed and retrieved the original painting.

"Let's hope they don't see us," muttered Drew, looking anxiously at the castle windows in the gathering gloom. They manoeuvred the bulky painting as quickly as they could back across the grass and inside. Regaining the safety of the library, they quickly removed the forged painting and repositioned the original above the fireplace. Then they took the forgery back to the shed, wrapped it in the same black plastic and hid it again.

"Right – you stay here," said Drew.

"I'll get back inside before I'm missed. McHarg's getting me back – washing up duty."

***

A fish broke the surface of the loch with a splash as she sat down on a rock, causing Rebecca to jump. She smiled at her own edginess, gathering her coat about her against a chill breeze coming off the black waters. Night was not far away now, purple dusk enshrouding the hillsides. Rebecca could no longer distinguish the mass of Shadow Island against the hillside on the far bank. Once again, she was drawn to the beauty and stillness of this country.

Something swooped just above her head and she jumped again as it flew off towards the trees. It was a bat. Rebecca recoiled instantly, shuddering.

She had only been sitting on the bank a short while, when she was disturbed again.

"Becca! Becca!" Startled, Rebecca heard the voice which had called to her high on the mountain. Her pulse quickened. She jumped to her feet, summoning her courage, determined that this time she would discover who was calling and why.

"Who is there? Who are you?" Her own voice, loud and unfamiliar.

Silence. Mist had descended once more, thick and swirling, enveloping her, impenetrable.

"Becca! Becca!" The voice was closer. Once again, Rebecca could hear the sound of oars, splashing through the water. She strained her eyes into the mist, desperate to catch a glimpse of the boat, of someone.

"I can't see you! Show yourself! Who are you?" she cried out, as the splashing became louder.

A long, mournful howl.

A shiver ran down Rebecca's spine. Her feet were rooted to the ground, her mind racing. Eyes wide and wild, she looked rapidly to either side and behind her, fearful of something leaping out of the mist at her.

What manner of creature could have made that noise?

An eerie, creepy stillness followed. Rebecca wrung her hands together. They were clammy with sweat.

The sound had come from the water. As it died away, Rebecca could see sinister shapes emerging from the mist, no more than ten metres off shore.

She shrank back into the shadows.

"Becca! Becca!" The voice was quieter, and Rebecca could now make out a huge figure, standing in the bows of a great boat.

With an instant chill of dread, she recognised the warrior from the painting in the Great Hall. Behind him, shapes moved at the oars, their faces shrouded in darkness.

Was this the Ghost Ship?

Next to the warrior, the white eyes of the Wolf stared unblinkingly at her. Rebecca could not breathe.

Hakon raised his great nose almost imperceptibly, as if sniffing her scent. His grey and white coat was beautiful. To see the beast so close was amazing, yet terrifying.

Rebecca had to summon all her strength and willpower to speak. "What do you want of me?" Her voice quavered and died.

The boat came to rest at the water's edge but neither the warrior nor the wolf moved.

"Go to the Sanctuary, Becca. Intruders disturb my lady's rest. You will do what must be done. You understand. You have seen the signs. Only you can do what must be done."

The warrior and Hakon stared at her, the wolf's eyes piercing into her very soul. Rebecca took a pace forward, her courage returning. But as she did so, the mist swirled around the Ghost Ship again and enveloped it.

"Wait! But wait ..." Rebecca cried out in vain. "I don't understand what you mean ...tell me!"

Her words hung in the silence over the loch. No reply came. Once again, as quickly as it had come, the mist receded and Rebecca stood alone at the edge of the water, watching ripples flickering gently in the moonlight.

***

Rebecca heard a rustling in the trees behind her. Still shaking, she turned swiftly.

Drew emerged, his face grim.

"Bad news, I'm afraid –" he started to say, stopping when he saw her ashen face.

"What's the matter?"

In a garbled rush, she told him what had just happened.

"Are you sure you didn't drop off?" Drew shook his head, when finally she had finished, his face registering a mixture of amazement and disbelief.

"It was just now – how could I be dreaming? I thought you would believe me, even if nobody else did. Didn't you see or hear anything?"

"No, really, I didn't. I saw Willie go off on the boat but no mist ... there was no mist."

Rebecca sat down on a rock at the edge of the water, frowning. Drew stood a few feet away, looking across the loch into the night. "The Ghost Ship ... I do believe you, really. It's just so strange, that's all. Spirits from the past? Ghosts talking to you? Why?"

"If I knew that! It's me it's happening to – how do you think I feel? Something is going on here and I seem to be part of it." Her tone bordered on anger.

"He seems to want you to do something. You really don't know what?"

"I haven't a clue. 'Go to the Sanctuary. You will understand, you will do what must be done.' That's what he said but I do *not* understand."

Drew paced up and down, deep in thought, his eyebrows furrowing together.

"I overheard Sibley talking to Henry about a 'Sanctuary', part of this McOwan Art Collection, or something. Perhaps it's the same one?"

"Maybe." Rebecca was distracted.

"'You have seen the signs,' he also said. What signs? Perhaps he meant the journal and the key? Becca wrote about the Princess and the place where she was buried, guarded by a warrior and a wolf. Am I meant to read and discover something?"

"Sibley had a list of all the artefacts and paintings. It's on the library desk. Let's go and see if it says anything about a Sanctuary." Drew stood expectantly, looking down at her. Rebecca sighed and got to her feet, nodding silently.

"Oh – first though, I have to tell you what I was about to say. You stopped me with your spook story. I went back to the shed just now and the painting has gone!"

Rebecca looked at him in pained disbelief. Drew gave a rueful smile.

"The crooks must have slipped back earlier than we thought."

"Damn! That ruins everything. Uncle Henry certainly won't believe us about Sibley now. Oh no, and we had him! I should have listened to you."

Rebecca paused for a moment, looking at Drew.

"Don't say you told me so, please."

"Wouldn't dare," Drew smiled wryly.

"What if they were waiting and watching – what if they saw us?" Rebecca's face registered sudden alarm. "They might think we are on to them. They wouldn't do anything, would they?"

Drew frowned.

"No way. Sibley wouldn't want anyone alerting Henry and if anything happened to us, Henry would stop this McOwan Collection business straight away and the thieves would have to back off. They might keep an eye on us though, to see how much we do know." Rebecca shuddered.

***

Having slipped quietly and unseen back into the castle and the library, Drew was poring over a small booklet entitled 'The Machoiann Collection'. Rebecca's attention had been momentarily drawn back to the painting in the Great Hall, which she had first looked at on her arrival. Now the inscription began to make more sense to her.

> *Gathering mist hides a clear silver pool*
> *Where the taunt of bold Hakon doth play ye the fool*
> *Whispering waters, Phoebus in cloud*
> *Where time has stood still in yesterday's shroud*

She had now heard the taunt of Hakon for herself. She had

heard the whispering waters and seen the clear silver pool in the mist up the mountainside.

Looking at the painting, she wondered whether it was the work of Becca, rather than Donald as her uncle had suggested. Becca, too, may have encountered the Warrior and Hakon. Perhaps this had contributed to her disturbed mind.

The white eyes of Hakon stared down from the painting.

Rebecca decided to read more of the journal that evening.

As she entered the library, Drew turned and showed her the page he was reading. Rebecca snorted contemptuously as she read a foreword by Simon Sibley, phrased in his pompous, self-important style and laying the major share of credit for the research at his own door. The work of other experts, by Sibley's measure, appeared to register on the lesser side of slight.

"He's even spelt the name McOwan wrong," said Rebecca dismissively, pointing at the heading 'The Machoiann Collection'. Drew gave a short laugh.

"That is actually the right way, or should I say, the Gaelic way. It doesn't look one jot like it sounds. Like our mountain – pronounced 'Larven' but spelled L-a-d-h-a-r B-h-e-i-n-n."

"And when you say 'gallic', I suppose you mean 'gaylich'?"

"Nope – correct pronunciation 'gallic', spelt g-a-e-l-i-c. 'Gaylich' is Irish."

Rebecca snorted.

"Well, thanks for the spelling lesson but let's get back to the point."

"Yes, ma'am." Drew tugged his forelock. She ignored him and started flicking through the booklet. After a couple of pages, her eyes widened and she grabbed Drew's arm.

"Here! 'The Sanctuary. Unattributed, probably first half of the eighteenth century. Subject matter unknown.'" Her face fell.

"Well that tells us practically nothing, Mr Know-it-all Sibley."

"It isn't the only one that's 'Unattributed' – look. " Drew was flicking over the pages and pointing to other entries.

"There must be ten more at least. Are any of them …"

His voice tailed off as he read. He flicked quickly back and forth through the pages.

"What?" Rebecca was impatient. "Tell me! Tell me!"

"Well …" Drew looked up thoughtfully. "There are no entries attributed to Becca and yet we know she painted at least half a dozen or so that are here in the castle."

"Well maybe Sibley doesn't consider her worthy of a place in his collection."

"I doubt that. I don't know much about art but one of Dougie's pals studied art history and he reckons they are the best things here."

He paused and sat down in the window seat. Outside it was now pitch black.

"Is this one of hers?" Rebecca was looking at a painting on the wall near the window. It depicted a woman's face, screaming at someone or something which was not part of the picture. Drew came over and scrutinised it over her shoulder.

"Aye, there's her signature, I'd say. R.M. Wonder who the woman was?"

"Maybe it's a self-portrait," said Rebecca, staring at the picture. "You said she went insane."

Drew was back scanning the booklet. He tapped it with his finger tip.

"There's one here called 'Rage'. Unattributed. Perhaps that's it."

Rebecca was still looking intently at the painting. She was strangely drawn to the anguish and pain that seemed to reach out from this woman. The face was lined and gaunt, the artist having made little attempt to portray it as attractive in any way. If Rebecca had truly been insane, could she really have created something as eloquent as this? Perhaps the painting allowed her to express the torment and anger that raged inside her. She inclined her head to one side.

"It's like the painting in the gun room, of the woman tearing out her hair. Do you think it *could* be a self-portrait?"

"Giving expression to the inner demons, you mean? Aye, could be I suppose. Looks a bit like you, actually."

"I have to get the journal," said Rebecca, suddenly making for the door.

"I have to see if she talked about her paintings and what she is trying to say in them. And to see what this Sanctuary business is all about. Maybe it's all tied up with these strange mists and I'll find out what the warrior is asking me to do."

Drew came over to the door and took a quick look outside to check nobody was about.

"I'll be off. Willie will be back for McHarg soon and I can hide away aboard. I'm going to do some asking around in the harbour tomorrow, see if anyone knows just who these divers are and what they are up to."

CHAPTER 9

LOCKED IN THE CRYPT

"So why are you in such a fine hurry to bolt your breakfast this morning?

Some tomfoolery, I'll be bound. Young flipperties, you girls these days." McHarg's lips had pursed into a thin red line. As she stood at the sink, the disapproving set of her head was now becoming familiar.

"I'm going over to Stoul in the boat ... to church." Rebecca smiled mischievously.

The brush dropped from McHarg's hand into the water. Eyes wide, she favoured Rebecca with what constituted the closest she was likely to get to a beam of pleasure.

"It's heartening that you will be venturing to the Lord's house. The path of righteousness leads to His door." McHarg's face shone for a second and then she resumed washing up, her expression settling back into its usual severe set.

Rebecca bit her tongue to stifle a giggle. Through the kitchen window, she glimpsed Drew going into the boathouse to wait for her. She looked away, down at the floor and back at McHarg and saw a frown hovering at her brow. It was but momentary, however, the naturally suspicious nature for once quelled by the joy of one young "flipperty" at last finding the true path.

"And will young Campbell be joining you at the kirk?" The suspicious nature had not vanished altogether then, Rebecca smiled inwardly.

"Yes, he will, Miss McHarg," she replied, noting the repeated astonishment on the other's face with some satisfaction.

"The Lord's house is a solemn place." The severe set was back. "You're not to be causing shame to your uncle, and you can warn young Campbell that he'll have me to deal with if I hear of any malarkey. I shall be along to the kirk later and I will be speaking with the minister, you can be sure of that."

The icy stare threatened to freeze the dirty crocks.

Uncle Henry had been observing all this from behind his newspaper, amused. Rebecca caught his gaze. Her eyes narrowed.

"What?" she whispered, seeing a quizzical look come into his eyes. For fear of giggling, she quickly shovelled a spoonful of cereal into her mouth. Uncle Henry held her gaze for a few seconds longer and then looked down.

"No matter," he said, softly.

***

On leaving the castle and finding Drew waiting, Rebecca had grabbed him by the arm and propelled him unceremoniously aboard the boat.

"Well, I'm glad you told me where we're going and why," said Drew, ironically, as they cast off. She looked up apologetically.

"Sorry, didn't have time to explain, in case somebody asked you."

"Yeah, but I don't know where –" He was cut short by Rebecca's upraised hand.

"I know – sorry. I couldn't tell you and if you had been asked and not known, it would have been too complicated. We're going to Stoul, to the church."

"The church!" exclaimed Drew, recoiling in horror. The boat swerved momentarily.

"I never go to the kirk! That's for Wee Frees, guitar-playing

82

hippies and old grannies like McHarg. And I swear they are weird … they probably do sacrifices and stuff."

Rebecca laughed at his horrified expression.

"Steady! Keep your forelocks on! Well, we are going today. A lot of good people do go to church, you know – even young people. Anyway, I thought you were all God-fearing up here, like McHarg?"

Her eyes could not hide a merry glint. Drew was frowning, his eyebrows locked together.

"She's batty! The one thing most likely to keep anyone away is her and her Wee Free pals." He shook his head slowly.

Rebecca laughed.

"Just what is a Wee Free?"

"Zealot – Free Church of Scotland-goer. They call Sunday the Sabbath, wear ties all day and frown if you smile before sunset."

"Well, we are going because of what I read in the journal last night," she said.

"I'm not the only who's witnessed these strange mists and had visits from Hakon and the warrior. Becca my ancestor did too. You said she was s'posed to have had strange dreams and hallucinations. Well, she writes about exactly the same things as I have seen. She was out on the loch in a boat one day and got lost in a thick, sudden mist. She ended up drifting out to sea. She met what she called a huge Norseman, who summoned her to the 'Sanctuary'!"

Rebecca paused, to check Drew had registered the significance.

"The Sanctuary, Drew! The same as the warrior said to me."

"Yeah but what is it? We still don't know what he was on about".

"But I think I may do now, listen." Rebecca took the

journal out of her bag and turned to a page she had marked. She began to read.

" ... *You will understand that I was disquiet, that my fright at the sudden encounter with this terrible looking fellow had all but overtaken me. Yet, still I listened as his cold, chilling voice bade me follow him to the entrance to this Sanctuary, as he called it. I asked him where it lay.*

'You will find the door twixt the grave of your ancestor and the sword of burial. You must seal it from the invaders so that my lady's rest is not disturbed.'

Rebecca paused for dramatic effect. Drew looked at her impatiently.

"Well? Did she follow him? Did she find this place?"

"No. She was too frightened and the mist receded, just like with me. But that's why we have to go to Stoul. Uncle Henry says that is where the family crypt is. We have to go to the church and find the crypt, the graves and this door."

She looked up at him, closing the book. Drew rolled his eyes.

"Aw great! Not only do we have to go to the kirk, but we have to go poking about in the creepy part where all the dead people are. You sure know how to show a guy a good time, Rebecca McOwan."

He paused for a moment, before regarding Rebecca thoughtfully.

"One thing though. Interesting choice of phrase used by this Norseman. 'Your ancestor'."

Rebecca looked at him, puzzled, not comprehending his meaning. Drew elaborated.

"Singular. Ancestor. It might be nothing but the kirk at Stoul has been the burial place of your ancestors for hundreds of years, I think, right back beyond William Wallace and Robert the Bruce. There must be loads of graves there. Seems odd to imply only one. Maybe there's another one somewhere else."

"But he might just have meant a particular grave next to this sword. I'm sure we'll find something, I just feel it." Rebecca's eyes burned brightly as Drew brought the boat alongside a small jetty.

***

Walking fast, they climbed the path from the landing stage over the crest of a hill towards the small village of Stoul. The early morning sunshine caused the windows of the cold grey church to sparkle. Rebecca could see a smattering of people making their way from the direction of the village.

"So just how are we going to do this with nobody seeing us?" Drew was frowning. She noticed his eyebrows nearly meeting in the middle again.

"Do you know that when you –" Rebecca stopped in mid sentence. Drew's frown was replaced by puzzlement for a moment.

"What?" he asked, after a pause.

"Nothing," said Rebecca, hurriedly changing the subject.

"Look, let's sit on the back row and try and slip off unnoticed. This entrance or whatever must come out somewhere in the crypt, 'cause that's where all the McOwan chieftains are buried. We have to get in."

"We should wait until the end when everyone has gone." Drew had reached the stone wall at the lane to the church. He peered over.

"I expect they'll all go off for a sherry with the vicar after the service," said Rebecca.

"That's what mother always does at home."

Drew turned and scowled at her.

"This isn't England! No self-respecting Scot drinks sherry. And it's not the vicar, either – he's called the minister. Look, we'll just have to duck under the pew at the end and wait until everyone has gone out."

"McHarg drinks sherry, I've seen her," said Rebecca, smarting slightly. She made a face at Drew's back.

"She's no' a Scot, she's from another planet," muttered Drew. "She thinks Catholics are aliens. Come to think of it, she thinks Campbells are aliens".

They had arrived at the churchyard gate. People were standing around the entrance, talking in polite murmurs. They were all dressed in their Sunday best, among the gravestones. Rebecca scanned the outside of the church for signs of an entrance that might lead to the crypt.

"Do you know where the crypt is?" Rebecca asked Drew.

"Nope."

"Oh great!"

"I told you – I don't come to the kirk. There are doors inside but I don't know where they go… Probably to the minister's sherry store".

"Stop it!" hissed Rebecca.

"If you make us laugh, we're done for! We've got to be inconspicuous."

"I can't spell that – I'll just stay out o' the way."

Rebecca kicked him on the ankle.

"Ow!" He grimaced. "Do that and we'll certainly get spotted. People are looking."

Drew made an almost imperceptible movement of his head towards a small boy and his sister who had turned to watch them, alerted by Drew's yell. Rebecca smiled sweetly. The girl smiled back and looked away. The boy carried on staring, so Rebecca put out her tongue instead. The boy giggled and nudged his sister. This made Rebecca laugh too.

"Oh brilliant – now we've got an audience," muttered Drew. "Come on."

He grabbed Rebecca's elbow and led her into the dim interior of the church.

It was very old, dating from the early 12th century, with plain white walls and a cold tiled floor. The pews were laid out in conventional style, a central aisle leading towards a covered altar at the front, beside a wooden pulpit. Three doors led off in different directions, one on either side, and in the rear corner a smaller door. Drew pointed at the door in the centre on the far side and gestured that Rebecca should inspect it, while he headed for the other. Rebecca looked quickly to check that nobody had followed them inside before rounding the end of the pews. She tried the heavy iron latch. It would not budge. Checking over her shoulder again, she rattled it as hard as she dared but still it did not give.

Drew appeared at her shoulder.

"Just the door to the minister's room that side. Don't worry, he didn't see me. This won't open? Let me try." He grasped the latch in both hands and tried to force it up. There was a loud grating noise and it gave slightly but still refused to open.

"It must be locked," whispered Rebecca. "Where would we find the key? Maybe in the minister's room?"

The low murmur of voices drifted into the church behind them. Rebecca looked round.

"People are coming in – leave it!"

She dragged Drew away. The rest of the congregation was coming through the main door. As yet, nobody was looking their way. Rebecca and Drew slipped quietly into a pew at the back and sat down. Drew picked up a hymn book from the narrow shelf on the back of the pew in front and pretended to be reading.

"Master Campbell, how nice to see you – you've not been

a regular visitor." A voice came from the doorway at the side of the church. Rebecca and Drew turned simultaneously to see who was speaking. Drew coloured, self-consciously. A dark-haired man in his late twenties, dressed in a dark suit was smiling at them. He was quite good looking, decided Rebecca, in an understated sort of way.

"Hello, I'm Tom Gordon, the minister here." He was smiling at Rebecca. She blushed. His eyes were wide and unblinking.

"Oh! Er, Rebecca McOwan, I'm, er, staying with my uncle–"

"Ah, yes, Henry. A fine golfer … a Sunday golfer, I think. And are you enjoying your stay in the Highlands?"

"Yes, thank you, very much indeed." Rebecca blushed again under the intense, smiling gaze, not sure if there was some sort of veiled reproof towards her uncle in the reference to Sunday golf.

"So, have you picked out something you'd like us all to sing, Drew? Or are you catching up on the latest Good News?"

Drew started, looking bemused. Tom Gordon pointed to the hymn book Drew was holding, his eyebrows raised.

"Oh, er, that is, no… no, Mr Gordon – minister … sir."

"Well, you're both very welcome." Tom Gordon nodded and passed on. He shook hands with some of the villagers entering the church.

Rebecca nudged Drew.

"He's young to be a vicar, isn't he? I thought they were all old, grumpy and whiskery. They are where I live."

Drew made a face.

"He's very young, isn't he?" he mimicked. "You blushed! You fancy him!"

"I do not!" Rebecca jabbed him. "You can't fancy vicars, anyway, can you?"

"I certainly don't," smirked Drew. "The young zealot, my Da calls him. He's from Fort William, went to St Andrew's University and came back with a degree and God.

Well, I guess we're stuffed now, with you making eyes at him, we can't go unnoticed any more, can we? We won't get away without you two wanting to say goodbye."

"I did not make eyes at him!" Rebecca snapped. "You'll just have to slip off during the service to look for the key and make sure he doesn't notice – nor anyone else for that matter."

"Why me? This was your idea."

"Because …you're the male."

"Oh, and what ever happened to equality, then, Ms modern London lady?" It was Drew's turn to sneer.

"Women are the brains, men are the brawn. Behind every man, there's a woman telling him what to do – so my Aunt Kitty says," Rebecca said airily, smiling to herself. "And you're Scottish and downtrodden, as you're so fond of saying. Anyway, I thought you weren't scared?"

"Aw hush, will you?! I'll go, I'll go!" Drew held up his hands in resignation.

"Wouldn't want you to show yourself up in front of lover boy, anyway."

He ducked quickly to avoid a swipe from Rebecca. Since the congregation was now seated in front of them, Drew shuffled slowly along to the end of their row, nearest the wall and the door in the corner. As the organ struck up and the minister stepped forward, the congregation rose for the first hymn. Seizing the opportunity, Drew ducked below the level of the pews and scuttled on hands and knees towards the door.

Rebecca watched him go, nervously. She darted a look at the minister but neither he nor anyone else seemed to have noticed anything amiss. She watched the door close behind Drew. Turning back to her hymn book, hoping desperately that he would be back before anyone noticed, she tried to join in with the singing. However, when she opened her mouth, only a hoarse croak came out. She shut it again, rapidly.

The hymn ended and the congregation resumed their seats. Now, surely, the minister would see she was alone. Rebecca looked down at her hands, not daring to raise her head in case she caught Tom Gordon's eye. He began his sermon.

Rebecca was certain that at any moment they would be found out. She strained her ears to listen out for the door opening behind her. Every so often she glanced over her shoulder but the door remained resolutely closed.

She noticed the little boy was watching at her again, smiling. She put her tongue out at him, hoping it would cause him to look away. Luckily at that moment, his mother pulled him sharply round by the collar, scolding him through clenched teeth.

"Hsssst!"

Rebecca started at a sudden noise. Drew was at the part-opened doorway, beckoning to her to follow him. She made a face and shook her head quickly, turning back to check nobody had observed.

"Hssssssssssssst!" This time Drew was much louder. He beckoned insistently.

Rebecca realised the only way to stop him was to do as he asked. Fortunately, just then, the organ struck up for the second hymn and the congregation began to stand.

It was now or never.

She took a deep breath, dropped to the floor as Drew had done and crawled quickly along to the end of the pew. Checking that nobody was looking back in her direction, she scurried round the corner and through the door, verse one ringing out behind her.

The door closed with a dull thud.

"Come on, I've found it!" Drew was hurrying down a low passageway towards another door at the far end. Behind this, a stone staircase spiralled down into the gloom. The only light came from an arrow-slit window, the ceiling barely inches above their heads. Unhesitatingly, Drew headed down the steps two at a time. Rebecca followed him, more slowly, arriving in a slimy underground passageway. She uttered a cry of annoyance as her face was instantly covered by a huge cobweb.

Drew took a torch from his pocket and switched it on. The beam illuminated an iron gateway to another chamber. Drew was already at the gate. As he pushed it open, there was a loud grating noise that Rebecca felt sure must be audible from upstairs, although the hymn-singing was now muffled.

She winced and followed.

"Mind your head just here," came Drew's voice, as the torch beam was suddenly swung round into her face.

"Mind, I can't see with the torch –*ow!*" A sharp thump on her forehead told her she had come into sudden and painful contact with whatever Drew had been trying to help her avoid. "Ow!" she glared at him. "If you hadn't been shining that flippin' thing in my face, I might have seen that!"

"Sorry! Look here, this is the crypt – see the inscriptions … William Stuart McOwan, Laird of Rahsaig, born August 14th 1836, died June 21st 1898 … and here's his wife Mary, nee Balfour. What does nee mean?"

Her eyes growing accustomed to the gloom, Rebecca made out headstones and graves numbering upwards of thirty in this low chamber.

"It's French. It means that was her maiden name. It's eerie down here," she said, shuddering and drawing her jacket about her.

"Like some spooky ghost film."

"One of those ones where vampires emerge from the graves

and start sucking your blood, you mean?" said Drew, waving his arms above his head as if about to swoop down on her. The torch beam danced wildly.

"Stop it! I mean it, this place is really creepy – and it's cold and smells of mouldy corpses. Let's find the entrance to the Sanctuary and get out of here. I don't want to hang about any longer than we have to."

Rebecca and Drew examined the gravestones for names and the walls for anything resembling a doorway. As they searched, there were inscriptions going back to the Middle Ages, barely legible in places but recording the names, births and deaths of McOwans who had lived their lives long, long ago. There were others too: McDonalds, McLeods, Stuarts; all of them people who had amounted to something significant in their time.

"Not too many poor people in here," said Drew in his habitual mocking manner.

"You had to be at least a laird or a laird's wife to get your bones in this chamber."

"Well I can't see a doorway next to a sword anywhere," said Rebecca, dejected.

She sat down heavily on a gravestone. At that moment, there was a muffled grating sound at the door through to the church upstairs. It closed with a dull thud, followed by what seemed to be the sound of a key turning.

Drew jumped up and dashed through the chamber to the door.

"Hey! Wait!" he cried out.

"Shhh!" Rebecca rushed after him. She grabbed him, trying to stop him from hammering on the door.

"It might be the thieves, following us!"

Drew regarded her for a second then shook his head decidedly.

"We'd have seen them in the kirk, or on the loch. No, look

at the time! It must be the minister locking up after the service. We could be stuck in here for hours.

"HELP! OPEN THE DOOR!"

He hammered on the thick door, shaking the latch to see if it was indeed locked. It would not give.

"Whatever happens, we're in trouble," said Rebecca, biting her bottom lip.

"Reverend Gordon is going to be none too pleased when he finds us down here."

"Why shouldn't you visit the graves of your ancestors?" asked Drew, a sudden impudent smile breaking out over his face. They heard the key being reinserted in the lock and the door slowly opened again. Tom Gordon's face peered through.

"Young Campbell … Miss McOwan … you'd best be coming out." He paused for a second, clicking on a light. "And then you can be telling me what you were doing down here in the middle of morning service."

Rebecca swallowed nervously, glancing sideways at Drew as she passed through the doorway, not daring to look at Tom Gordon. To her amazement, Drew made no move to depart and was, instead, smiling at the minister. She feared the worst as he launched into his defence.

"I was showing the laird's niece where her ancestors lie. She was keen to visit the graves to pay her respects."

Rebecca closed her eyes, expecting a sharp rebuke to follow.

"Is that so? You did not mention it when you arrived. I would be happy to show you the crypt myself, Miss McOwan, follow me, please. The history is just wonderful."

To Rebecca's astonishment, Tom Gordon was now smiling at her. He placed a gentle hand on her back to invite her back into the crypt. Rebecca stole a quick glance at Drew, who smiled smugly back, out of sight of Tom Gordon. For the next few minutes, the young minister explained the history of the crypt and recounted the details of some of its inhabitants. He was most affable and was extremely well informed. By the time they re-entered the church upstairs and emerged back into the daylight, Rebecca was completely disarmed. She felt bold enough to ask the question which had been burning inside her.

"Do you know of somewhere called the Sanctuary, minister?"

Tom Gordon looked blank.

"Most churches are places of sanctuary. As to one place with that name, no, sorry."

As they made their way back over the hill to the boat, Rebecca was conscious that Drew was chuckling to himself. Guessing at his thoughts, she frowned and favoured him with a cold stare. He looked up innocuously.

"What?" he said, mustering as much innocence as he could. Rebecca was not taken in.

"You know very well what. You are going to tease me about the minister, only you probably can't think of anything sharp enough to annoy me."

"Ouch! Doesn't look as if I need to! Methinks the lady doth protest too much! And while we're at it, I would point out that it was only my incredibly quick thinking which dug us out of the hole you had got us into."

"Oh shut up, Campbell! Anyway, it's all pretty pointless, since we didn't find anything. We're back at square one."

CHAPTER 10

THE STORM

Salty Galbraith was the kind of Scotsman who featured in old postcards, caricaturing the wild Highlander of yore. A long red beard obscured his face below his nose, as well as a fair proportion above. A pipe protruded from somewhere in the middle. His eyes had been beaten into leathery slits in his ruddy visage by years at sea, squinting into the teeth of the gale. He sported the traditional kilt, which had the considerable benefit of hiding his whiskery knees from the world. To those who knew him, he was a man of few words; to strangers, he was silent.

"Afternoon, Salty. Beautiful day!" chirped Drew, airily, striding along the jetty and jumping down onto the bow of the boat where Galbraith was standing, filling his pipe and eyeing the world with silent disdain.

The *Hebridean Princess* was a vessel of some thirty metres, which had been making the crossing from Arisaig to the Islands of Rum, Eigg, Canna and Muck, for over thirty years. Galbraith was not the skipper. That honour belonged to Murdo Stuart, currently busy in the wheelhouse on the radio.

Galbraith chose not to register Drew's presence. His countenance changed as Rebecca's uncle appeared, however, drawing an almost imperceptible nod of recognition from the whiskery seaman. Henry nodded firmly and climbed aboard.

"Good to see you, Salty," he said. Galbraith gripped him in a firm handshake, looked him witheringly in the eye and grunted something gruff and incomprehensible. Once out of earshot, Rebecca nudged her uncle and whispered

"How come you're so honoured?"

Henry looked puzzled. Rebecca elaborated.

"He completely ignored everyone else but was almost gushing with you."

Henry smiled and waved her playfully forward.

"Mind your manners, you," he said, solemnly. "He may look a bit odd but a finer seaman you will never meet. A living legend in these parts. Nobody knows how long he's been sailing, because there's nobody left around here who can remember a time before. He taught me to sail when I was a lad and he was a veteran then. If the weather turns, you watch who the skipper turns to."

"But he looks really old," said Rebecca, eyeing the veteran sailor sceptically as he tied ropes at the stern.

"He is old," answered her uncle. "But that means he's experienced."

Rebecca detected a ring of reproof in Henry's tone and decided not to pursue it.

Minutes later, with gulls squawking overhead, the *Hebridean Princess* cast off from the pier. The majority of the passengers were, like themselves, bound for Rum Castle to see a performance of Shakespeare's Hamlet, to be put on in the grounds. Rebecca had not seen a Shakespeare play before and was not overenthused at the prospect but had been persuaded by Henry to try it. There was also the opportunity to explore Rum Castle and the boat trip was something Rebecca knew she definitely would enjoy.

The first half mile led out through the Sound of Arisaig, winding between small rocky islands. The hills and mountains behind them lazed in the afternoon sunshine. Seals basked on the rocks, their black, unblinking eyes following the boat with apparent disinterest. Henry pointed at some of the birds flying overhead and became rather excited about something he spotted in the distance, called the 'Great Northern Diver'. This elicited laughter from Rebecca. The sun turned the seas a brilliant azure blue and a brisk, fresh breeze carried a refreshing salty smack.

All in all, it was an idyllic afternoon.

"Now tell me that you still miss London," said Drew at Rebecca's shoulder.

"London can have nothing that's a patch on this."

Rebecca rested her chin on the boat rail, her gaze locking on a nearby seal.

"I s'pose it's not that bad all the time," she said and paused. "When I came here, I admit, I was pretty much expecting the worst. It was pelting down with rain, cold, bleak, remote and hardly the centre of the universe. Scotland has only ever been a place on the weather forecast with big black clouds over it. I was coming to stay with an uncle I'd not met for years, in a place I'd never seen. My brother was off to the Med, my parents to the Caribbean – how would you feel?"

She paused for a few seconds.

"But now … it's growing on me."

Drew was silent for a moment, before chuckling.

"You know what? I've never been to London," he said. Rebecca looked at him in disbelief.

"Seriously," he went on. "Actually, I've never even been to Glasgow. Fort William is the biggest town I've ever seen. And I tease you!"

"I guess that makes us even," smiled Rebecca. For the next few minutes they lapsed into silence, enjoying the scenery and the anticipation of sailing to the little islands of the Inner Hebrides.

"So, let's take stock of things," said Rebecca after a while.

"The thieves got away with the forged 'Flight of the Bonnie Prince'; Sibley went to Rum Castle and is now on his way to Barradale; we think they are stealing valuable artworks, replacing them with forgeries and that Sibley is involved; and the thieves may be operating from a boat and using diving equipment."

"And what about your creepy ghost friends?" asked Drew.

"I can't help thinking it's all somehow linked together," answered Rebecca. "Becca's journal; the paintings that look like me; the key to Becca's locker being left in my room; signs leading me to read and find things; and the fact that she had the same experiences with the Warrior and the Wolf. Somehow, what the thieves are up to is disturbing something from the past."

"And the past is speaking through you," said Drew, slowly. Rebecca shuddered.

"Blimey ... It's a bit spooky when you put it like that."

***

They rounded a huge buttress of vertical cliffs at the north-east of the Isle of Eigg, the halfway point of the voyage. Clouds were welling up, grey and impenetrable. The blue skies of the trip so far had vanished. The air had freshened considerably and, without the protection of the land mass of Eigg, the sea took on an entirely different character. The swell grew more intense and it was not very long before the boat was rolling and churning. Every so often, it would pitch into a wave causing a great plume of spray to crash over the deck.

The passengers gradually sought shelter in the cabin. Only a few, hardy souls remained on deck, braving the elements and rapidly falling temperature. Henry had disappeared inside some time ago and Rebecca now raised her eyebrows at Drew.

"Where's your stamina? First little bit of weather and you want to go inside. Salty will see us through." Drew nodded his head towards the wheelhouse. Looking up, Rebecca saw her uncle's prediction had proved correct. The old seaman was now wrestling with the wheel, a broad grin creasing his whiskery features. Occasionally he would emit a great roar as a particularly large wave bore down. Undeniably, their passage became steadier after he took the helm.

As another huge plume of spray doused them, though, she did not hesitate. "Well, I'm going inside!" she shouted above the roar of the sea and wind. "You suit yourself, Campbell."

Minutes later, aided by a steaming mug of tea, procured from the galley by her uncle, Rebecca was beginning to thaw out. About thirty people were crowded into the cabin, more than a few of them clearly not relishing the rolling of the boat. Occasionally, somebody would disappear outside and return a few minutes later, looking decidedly pale.

Oblivious to this, Rebecca grabbed a marmite sandwich and took a large bite.

Next to her, one man obviously not enjoying the trip and looking somewhat green around the gills, gulped and made a sudden dash for the door, clutching his hand to his mouth.

Rebecca quickly polished off the sandwich. Henry grinned. "That's showing off."

"So, has Mr Sibley identified everything in the collection?" she asked, changing the subject, her eyes fixed on her lurching mug of tea but her attention hanging on her uncle.

"I should think he's barely halfway through," answered Henry. "He has several houses to visit while he is up here."

"Has he finished at Rahsaig?" asked Rebecca.

"I'm waiting to see. He's verified the known works but I want to know what he thinks of some of the unattributed paintings."

"Do you mean Rebecca McOwan's paintings?" Rebecca held her breath.

"If that is who painted them, then yes. It's not certain and that's one point it would be interesting to get clarified. When the old manse burned down, some paintings went missing. No records were ever taken so we don't know what was lost."

"When was the fire?"

"1929. My father was too young to remember and my grandfather was hopeless with paperwork, so not much is known of where everything ended up."

Rebecca wanted to tell her uncle what she and Drew had discovered and to lay their suspicions before him but the experience with Constable Lennie had shown that Uncle Henry was a man of logic. She feared he would discount her theories and, in any case, explanations would necessitate divulging her strange experiences with Hakon and the warrior. She was certain that he would dismiss these as flights of fancy.

"What is there of the collection on Rum, Uncle?" she asked.

"For goodness sake, call me Henry," he smiled at her. "You make me feel old! Well, the Castle on Rum was once home to Lachlan McOwan, our Donald's brother, and the less honourable branch of the family. He won it in a wager with the owner, a McLeod. The McLeod was a bad lot too, much given to drink and gambling. He is said to have sold out to the English in 1746 after Culloden and he came to a murky end because of it. Nobody asked too many questions, I think, but it's fairly certain the locals did for him. Anyway, Lachlan swiped many of the family treasures and heirlooms and took them off to Rum with him. Most of the family silver is there. A few interesting other pieces too – some from your Princess legend."

Rebecca was agog. Henry continued.

"You remember the painting in the Great Hall? Well, a collar studded with jewels, said to be that of the wolf, is there, together with the Princess's burial mask."

"Can we see them?" Rebecca could hardly disguise her excitement.

"Yes, they're on display."

"Lachlan came to live at Rahsaig after Culloden, didn't he?" said Rebecca.

"After the death of Donald, he made himself Laird. I found an old journal written by Rebecca, Donald's daughter. She says nobody was left to oppose him. Lachlan banished her and her brother. He stole young Donald's birthright."

"I should be asking you about the family!" exclaimed Henry, smiling.

"This journal sounds interesting. So what else does Rebecca say about Lachlan?"

"Not much, other than he had been her father's good-for-nothing younger brother, who left home at sixteen to seek his fortune but would return when he needed money to borrow from their father. Rebecca hated him for the way he treated little Donald and herself. He imprisoned them in the manse, which is where she supposedly went insane."

"You don't believe it?"

"She doesn't seem mad in her journal. And her paintings are superb."

"You can still do amazing things when your mind is disturbed. Genius often lives on the edge of madness." Henry offered more tea, which Rebecca accepted gratefully.

"So is Rum Castle owned by our family now?" she asked.

"Unfortunately no, for it is magnificent and the island is a rare spot. As beautiful a place as I know on God's earth, although the rainfall is heavy, even for Scotland." He smiled.

"That is saying something," grinned Rebecca. "Even Drew admits the rain is bad here, although I expect he blames the English for it."

***

The boat ploughed on relentlessly through the churning seas, the hills of Rum now looming much larger and closer. In the galley the loudspeaker crackled into life, Murdo's whistling tones alerting the passengers to the possibility of disembarking into dinghies, should it prove too dangerous to put alongside the jetty. He requested that everyone put on a lifejacket, which was the cue for some nervous laughter and weak attempts at humour.

Conditions on deck had been made treacherous by the spray and driving rain, whipping down the Cuillin Sound from Skye. The storm was definitely gathering strength. In the galley, Murdo was talking to the coastguard over the radio, requesting updates on the weather. The afternoon already resembled evening, darkening skies bringing a premature end to the daylight.

The door to the galley was flung suddenly open, prompting a soaking for anyone in the immediate vicinity. The wind seared inside, bringing with it a bedraggled figure, which Rebecca recognised as Drew. He managed to close the door behind him and stood before Uncle Henry and Rebecca, dripping, gasping and laughing. His face was ruddy and alive.

"I think it means it out there, you know!" Drew unfastened his jacket and shook the water from his head, like a dog emerging from a river.

"Oh, thanks for that, I'm sure!" cried Rebecca, as spray hit her full across the face.

"Pillock!" added Uncle Henry, who did not escape, aiming a mock punch at Drew.

"Sorry!" said Drew, cheerfully. "I've come for my lifejacket."

"With any luck you'll sink under that weight of water," grumbled Uncle Henry, wiping his eyes.

***

The passengers edged warily along the slippery deck, shielding their faces against the driving rain, not helped by the rolling of the boat in the swell. They clung to the nearest solid object. Rebecca, Uncle Henry and Drew found themselves on the leeward side, where there was some shelter from the force of the elements.

"Your first Hebridean storm, niece!" laughed Uncle Henry above the roar of the wind.

"How do you like it?" Rebecca shot him a look of contempt.

Under Salty's expert steering, the boat edged closer to the small jetty at the end of Loch Scresort, an inlet of normally tranquil water below Rum Castle. It afforded some relief from the heavy seas but the swell was still enough for anxiety on the bridge. Waves surged against the jetty, dousing the cobbles. As the boat came within a few feet, one of the crew boldly leapt ashore, tightly grasping a rope. As he looped the end over an iron bulwark, two other crewmen scrambled along, dropping air-filled rubber buoyancy balloons over the side to cushion any impact against the sea wall. Murdo was at the gangplank, waving the passengers forward.

"Quickly, please folks! When I give the word, you're going to have to walk the plank and jump, one by one! Steady as ye can, Salty, man!"

"This should be fun!" shouted Drew as the first few passengers began, hesitantly, to shuffle forward. Murdo Stuart grasped them by the arm and with a yell of encouragement, launched them towards the jetty. The first man stumbled on landing but regained his balance and lined up to help the next. Many people were tentative and nervous and had to be coaxed and cajoled by Murdo.

"Anyone who doesnae fancy the jump can stay aboard but we're headed back to Arisaig!" He cried. Despite the churning seas, several souls were inclined to accept this proposal and retreated to the safety of the galley. Rebecca found herself at the front of the queue.

"Ready, lassie?" said Murdo, holding out his arm. She had not been exactly relishing the prospect and gave a quick nervous smile.

"What the heck, I'm soaked already," she said, with more bravado than she truly felt. She would privately admit to a healthy respect for the sea. Taking a deep breath, and wondering, fleetingly, on how many more occasions during this holiday she would have to confront her fears, she stepped forward and grabbed Murdo's arm to steady herself.

"Steady there, lass, wait till she rolls up again and then – jump!"

Rebecca started to ask why it was that men always gave boats and vehicles female identities but was cut short as Murdo shouted "jump!" The boat pitched towards the jetty and she leapt into the air, landing with rather less aplomb than she had hoped in front of the watching audience. As she tried to stand up, she stumbled and twisted awkwardly on her ankle, letting out a sharp cry of pain.

"Very elegant, milady," shouted Drew, landing next to her. Rebecca was peeved to observe his sure-footed landing, which only increased her own embarrassment. He bent down to help her. Gingerly, she put the damaged ankle to the ground, but a sharp stab of pain caused her to stumble again.

"Come on, let's get you inside," said Henry at her other elbow. "We'll get some ice to stop the swelling."

"Or you could dip it in the sea instead," offered the ever cheerful Drew, helpfully.

CHAPTER 11

RUM CASTLE

The castle on the Isle of Rum had been destroyed and rebuilt more than once during the centuries, as the island had been fought over by generations of Clans. It now stood on the shore at the end of an inlet called Loch Scresort.

The McOwans had been Lairds of Rum for a while in the time of James, or Bloody Jim McOwan, Donald's great-grandfather. The island changed hands several times during skirmishes with the McLeods, until the McOwans finally lost control on the death of Lachlan in 1751. In more recent times, it had, since 1947, been owned by the Balloch family of wealthy Edinburgh bankers.

Ungracious questions had been asked in the local area as to why Hamish and Ludmilla Balloch, the present owners, had invited the touring Camden Players from London to perform in the castle grounds. It was muttered that they would have difficulty locating the theatre listings in the newspaper, let alone read Shakespeare. The Ballochs made little contact with the local community, keeping themselves to themselves and discouraging visitors to Rum with large fences around the estate and charging admission fees. Consequently, the locals were rather inclined to find fault with them.

After a brief introduction to the Ballochs from Henry, Rebecca was shown into a small sitting room. A bucket of ice and a towel quickly appeared and she sat, applying a cold compress to her injured ankle. It was apparent that the room was serving as a temporary costume and prop store to the actors.

Large wooden boxes spewed forth piles of clothing, seemingly opened in great haste. Labels on them referred to scenes, sets and characters. 'Hamlet' read the label on one casket, 'Ophelia' on another. Her attention was drawn particularly to a casket marked 'Ghost'. She hobbled over to it. The chest contained a long grey shroud and a black mask with brass cheekplates and eyelets, sufficiently ghoulish to evoke a shudder. She closed the lid. As she looked up again, Drew stood in the doorway.

"Rumour is we'll be staying here tonight. A big storm is forecast and, if that hits, no boat will leave Arisaig tonight – far too dangerous. Force nine, they reckon."

"Are there enough rooms and beds here for everyone?" asked Rebecca.

"Doubt it. There must be fifty of us. We'll end up crashing on the floor – play up the injured ankle and they'll probably take pity and give you a stateroom."

Rebecca put out her tongue at him. She paused, before a look of intent came over her.

"At least it will give us a chance to do a bit of snooping around, although you'll have to do it. I can't get about unless this ankle improves dramatically." She lifted up the cold compress to inspect it. She shrugged. "At least it hasn't swollen up too badly."

"The play will not take place in the grounds, you will no doubt be surprised to hear," said Henry, ironically, from the doorway.

"The cast are improvising, as befits the true dramatist, and will use the ballroom instead. Due to start in ...one hour exactly." He tapped his watch and smiled.

"And I was so looking forward to a warm summer evening outdoors," said Drew.

"Is it true that we are to stay here tonight, Uncle dear?" asked Rebecca brightly. "And miss dear old Miss McHarg's cheerful company tomorrow at breakfast?"

"That will do," reproached Henry. "In answer to your question, it does look as if we will be here overnight. And, since the rain is not about to let up, I'm afraid that a walk round the island is also off. Mind you, we'll probably have a Hebridean storm to enjoy as well as the play."

"Every cloud has a silver lining, hey? Mind you, up here every cloud has another ten behind it – how can you stand the weather?" grumbled Rebecca.

***

With Rebecca restricted to her armchair, Drew slipped out to explore the castle. He was keen to discover the mask and collar, or anything vaguely connected to the McOwans. The poor weather having confined everyone indoors, he was far from alone wandering around and could therefore avoid arousing undue suspicion.

The ground floor rooms turned up very little of interest, so Drew went up the sweeping staircase to the first floor, where a gallery overlooked the main hall. An imposing statue of a Viking warrior dominated the head of the stairs. It was surprisingly lifelike and clothed in coarse woollen leggings and frock coat, with a heavy broadsword clasped in both hands, the point resting on the floor at his feet. Drew detected a passing resemblance to the warrior with Hakon in the Princess legend and decided to take a closer look. Below the statue was a plate which bore an inscription.

Knut the Strong, fabled Viking bodyguard of Princess Immelda of Norway. Legend has it that he guards an unknown cave where his mistress was buried, together with the fierce wolf Hakon. The Princess was drowned in Loch Nevis, on her way to her marriage to the Machoiann, Angus of Rahsaig in the Eighth Century.

"Are you the guy who's been scaring our English?"

whispered Drew, leaning close to the statue. The visor looked back at him, impassive. "Pick on someone your own size, Knut the Strong."

"Not one of our interactive exhibits, I'm afraid, sir," said a kindly voice. Drew straightened with a start and coughed self-consciously. An elderly lady, whose sweatshirt sported the legend 'Rum Castle Guide', was smiling indulgently at him. She reminded him of an aunt who lived in Fort William and always fed him ginger cake.

"Oh! Ah – just messing with old Knut, here." Drew smiled weakly and turned quickly to go back down to the hall and hide his embarrassment among the people milling around. He was glad that Rebecca had not witnessed his gaffe but, on reaching the bottom stair, ran into a smirking Henry.

"Scaring statues and old ladies, hey Drew?"

Drew blushed and bade a hasty retreat into an adjoining room. Once through the door, he realised this was the main drawing room which he had missed earlier. There was a grand piano but what immediately caught his eye was infinitely more interesting.

Next to the fireplace in a glass display case was the wolf's collar.

He moved quickly forward and read the legend next to it.

Eighth-Century Viking – Collar of fabled Hakon the Wolf, guardian to the tomb of Princess Immelda of Norway. Believed to have come to Rum with Lachlan McOwan in 1739.

Red and green gemstones were sewn into the worn and faded leather collar. It looked identical to the painting at Rahsaig. Alongside it was another display case with something else that grabbed Drew's attention.

Viking burial mask, Eighth Century. Reputed to be that of Princess Immelda of Norway.

The mask was eerie, made of leather and bronze, dulled in colour by the passage of time. There were openings for the eyes and mouth and simple, subtle patterns etched into the cheeks and forehead. At the corner of either eye, Drew noticed faint circular patterns.

***

Drew arrived back in the sitting room to find Rebecca in a state of great animation.

"Come in, quick! Shut the door!"

"What is – " Drew began as he hurriedly clicked the door shut. Rebecca did not wait.

"You'll never guess what I've found – this is the actors' costume store – just open that!" She pointed to a chest by the window, her face shining with excitement. Drew raised the lid. Inside, under a grey blanket, was diving equipment.

"There's a full suit here, and a tank!" He turned to look at Rebecca in astonishment.

"Now what on earth would a diving suit be doing in the costume store of a theatre company, putting on Hamlet?"

"We read Hamlet at school last term and I don't remember there being a part for a diver," said Rebecca. "Maybe our thieves are here? They might be involved with the Players."

They looked at one another, barely able to contain their excitement.

"Do you suppose they are after anything here on Rum?" Drew took a few paces towards the window. He looked at the diving equipment and then back at Rebecca.

"Sibley's been here and the mask and the collar are here, aren't they? Did you see them?"

"Aye, in the drawing room."

"I spoke with Uncle Henry while you were out and the

latest plan is for the boat to pick up *everyone* tomorrow morning, actors included. That means if it is something to do with the Players and they intend to steal anything, they'll have to do it tonight. We must stay up and keep watch – all night if necessary."

"But first we've got this Shakespeare to get through," said Drew, moodily.

"Shakespeare is all sex, murder and intrigue, according to Uncle Henry," said Rebecca. Drew brightened in an instant.

"Oh well that sounds all right – maybe it won't be so bad after all!"

***

A bell shrilled loudly in the hall where the audience were awaiting the performance.

The storm raging outside had fuelled the sense of drama and atmosphere and, despite their apprehension at the prospect of three hours of Shakespeare, Rebecca and Drew were both in a state of great expectation as the opening curtain-up drew closer. Rather than being due to a sudden appreciation for the Bard, this owed more to their recent discoveries.

"Three minutes to curtain up," called a voice from the entrance to the ballroom.

"We should find our seats," said Henry, who had appeared next to them and now helped Rebecca limp through the crowd of people gathered in the hall. They made their way into the makeshift auditorium and sat down. Rebecca leafed through a programme absently. Suddenly, she caught her breath and grabbed Drew's arm.

"Look!" she whispered, urgently. She pointed to a photo of the cast. Drew looked, uncomprehending and shrugged his shoulders.

"It's him!" she hissed. "That's the face I saw at the window, I'm sure of it!"

Drew started in astonishment.

"He's in the play?"

"He must be! And that would explain the diving gear, don't you see?"

"Shhh!" Her voice had risen. Drew looked swiftly around to check that nobody was listening to them. Henry was deep in conversation with a man at the end of their row.

"If you're right, we could really be onto something here." Drew's face was serious and the gravity of the situation that was starting to unfold began to dawn on Rebecca.

"We are going to have to be really, *really* careful."

The lights dimmed, the curtain rose and the play began. Rebecca was agog to see whether her intruder of a few nights ago would appear and scrutinised each new arrival on stage intently, paying little attention to the play itself.

There is an early scene where the ghost of Hamlet's father appears. When this scene began the figure of the ghost suddenly rose from a seat in the audience and walked right past them. It was Drew's turn to gasp. He turned and whispered excitedly.

"The ghost is wearing the mask!"

Rebecca look at the black and brass mask but the ghost was past her too quickly to be able to identify the markings Drew had described.

"We'll have to check their props store," she whispered. "I looked in the box marked 'Ghost' and there was a mask there too. Perhaps they'll swap a fake one for the real one."

The scene continued but unfortunately the ghost did not return and quickly left the stage at the back. By the time the interval arrived, Rebecca had not seen her intruder and was becoming frustrated. After the lights came back up, she stared at every person who came by, until Drew had to nudge her.

"Stop it!" he growled. "You'll have people wondering what's wrong with you. And suppose the guy sees you? He'll recognise you too, won't he?"

Rebecca's face went white and a shiver ran down her back. She looked at Drew in alarm.

"I hadn't thought of that. You don't think he's seen me already, do you? Perhaps that's why he hasn't appeared."

"Don't be daft. Look, let me see that programme again."

They pored over the programme, flicking back and forth to find any references to the cast, or photos. All of a sudden, Rebecca gave a hollow laugh and tapped the bottom of a page. She pointed to an advert.

"Well, well! Sibley's Antiques of Holborn Passage, London, are the gracious sponsors. What a surprise! He's definitely tied up in this. There are just too many coincidences."

"Ha! They have invited two performers from a French Mime Company to join them on the tour... " Drew broke off in mid sentence, gave a low whistle and pointed at the other page.

"That's why we haven't noticed your man yet. Look, he's the ghost."

He pointed at a picture of the intruder identified by Rebecca. "So he's the one wearing a mask. Convenient for stealing the real one, hey?"

"Perhaps he has already switched them." Rebecca looked closely at the photo. "This one doesn't have those markings you mentioned."

Drew looked over her shoulder. "I'll nip out and see if it's still there. I bet they are after it. It's over a thousand years old, according to the legend and that must make it worth a fortune."

He did his best to leave the room unobtrusively. Many of the audience had moved outside to the hall, talking and sipping at drinks. It was not difficult to slip through unnoticed. The drawing room was still open, so he went inside, trying to adopt the casual air of somebody wandering around, disinterestedly whiling away the interval.

He breathed a sigh of relief. The genuine mask was still in its place.

The bell shrilled, recalling the audience for the second half. Drew waited as long as he could, half in the hope that the ghost might appear and attempt to swap the masks. The hall was empty by the time he eventually re-emerged. As he passed the end of the stairway, he looked up at the gallery above and his eye fell on the statue.

Back in his seat, Drew tugged excitedly at Rebecca's sleeve.

"What is it? Has the mask been switched?"

"No, it's not that."

"Then what are you so worked up about?"

"You remember I told you about the statue of old Knut?"

"The one you talked to?"

"You've been talking to Henry. Anyway, never mind that. I just saw it move!"

Rebecca's mouth fell open slightly. She regarded Drew with disbelief.

"Drew, statues do not move. That is why they are statues. They stand still ... like statues."

"I know that! I swear to you, Knut scratched his ear."

"Shhh!" A lady behind them hissed loudly. Henry turned and frowned disapprovingly at Rebecca, who reddened. Desperate to exchange theories, they were compelled to watch the second half in silence. Each was thinking up wild elaborate theories as to why a statue might move. Little of their attention was devoted to the dramatic conclusion of Hamlet, their interest not even kindled by the bloody, climactic swordfight.

When the performance finally ended and they rose to leave, they were at last able to whisper to one another.

"Either you were seeing things, or the statue isn't real." Rebecca was the first.

"It isn't real and I'll tell you what I think it is." Drew opened the programme and flicked through the pages until he came to the picture of the entire cast. He began to read.

" 'The Camden Players are delighted to welcome our friends Serge Balatte and Auguste Lemerre from the famous Parisian Troupe of St Denis, artistes schooled in the renowned tradition of French mime.' There!"

Rebecca looked at him as if he had taken leave of his senses. Drew tapped the page, as if for emphasis.

"Mime artists! Knut is a Frenchman in drag. These guys can stand stock still for hours. Your thief stands still all day, then goes stealing after everyone has gone to bed."

"Surely not? You're just trying to justify why you were talking to a statue. Think about it – they would have to replace the real statue without anyone noticing, hide that somewhere and then stand there all day, right through until nightfall when they could swap it back. I mean, the guy couldn't even go for a pee!"

"Well maybe he has a pee bag strapped to his leg – I don't know but, if it isn't an actor, and I did see it move, then that means it's something else … something supernatural …"

They looked at each other for a second or so before shaking their heads in unison, dismissing this immediately.

"I'm going to go and prod him," said Drew. "That'll prove it."

"Mind the pee bag," murmured Rebecca.

Just at that moment, Henry broke off from a conversation he had been holding with Hamish Balloch and came over.

"Right, you two. Time to sort out the sleeping arrangements."

Rebecca opened her mouth to protest at this inconvenient

interruption but closed it when she saw the look of intent on her Uncle's face. Ludmilla Balloch had appeared at Henry's shoulder and was studying them with a look of such intense condescension that Rebecca found herself looking down at her feet, to avoid the gaze. Drew, however, seemed quite oblivious, his attention diverted to their fellow audience members. He was wondering where they would all be able to sleep.

"Mrs Balloch will show you to your rooms."

Ludmilla stood expectantly, the look of superiority unwavering. She gave the impression of someone used to issuing rather than receiving instructions and possessed a manner which could definitely be described as haughty. The generosity and hospitality of her husband in opening their home to the players and audience for the night might not, Rebecca suspected, have enjoyed his wife's complete approval. Having studied Rebecca and Drew intently, she raised her eyebrows a fraction of an inch, turned abruptly on her heel and strode off towards the stairs.

"I guess that's our cue to follow," muttered Drew, out of Henry's earshot.

CHAPTER 12

IN THE DEAD OF NIGHT

A large grandfather clock at the foot of the stairway struck midnight, the chimes reverberating through the darkened castle. As the last note faded, silence fell.

The thick stone walls muffled the noise of the storm, although did not stop brilliant flashes of lightning penetrating inside. The storm's ferocity had waned; nevertheless it was raining steadily and the wind still howled round the castle walls.

Rebecca got out of bed, put on her jumper and limped over to the door. As Drew had guessed, she had been fortunate enough to be allocated one of the few single rooms. Elsewhere, most people were billeted together. Drew was in a room with ten others, the largest group of all, camping out on a mattress on the floor. This situation had dismayed them both, due to the severe limitation it put on his ability to slip out unobserved.

They had been desperate to see the man who had played the ghost of Hamlet's father, to ascertain if he was the intruder from Rahsaig. Neither could claim a positive sighting before they were forced to turn in but Drew was hopeful that one of his room-mates might prove to be the man himself.

Rebecca's ankle was still painful, although she was now able to put her complete weight down and could walk slowly. She was determined to stay awake, in case the thieves made any move that evening. She left her door slightly ajar, pulled up a chair and sat where she could see the top of the stairs. She retrieved her duvet from the bed and wrapped it around her shoulders and legs to keep warm. It was cold in the castle, and she could see condensation as she breathed out. As she peered through the door, a head popped round, causing her to cry out in surprise.

"Shhh!" Drew came quickly through the door and pushed it to.

"What on earth … !"

"Shh! We don't want to be heard, do we?" he hissed.

"We don't want to be discovered, either, do we? What will Uncle Henry say if he catches you in my room in the middle of the night?"

Drew paused, sudden realisation dawning. Rebecca thought she detected a slight blush.

"I hadn't thought of that. Don't s'pose he'd be too pleased, would he? Nor Mrs Balloch!"

"It's no joke – and I can't say I'm too pleased about having some hairy Scotsman barging into my room, either. Where are your manners – don't you knock? Anyway, how did you manage to get out of your room without being seen?"

"No problem, as it happened. The door doesn't shut because the lock is broken and I am sleeping right at the end. The guy next to me was this great fat geezer who was snoring loud enough to wake the dead. He blocked me from sight from the rest of the room. It was really easy to slip out. So – anything gone bump in the night, yet?"

"Nothing – except you." Rebecca hunched back into her chair and pulled the duvet around her. Drew pulled the door open and peered out.

"Right. You stay here and keep an eye out. I'm going down to look for ghosts."

Before she could open her mouth to protest, he was at the top of the stairs. She watched him crouching low and checking there was nobody about before he edged forward and disappeared from view. She left the door open a narrow crack and sat back to keep watch.

Drew had slipped back into his clothes before leaving his room but had left off his shoes, for fear of making a noise. As he tiptoed down the icy cold stone stairs, he was beginning to regret this.

Halfway down, his eyes gradually becoming accustomed to the gloom, he peered around the hall. The moon provided no light tonight. Shadowy pools lurked in every corner and doorway, impenetrable and unsettling. Drew did not sense that he was being watched but something indefinable made him feel uneasy. His pulse quickened as he reached the bottom of the stairs and he went quickly over to the door to the drawing room, seeking the safety of the shadows. Nothing was stirring anywhere in the castle. It was so quiet that he felt sure he would have heard someone turn over in bed in one of the rooms upstairs.

He made a quick tour of the drawing room. Nothing was missing. Through the window, the sea had calmed a little, although there was still a heavy swell.

Drew came back out into the hall and sat down on a chair against the wall. His eyes roamed around the gloomy interior. He was disappointed to find nothing, although he was not altogether certain what he would have done, had the thieves been at large.

As he looked upstairs, though, he realised at once what had caused his unease.

The Statue of Knut was no longer at the head of the stairs.

Drew leapt to his feet. The plinth on which the statue had stood was still there but the statue had gone.

What was going on? Despite what Rebecca had told him about her encounters with the ghostly Viking and Wolf, Drew would not believe that anything supernatural was at play. He firmly believed a moving statue could only be one of the thieves dressed up.

His grandfather had always told him that a logical explanation exists for everything. "When you have discounted the impossible, whatever remains, however improbable, must be true."

Drew turned suddenly at a noise from the end of the passageway.

Ducking back into a recess, he peered cautiously out, the blood thumping in his temple.

He strained his eyes but it was too dark to see any further than a few feet away.

Something heavy was scraping across the wooden floorboards, coming his way.

In panic, he realised it was now too late to flee for the safety of Rebecca's room without being observed.

The noise was closer and louder.

A shadow fell over him.

In trepidation, he slowly looked up at the huge figure of a Viking.

Drew gave an involuntary gasp. His heart hammering in his chest, he pressed himself back into the recess as far as he could. He held his breath and shut his eyes tightly, praying he would not be discovered.

Time seemed to freeze.

After what to Drew seemed like a lifetime, the shuffling footfall moved on past him. It gradually died away along the passage and he felt safe enough to open his eyes. He peered carefully around the edge of the recess, just in time to see the Viking lumbering around a corner. He leaned against the wall and took a couple of long, deep breaths. Gathering his wits again, he rushed up into Rebecca's room and pulled the door almost to behind him. He turned to make sure he had not been observed.

"What – who – er, oh it's you" said Rebecca, who had clearly been asleep. She quickly rubbed her eyes in an attempt to hide the fact. Drew was too excited and breathless to have noticed, however, and immediately launched into the tale of the moving Knut.

"It has to be one of the thieves," he said finally.

"But are they stealing the statue or is the man pretending to be the statue the one doing the stealing?" He kept an eye out through the crack in the door as he whispered.

"You saw nothing downstairs?"

"Nothing. The mask and collar were still there, there was no sign of the real Knut and nobody was about. It would take at least two blokes to carry that thing."

"Why would they steal it?" Rebecca furrowed her brow.

"It isn't old or supposed to be valuable, or anything is it? If you ask me, I think it's just put on display to show what Knut looked like. The clothes are probably worth more than the statue. I hate to say it but your mad idea about Knut being a thief must be right."

Drew turned back to face her.

"He can't be working alone, because he'll need help to put the real one back."

They were quiet for a few moments, puzzling what to do next.

"Are you sure the mask and the collar are still in place?" whispered Rebecca.

"Well, it was dark but I'm fairly sure. I could go down and check again." There was a slight nervous edge in his voice as he suggested this. He turned back to the door and peered out through the narrow opening. All at once, his arm started waving frantically, beckoning Rebecca forward.

"What on earth –" Rebecca started to speak but what she saw through the gap in the doorway caused the words to stop in her throat.

In the shadowy passageway by the top of the stairs, Knut the Strong was standing just a few metres from the door. Rebecca gasped.

As they watched, the huge, menacing Viking turned and trudged slowly and silently towards them. The massive bulk was clothed in a long black sackcloth coat, with dulled steel epaulettes and armguards. The face was hidden behind a visor, attached to the famous horned Viking helmet. Rebecca feared it had heard them and was coming to the room.

But it stopped. For what seemed like an eternity, the warrior stood in the semi-darkness, staring intently down to the hall below. Behind the door, Drew and Rebecca hardly dared to breathe. The slightest creak of a floorboard or noise, now, would give them away.

A second man appeared out of nowhere and joined the Viking. He whispered something into his ear and disappeared swiftly downstairs. In his slow measured tread, the warrior followed.

Drew turned to Rebecca, his expression awestruck. For a few seconds, neither of them could find anything to say. Eventually, Rebecca shook her head in disbelief. "You have to pinch yourself to remind you it's a Frenchman dressed up," she breathed.

"I have to go back down and see what they're up to. We have to know."

Drew looked none too certain that he felt this was sensible. Rebecca puffed out her cheeks. There did not seem to be any alternative. She put a hand on Drew's arm.

"Don't do anything daft. And whatever you do, don't let them see you. We can go to Uncle Henry in the morning and get the police involved."

She eyed him anxiously as she said this. For the first time that she could remember, his usual light-hearted air seemed to have deserted him and he looked uncertain. He set his face into a determined grimace and put a hand on the door handle. With just a fraction of a second's hesitation, he was gone.

CHAPTER 13

STEALING STATUES

Rebecca woke with a start. She was still huddled in her chair and wondered how long she had been asleep. Her neck was painful and stiff. The room was very cold, although from the noises now emanating from the radiator, she guessed the heating was starting up. She wondered where Drew was and checked her watch.

Horrified, she saw it was now just after seven in the morning.

What had happened? Why had Drew not come back and woken her?

Light was seeping through the thick curtains at her window. She leapt to her feet, forgetting her injured ankle and immediately crumpled as a stab of pain shot up her leg. She just managed to grab a chair to prevent herself falling to the floor. She hobbled to the door and looked out. Sunlight was streaming onto the landing and she could make out voices downstairs. Hamish Balloch and his wife were talking about the breakfast arrangements for their impromptu guests and instructing the cook to make preparations. Rebecca shuffled over to the balustrade at the top of the staircase and peered down.

There was no sign of Drew but the statue was back in place.

She was about to go inspect it when her Uncle's voice stopped her short.

"My! Up and about early, aren't we?" he said, cheerfully. "I thought I should go and help with the feeding of the five thousand – show willing and all that. How's the ankle this morning?"

"Er, oh, sore but better, thanks," Rebecca stuttered, unnerved by her uncle's unexpected appearance and his liveliness at such an hour. She smiled weakly.

"I – I was looking for an empty bathroom".

"Down the end there and on the right, I think, for the ablutions," he offered helpfully and went downstairs.

Rebecca paid rather less attention than usual to bathroom preparations that morning. She was desperate to know what Drew had discovered and what had happened in the night. She was annoyed that she had let herself fall asleep and also that he had not woken her to tell her anything. This led her to an entirely different concern, that perhaps he had not been able to tell her because he had been discovered and prevented from returning upstairs. A feeling of alarm gripped her, as a vision of Drew lying somewhere, having been hit over the head, passed through her mind. Or perhaps he had been discovered and taken prisoner?

"Now you are being silly," she muttered. She must remain calm and rational. The more likely scenario was that he, like herself, had simply fallen asleep somewhere. Dismissing her fears as the product of her active imagination, she faced the bathroom mirror.

As she returned from the bathroom, fully dressed, Rebecca's attention was drawn once more to the statue of Knut. She took a deep breath and went over to examine it more closely. A few paces short of it, she hesitated, suddenly fearful.

What if it was still a man in disguise?

She stopped, eying the statue warily, wondering whether she should wait for somebody else to come by. Narrowing her eyes, she scanned for anything which would give it away. Knut the Strong remained absolutely still, without a tremor of movement and stared back from behind his steel visor.

If it was one of the French mime artistes, he was an excellent actor.

Rebecca was almost certain, however, that this was the real statue. Where there should have been flesh around the neck below the visor, she could only detect a grey substance, which did not look human. Holding her breath, she took a pace forward and reached out her hand – cold and definitely not a man.

Breathing a huge sigh of relief, Rebecca stood back and smiled at her own fears.

The thieves must have replaced the statue during the night, she reasoned. She frowned. That would mean, surely, that they had achieved their aim and that Drew would almost certainly have seen them doing it.

Where was Drew? Rebecca was peeved he had not yet appeared. If the thieves had been successful, this would mean the mask and collar had been replaced.

Her attention was drawn by more people talking. An enticing smell of frying bacon wafted upstairs and she realised how hungry she was. Some people passed by behind her on their way downstairs and she started to follow them.

Rebecca entered the dining room, where breakfast had been laid out on a long table. Given the unforeseen circumstances which had compelled the audience to stay overnight, Rebecca marvelled at the extent of what was on offer this morning. There were cereals, breads, jams and marmalades and a very impressive array of hot dishes. She noticed a large dish of bacon, which she had smelled upstairs and made herself a bacon roll. Over by the window, her Uncle was chatting to some people she did not recognise. There was still no sign of Drew.

She was becoming quite concerned now.

Another group entered the room, leaving the door open behind them. Rebecca began to grumble inwardly at the draught of cold air, when she saw two men struggling across the Hall with one of the large wooden boxes of theatre costumes.

They came out of the room which had served as the store and were making their way towards the main door. The box was evidently very heavy, as it seemed to require a significant effort to move it.

Rebecca was about to turn away when, from behind them, appeared the shaggy head of Drew. He did not see Rebecca, rather more preoccupied with what the men were up to and who was in the hall. She watched, barely able to suppress a giggle as he tiptoed out of the door, hopping quickly and rather comically in just bare feet on the cold floor. He disappeared from her line of vision in the direction of the stairs.

Rebecca turned towards the French windows, relieved he had come to no apparent harm. Outside, the sun was beaming down, the storm having blown itself out during the night. A man opened the French windows and Rebecca followed a group onto a large raised patio area, looking down over a stone balustrade to Loch Scresort and the sea. She was now able to admire the full splendour of the Island of Rum.

"This island is a bit of a well-kept secret," said Henry, gravitating towards his niece as she limped down some steps and onto the lawn, biting into her bacon roll as she went.

"Not many people come here, since there are no hotels on the island. There are some beautiful mountains, though, just above the castle here."

He paused to look up at the mountains, soft and green in the morning sunshine.

"The Rum Cuillin – where I saw my first Golden Eagle. Came over the top of a ridge and there he was, not twenty metres away, a real beauty."

Rebecca smiled to herself. She took a long breath of fresh morning air.

"A rare spot, though – as you like to say." She tried to mimic his accent.

"So where's our Campbell this bright, sunny morn?" asked Henry, triggering an immediate gulp from Rebecca.

"Oh, er, he's ... I think he's overslept... haven't seen him yet." She did not sound terribly convincing, even to herself. Luckily, at that moment, Drew appeared in the doorway of the French windows and waved merrily. He bounded down the steps.

"And a braw bricht mornin' to ye!" he chirped, in his best Rob Roy accent.

"How are we today? Where did the storm go?"

"Did you sleep okay, young Drew? You certainly slept long enough – the boat's due soon. I'm going to get one of those bacon butties Rebecca has. Can I get you one?"

"Aye, that'd be great, thanks." He paused until Henry had moved out of earshot and then turned, animatedly to Rebecca.

"So, what happened then?" She asked in a low whisper.

"Well, you are not going to believe it. I've only just got out of the room – that's why I'm late down."

"I know. I saw you coming out after those blokes with the crate."

"Yeah, well, I went down last night and waited in the drawing room. I don't know where those two guys went. There was nobody around for ages but the mask and collar have been swapped! My, it was cold! I didn't have anything on my feet, either."

Rebecca suppressed a smile, remembering his exit from the costume store just a few minutes previously. Drew continued.

"I did some poking about in that store room. Well, I found Knut there, the real Knut – that is, the real *statue* of Knut. They put him behind the curtains. So I figured that if I waited, they were bound to come back. I hid behind that screen thing in the far corner and covered myself over with some bits of the costumes. Anyway, about two o'clock, I know it was then because the clock in the hall had just struck, I heard voices in the hall. Sure enough, two blokes came in."

"Was one of them the ghost?"

"It was too dark to tell. They had torches too. I kept my head down but I could just about see what they were up to. One had just swapped the mask and collar and I saw him put them in a crate. They got old Knut out from behind the curtains and took him out. They were very quiet. I guessed they were taking him back upstairs. They were soon back. One of them was one of the French geezers – he had this really thick accent but the other was English. Then – and this is the bit you'll like – they started talking about the robberies. We have been right all along. They are forging things and stealing the originals. The idea is that nobody notices the real ones have gone until it's too late. And, here's the thing; Sibley *is* in on it. I heard the English one say that something had to be at Sibley's shop by such and such or it would miss the shipment abroad."

Rebecca let out a short yell of triumph.

"I knew it!" she smiled, her eyes ablaze. "Go on – what else?"

"They're doing the forgeries at the old ruin near Rahsaig. We'll have to go and suss it out. Some bloke is camped there, doing the paintings. It's the perfect place, if you think about it. Halfway between Loch Nevis and Loch Hourn in the middle of nowhere – nobody ever goes up there."

"So is that where the boat we saw was headed?" They wandered slowly round the velvet lawns, careful not to stray into earshot of any of their fellow guests. Rebecca kept a watchful eye on the French windows for the return of her uncle.

"Must be. Those blokes are going to the Manse tomorrow to pick up some more stuff and take it to what they called the 'loading point'. They didn't say where that was. They mentioned Barradale and a cave. Maybe that's the same cave we've been trying to find, if it's the one your friend Knut keeps freaking out about. We've got to go to the old ruin and catch them red-handed. Hmmm…" He paused.

Rebecca looked quizzically at him.

"What's the problem? We know, or rather you do anyway, where the old ruin is?"

Drew bit his lip pensively.

"For sure. Problem is, it's a day's walk at least to get there and the countryside isn't a park. We'll have to camp out. I'm not sure how keen Henry will be on that, given the speed storms whip up round here and your ankle. And besides, I've work to be getting on with for Henry on the estate."

"I'm sure Uncle Henry would rather you solved the problem of looking after his niece. Camping out sounds a bit of a lark."

"It might work if we get Dougie along with us," said Drew, looking seriously at her.

"I'm a bit nervous of what we're getting into. Dougie knows the country round here better than anyone and Henry trusts him too. He mightn't think twice if we said we were going off with Dougie, whereas I doubt he'd let you and me go alone. It's been a laugh but there's a lot of money at stake here and these guys sure won't think it's a game."

"Can you persuade Dougie, then? Will Uncle Henry allow it? I thought Dougie has a job to do, too."

"Dougie's a cinch. He's supposed to be heading up into the hills anyhow, tracking the McOwan deer, now he's finished with Barradale's. Once he hears about all this, we won't be able to stop him."

CHAPTER 14

THE PLEDGE

Bright August sunshine shimmered across the waters of Loch Nevis as Henry steered the boat carefully into the boathouse at Rahsaig.

The journey back across from the Isle of Rum had been enjoyable but largely uneventful. Drew had bade them farewell in Mallaig.

The cargo of props and costumes had been deemed too heavy for the *Hebridean Princess* to carry, when one took into consideration the theatregoers and the players themselves, who must also be transported. The Camden Players gallantly elected to stay on the island, to be picked up later on. Rebecca and Drew had thus been denied a further opportunity to make a positive identification of the man Rebecca had seen at the window of the castle. This had not caused them undue concern, however, since they knew the thieves intended to go to the old ruin the next day.

Rebecca jumped onto the wooden landing stage and threw a rope around the forward landing rail. She pulled the boat up to the edge of the jetty and tied the rope off in a knot. She had by now become quite proficient in handling the boat and had earned her uncle's praise on several occasions. There had even been hints that he trusted her sufficiently to allow her out alone.

They made their way up the lawn and into the castle in casual conversation about the play and the events of the previous evening. Rebecca was careful to avoid mentioning the more dramatic occurrences during the night, or be tempted to divulge her theories about the art thefts. She was still unsure of her uncle's reaction and wanted to be certain of her ground before she attempted any explanations.

She was sure that Henry would have no hesitation in calling PC Lennie, once the truth revealed itself and from there, things would be sure to escalate. She had also learned from her uncomfortable experiences earlier that one had to have demonstrable proof before the police would take things seriously.

As they went indoors, a hooded figure detached itself from a tree it had been leaning against and disappeared at a run into the woods.

*****

Rebecca went up to her room in the turret of the east wing, grateful to be able to change out of the clothes she had been wearing for the last two days. She reached up to open a window. As she did so, she felt a sudden rush of air behind her.

The door to her room slammed shut.

Rebecca turned round, the hairs on the back of her neck prickling.

For the faintest instant, she felt as if she was being observed – then the feeling left her.

She shook her head and smiled.

"You really are imagining things, girl," she muttered to herself.

She busied herself with washing and changing, leaving her room for a few minutes to go to the bathroom.

As she came back through the door, she noticed the journal lying open on her table. Puzzled and certain that she had left it closed in her bedside drawer, she picked it up. In Rebecca McOwan's beautiful flowing script, the page was entitled

The Voice

Intrigued, Rebecca took the journal over to her favourite window seat and began to read.

The most dreadful foreboding has overtaken me. For some days and weeks now, I have been assailed by a man with a chilling voice, who seems to know me. He speaks to me from out of the dark and dreich mist but will not reveal himself. His voice is strong and I feel that I know it, though I know it not. It is as though I am in a dream, for when he leaves me, I have not been asleep but neither has he been with me. I fear I am losing my mind.

Rebecca was gripped. She thought immediately of her own voice in the mist.

Today he came to me as I stood at the edge of the loch. I could hear the stroke of oars in the water and once more he bade me guard his lady's resting place from the English soldiers. He calls this place "Sanctuary".

There it was again – the Sanctuary.

Each time, it is the same. I know not who he is, nor his lady, nor why he calls on me. I ran from the Loch and hid myself indoors, barricading the door behind me. Thinking I was safe, I went up to my room and looked down. From out of the mist at the edge of the loch there came the most chilling howl, from what manner of beast I knew not, until I saw a ghastly white wolf leap from the waters. The terrible creature launched itself at the castle gate and clawed at it with such ferocity that I felt sure it would give way.

And then, as quickly as it had come, the beast was gone. All at once, I heard the voice crying out to me.

"Becca! Becca! You must protect my lady! Keep the invader from her door! Only you can do this! Only you know the secret. The Sanctuary, Becca, the Sanctuary!"

And then the voice was gone and all was tranquil as before. I cannot rest. I understand not what the voice wills me to do, nor from where he comes to me. And I fear the dreadful beast. I am lost in a nightmare. Reason says it cannot be real. And so would I believe, were it not for the livid clawmarks of the beast gouged on the castle gates.

Rebecca paused, shaken. There could be no doubt that Becca was describing the same experiences as she had herself undergone. The coincidences were too strong to mean anything else. The same voice that beckoned her had called upon her namesake back in the eighteenth century. The reference to the "Sanctuary"; even what Becca wrote about the wolf seemed to describe identically the beast she had seen at the edge of the loch.

What Rebecca could not fathom was why they had been singled out?

And who had opened the book?

Even if one accepted, just for a moment, that something supernatural was at work here, and Rebecca was not prepared to admit that yet, why was it that the warrior called upon her and Becca? What would he have them do? In speaking of "my lady" he must mean Princess Immelda. "Disturbing her rest" suggested that her grave was being violated in some way. But where was the grave and who was violating it?

You will find the door twixt the resting place of your ancestor and the sword of burial. You must seal it from the invaders so that my lady's rest is not disturbed.

Local legends were contradictory on the location. She now knew it was not in the family crypt beneath the church at Stoul. Henry knew of no burial place on the estate, although he admitted that was unusual for noble Scottish families. Perhaps discovering the location of the grave might unlock the secret and find the answers to her questions.

Rebecca turned back to the journal and flicked over the page. To her great consternation, she found that but for a few more words, Becca had written no more. The last entry was a few simple lines and read:

It is a few days since my last entry. Were I to write here what I believe to be true, people would say it is too fantastic and would question my very reason. I must discover more and find some proof to affirm the imaginings of my mind. Tonight I will venture out and, God willing, find my answers.

And here, the journal came to an end.

Rebecca leafed through the remaining pages but they were all blank. A mixture of sadness, frustration and unfulfilment overcame her, as she realised that she could now learn no more. It was as if a voice had been switched off.

She looked out of the window, the very same window from which Becca had looked down and seen the beast leap from the loch, all those years ago. How calm and peaceful it now seemed across those same waters, how very different from that night.

"So now it's all up to me," she whispered to herself, staring out at the mountains.

"I must find the answers for both of us, Becca. I promise I will not let you down."

CHAPTER 15

THE LAST GREAT WILDERNESS

"The last great wilderness in Europe." Drew Campbell stood on a high, sunny hillside, surveying the great expanse of rugged, open country stretching for miles around. He spoke in the manner of one bestowing a gleaming nugget of information.

"That's what they call the Highlands. And they're not wrong. If you don't know what you're doing, you can get into real trouble out here. Eighteen people die each year on the mountains, you know."

"Well that's a nice, comforting thought as we head into the middle of nowhere, Drew, thanks!" Dougie Campbell spoke softly, clapping his younger brother on the back.

"Bleak."

"Beautiful."

From her seated position just below them, Rebecca studied the Campbell brothers with detached amusement. The camping expedition, sanctioned by Henry when he had been told of the inclusion of Dougie, had begun a few hours ago and already Rebecca had found much to amuse her in the way the two brothers interacted.

Dougie Campbell, by several years the elder, was very different from his lively, disrespectful brother. He exuded dependability and confidence, which no doubt explained how he had come to rise so far at such a young age, to be an estate ranger. It was a position of no little responsibility and, Henry had told Rebecca the previous evening, was normally only reached after many years.

There was no doubt that Drew looked up to his elder brother and respected him but he missed no opportunity to joke at his expense. Rebecca found Dougie's dry, subtle wit greatly to her liking.

"What is this Glen called?" she asked, looking at the ridge they had just climbed and somewhere behind which she had her first experience with the mist and the Warrior.

"Glen an Dubh Lochan," replied Drew. "Glen of the dark loch. Dark lake valley to the English."

"So Drew has told me a bit about what's been going on." Dougie sat down on a rock opposite Rebecca and slid his pack off his shoulders.

"You seem to have got our kid into a bit of a mess. Girls, hey? You'd better tell me what I'm getting myself into – and don't leave anything out."

Rebecca related the full account of her experiences at Rahsaig, aided by interjections from Drew.

They divulged all their theories about the thefts, Simon Sibley, the Camden Players, the divers, Becca's journal, the Warrior and the mists. When finally they finished, Dougie was lost in silent thought.

"You guys have been pretty busy," he said at length, a wry grin on his face.

"If half of your theories are right, then we are going to have to be on our guard. I'm not sure what I think about the ghostie part but you seem sure enough that something, shall we say 'odd', has been going on. Should be fun, though."

He paused for a moment.

"One thing we need to get straight right now is this: out here, I am in charge, okay? I don't want any arguing if I say we are going in a particular direction or complaining if you get tired. You only got this trip because Henry put me in charge. If you want my help, you do things my way, understood?"

Rebecca and Drew nodded readily, secretly quite glad to have somebody else taking the lead.

"And we are doing nothing remotely risky without involving the cops. Okay?"

Rebecca and Drew nodded again.

"Okay. So, I guess we'll be heading for the old ruin. Catch ourselves a forger."

Dougie swung his pack onto his shoulders and stood up. His eyes narrowed for a moment as he looked up the Glen towards the mountains, before he began to stride off along the rough stalkers' path. Drew and Rebecca picked up their own rucksacks and fell in step behind him. The camping trip had been planned quite hurriedly but, with Dougie's help promised to be an experience. Rebecca's previous contact with camping was limited to a wet week on the Isle of Wight. A few nights in the open in the wild, remote Highlands of Scotland might not be quite the same thing.

***

The route Dougie had laid out over breakfast would take them along the shore of the 'dark' loch of the glen's name. Dougie had decided to camp at its northern end. Next day, they would continue a few miles further to the Old Ruin, the main objective as far as Rebecca and Drew were concerned. From here, they would climb steeply up to a high ridge between Ladhar Bheinn and the neighbouring mountain Luinne Bheinn, from where they would descend into Glen Barradale and call Willie McHarg from a phone box near the shore, to arrange to meet his boat. Rebecca had reasoned that the area could not be too remote if there was a phone box, only to be told gently by Dougie that it was a Mountain Rescue Post. If this caused her concern, Rebecca's pride was not about to let this show.

After a long day walking through highland heather and rock, they reached the end of Loch Dubh in the late afternoon and set about pitching camp. They chose an area of flattish grass between two small rivers which flowed into the loch itself. Dougie was carrying lightweight tents, which he now began to unravel and spread out on the ground.

"Firewood, you two!" he said, briskly, pointing towards a small forest at the foot of the hillside close by. Although tired from a hard day's walking in the rocky terrain, Rebecca and Drew set off and began to build a pile of wood.

Pausing to catch her breath for a moment, Rebecca took in the surroundings. They must be the only people for miles. All day they had not seen a single person. There were several groups of wild deer roaming the hills and panoramic scenery. Out here, there was a sense of complete solitude.

Within minutes of their arrival, Dougie had erected both tents; a larger one for himself and his brother; and a single for Rebecca. Rebecca was a little doubtful that it would be big enough but, on opening the flap, discovered that its size was deceptive. She could lie fully extended with still a foot at either end. Dougie put down a bed roll as a cushion against the ground, onto which she now laid the sleeping bag she had been carrying in her pack. She lay back and briefly closed her eyes. Overcome by sudden tiredness, she was unable to stop herself falling asleep.

When she eventually emerged outside, an hour had passed. Drew sat a few feet away, busily coaxing the fire into a strong blaze.

"Where's Dougie?" asked Rebecca.

"Evening, sleepyhead. Away seeing to the food," replied Drew, his eyes not leaving the flames roaring away before him. Rebecca raised her eyebrows in puzzlement but did not reply. She looked down at Drew's rucksack, into which, earlier, she had watched McHarg pack copious provisions for the trip. Drew had complained about the weight on his back several times that day. Moments later, Dougie reappeared, two bright silver fish hanging from a string in one hand. From the other, he dropped a black fishing rod to the ground.

"Very impressive!" said Rebecca, smiling. "I didn't see you carrying a fishing rod, though, I'm sure?"

"Secrets of the trade. The rangers keep some bits and pieces in a shed up there in the trees, for when we're out here. You can't always carry everything with you. Stove too."

"What are they?" Rebecca asked, sitting down next to the fire.

"Trout – when the estate was a gentlemen's retreat, they were kept for the visitors to catch. There haven't been any visitors here for a number of years so the stocks are good. We always have fresh fish for supper when we're up here."

Dougie sat down and set about slicing and gutting the fish in expert fashion. A frying pan was produced and it was not long before the delicious smell of cooking wafted across their little camp.

"So is this *still* Uncle Henry's estate then?" Rebecca asked, looking up at the peaks and ridges of the mountains that surrounded them.

"Aye – just," answered Dougie, not looking up. "Most say Rahsaig ends at the Old Ruin, although Henry calls Ladhar Bheinn the boundary. Centuries ago there was a battle on the ridge between the McOwans and the McLeods of Barradale. The McOwan, Hugo, cornered the McLeod chieftain and threw him off the top. I think that made him the winner. They say Hugo was seven feet tall, so nobody was going to argue. The McOwans have always claimed the summit. There's a place up there called Dead Man's Crag, where it's supposed to have happened."

They enjoyed a supper of fresh fish and bread, huddled

around the fire and whiled away the evening talking and watching the sun set over the purple mountain tops. Rebecca did not even mind being the butt of some of the humour. There was an honesty and refreshing directness in the way the Campbells spoke.

"So, tomorrow we'll dig a bit further into this mystery," said Dougie, turning over the coals with a stick to put out the fire.

"I'd almost forgotten," said Drew, laughing.

"Now don't move suddenly, but there are a couple of people over the other side of the river," said Dougie, softly. "Might be your thieves, off to the ruin."

"What?!" gasped Rebecca, with a mixture of disbelief and incredulity on her face. Drew's face registered similar emotions. He tried to stand up to look, only to be dragged firmly back down by his brother.

"I haven't seen anyone – are you sure? Where?" said Drew, still trying to look past his brother. Dougie remained calm and unperturbed under their indignant stares.

"They are level with us. I don't think they've seen us yet."

"Are you sure?" asked Drew. "That'll blow it completely if they do."

"Why? We're just a few kids out camping as far as they are concerned. I spotted them a couple of hours ago, when I was fishing."

"Why didn't you say anything?" asked Rebecca, somewhat put out by this revelation.

"You two would probably have gone gallivanting off and blown our cover," replied Dougie, in what to Drew and Rebecca was an irritatingly patronising manner.

"We haven't done so badly up to now, actually," said Drew, in what he intended to be a tone of withering sarcasm. He and Rebecca exchanged a quick nod of satisfaction before turning accusing gazes on Dougie.

"Sorry – didn't mean to act the big brother there. You haven't done badly at all, I am the first to agree. Just thought it was for the best – if they'd seen you two, they might have recognised one of you. Me, they won't know from Adam."

Rebecca and Drew had to admit to the logic of this. They crouched down and followed Dougie's silent gesture towards the far bank. Two figures were just visible, making their way along the rough path below the trees where Rebecca and Drew had collected firewood. They did not give the impression of minding whether or not they were being observed, and were talking quite loudly. Dougie motioned for Rebecca and Drew to keep low and follow him, as he crept slowly forward. In moments, they had gained the comparative safety of a small hillock, from where they could see a long way up the glen.

"Do they look like our men?" Drew's voice was low next to Rebecca.

"I can't really tell. They could be, or they could just be two people out for a walk."

"Bit late for that," whispered Dougie. "If it is them, we don't want to stumble on them in the morning. We can watch from here to see where they go."

They lay low until the gathering gloom and distance travelled by the men made it impossible to see them any more.

"I don't think they'll return but we'd best keep watch tonight, just in case. Drew, you take first watch and wake me in …" he paused for a second to examine his watch "…two hours. Go on, Rebecca, you turn in."

"In a few minutes. I want to sit down and look at this sky for a while – it's unbelievable."

Rebecca pointed up. "I've never seen so many stars."

"Aye," said Drew. "No big city haze to obscure it, that's why it's so clear. Kind of makes you feel small and not very important, doesn't it? My Grandda says that when you look at a star, the light you are seeing actually left there thousands of years ago. Can't get my head round that one. I don't want you thinking it's always like this though ... it's sometimes cloudy, would you believe?"

The three of them lay on the ground gazing at the canopy of stars. Rebecca was awestruck by the sheer breadth of the sky. It took some time to be able to pick out the constellations, such as the Plough, with which she was familiar and had seen at home, since every inch seemed to be covered in stars.

"You can see some of the planets with the naked eye on a night like this. They look like stars, too, but that –" Dougie pointed to a yellowish light lower in the sky towards the horizon, "– that, I think, is Mars."

Rebecca followed the line of his arm.

"Mars is good but wait till you see the Northern Lights, Rebecca," said Drew. "Now *that* is really awesome, as the Yanks say."

"Northern Lights? What are they?"

"Sort of when the whole sky lights up in all the colours of the rainbow and glows and flashes at you. Some form of atmospheric, cosmic occurrence – I don't really know or understand but it looks pretty."

"Will we see that?"

"If we're lucky."

***

A man was running, frenziedly, through the heather.

Exhausted, he stumbled every few paces and scrambled back to his feet, terror etched into his eyes and face. He cast fearful glances over his shoulder.

Moments later, a huge wolf leapt over a rocky outcrop twenty metres or so behind him, fangs bared and its eyes ablaze.

The man cried out and stumbled backwards, putting up his hands to try and keep the animal at bay. The wolf stopped, cornering him. It uttered a low snarl, filling its nostrils with the scent of its quarry. Quaking in fear, the man edged back, his desperate eyes never leaving the wolf.

With a blood-curdling howl, the wolf leapt at the man, its huge front paws slicing through his shirt and into his chest. Screaming in pain, the force of the attack knocked the man over. Turning his head to take a look behind him, the awful realisation dawned that he was now at the very edge of a cliff, high above the sea.

The wolf's attack was too powerful for him.

In the next instant, he plunged over the precipice onto the rocks below and was lost in the pounding sea. As his dying scream faded on the breeze, the wolf remained at the top of the cliff, panting gently, its white eyes staring down impassively.

Rebecca woke up with a cry, clutching her heart, her breath coming in short sharp gasps. It took her a few seconds to realise that she was in her tent and it had been a dream.

She was just dropping off to sleep again when she heard a distant, forlorn howl from somewhere up in the hills.

CHAPTER 16

THE OLD RUIN

As the first shafts of sunlight glinted over the mountains, the campers were up and about. Early morning mist hung low over the glen, brushing the pine trees. Rebecca was struck once more by the silence and grandeur of the Highlands. As she packed her tent and sleeping bag, she looked at her watch and saw it was not yet seven. She yawned.

From over by the fire wafted a glorious smell of bacon frying.

"Drew has his uses," said Dougie, appearing at her shoulder and attaching her tent to his backpack, nodding towards his brother, busy with a frying pan over the fire.

"Have you seen the deer?" He pointed towards the slope above the wood. Narrowing her eyes, Rebecca made out at least a dozen does about a hundred yards away. Their coats were very effective camouflage.

"See how the stag stands a way off from his does?" Dougie pointed to where a large deer stood proudly aloof, a magnificent set of antlers on his head.

"Typical male! So stand-offish!" said Rebecca drily.

"If he makes a move, they'll all follow him."

"Typical females!" called Drew, chirpily.

"Aren't they worried we're this close?" asked Rebecca. "People shoot them, don't they?"

"Aye they do," answered Dougie. "Deerstalking, they call it, not to be confused with sad hats worn by style criminals. Sport, in inverted commas, for the rich. It's good sense to manage the numbers to preserve the natural habitat and the ecological balance. Whether it's humane to kill them rather than simply move them somewhere else – well, wiser folks than me can argue that one." He paused and studied the deer.

"You must have an opinion, though?" asked Rebecca. "I know I do."

"Aye, so do I," he answered, before giving her a smile. "But why should our opinions be anybody else's business?"

Rebecca was wrong-footed by this.

"Are you calling me a busybody?" she smiled, eventually.

Dougie smiled, his attention now back on the deer.

"They'll only worry if we make a move in their direction, if they catch our scent. Ah!" He stopped abruptly as the stag took a few sudden, quick paces.

"Something's disturbed them. Probably got a whiff of chef burning the bacon."

As they watched, the stag launched into a canter up the slope, followed immediately by the does, and disappeared over a small rise.

A few minutes later, the three were hunched around the fire once more, enjoying a bacon sandwich and the peaceful early morning in the Glen. After breakfast, they washed the pans in the burn, gathered their packs and set off along the rough track to the Old Ruin.

"Any sign of the people we saw last night?" asked Rebecca, scanning the undulating land ahead. Dougie shook his head.

"Long gone by now, I expect. They might have made the Ruin by nightfall, although they would have had to crack on some."

***

After several hours walking up the glen, Dougie led them off the path into some trees. They were just a little way short of the Old Ruin, nestling in a dip up ahead. They climbed higher, to give themselves a clear view of the house and anybody who might be about. Motioning to the others to be silent, Dougie crept forward to a stone wall at the edge of the trees, from where it came into view below them. They squatted down and peered cautiously over the top.

The Old Ruin was an austere, spooky place, uninhabited for many years. Jagged holes riddled the roof and the walls. Fractured, blackened timbers protruded, covered with moss and grass. No glass remained in the windows, which now formed blackened holes in the granite walls. Several sheds and outbuildings still stood nearby but everywhere appeared long since deserted.

"When was the fire here?" Rebecca asked.

"1929," said Drew, "destroyed just about everything. Two people died as well. They never repaired it. Nobody has tried to live here since."

"I'm not surprised. I wouldn't like to do the walk every day."

Dougie grinned.

"Quite a way, although in olden times they had the likes of the Campbell forefathers to carry everything for them. Same thing today – me and Drew carrying your luggage."

Rebecca smiled broadly.

"Just keep tugging those forelocks to me."

"Stay here until I call you down," said Dougie, getting to his feet, a note of authority entering his voice. Before Drew or Rebecca could protest, he made his way nimbly down towards the house, keeping to the trees for cover. He disappeared from view.

"Guess we'd better do as he says," said Drew, resignedly. "He'll only get stroppy."

"Brown-nose!" taunted Rebecca. "Hold on – I saw something! In one of the downstairs windows – there, look!"

A piece of cloth had suddenly appeared waving out of a window space just along from the front door. She grabbed Drew's arm as a man's head appeared after it.

"It's him, I'm sure!" she whispered. "It's the man I saw breaking into the castle! Come on, we'd better warn Dougie."

They were on their feet in a second and heading down through the trees as quickly as they could, trying not very successfully to avoid making noise that would alert attention. As they neared the bottom, they saw Dougie crouched behind the wall, scowling at them. He gestured to them to keep low.

"I thought I told you to stay put!" he hissed.

"I know but there's a man –"

"I know there's a man! I've been watching him and now he's probably seen us too, with you two crashing through the trees like elephants." Dougie quickly turned back. To their relief, the man seemed not to have noticed and was looking in a different direction. After a moment, he disappeared.

"What do we do now?" whispered Drew.

"*You* do absolutely nothing! *We all* stay put here until we know what's going on." Dougie's eyes did not leave the house. Two men appeared by the door to one of the outbuildings. One of them was the man Rebecca had recognised. As they watched, a third man appeared in the doorway. After a brief exchange, all three disappeared inside.

"We've got to find out what's going on," whispered Drew imploringly. Dougie gave him a look but his brother persisted.

"Look, we can go round the back and listen at a window but we have to find out what they are up to. Come on Doug, you know we do."

Rebecca and Drew both looked pleadingly at Dougie, who grimaced and then closed his eyes in apparent resignation.

"Okay," he said, "but – before you pair get carried away and get us all tied up and thrown in the loch – you don't make a noise and you stick right on my tail, clear? Step out of line and …" His expression left neither in any doubt of the consequences.

Slowly, silently, they crept over the wall, down the slope and circled behind the building. There was a bank which ran at the same level as a row of high windows. They scrambled quickly up it and Dougie edged along on his stomach, peering cautiously into each window until, all at once, he stopped and flattened himself on the ground. Slowly, he swung round until he was facing the other two, and gestured them to take a look. They could hear the sound of voices drifting up through the window below. Together, the three of them looked cautiously through the window.

The room, the roof of which was still intact, had clearly been inhabited very recently. Two of the men were on a bench by the door, talking, while the third stood at an easel, painting. There was a sleeping bag in the corner and some food. The room resembled an artist's studio, with pots of paints, canvases and brushes strewn over wooden tables and boxes. Rebecca nudged Drew and pointed at a pile of rubber divers' bags. As they watched, one of the men by the door turned and spoke to the artist. His voice was heavy with a thick French accent.

"Are you ready to come with us then, Godfrey? Monsieur Sibley wants to go through the plan before he goes back to Rahsaig. And we've got to get the ones you've finished to the cave, so you can help us carry."

The artist gestured agitatedly with his brush. "Tell him I will lose a day I cannot afford if I am to get everything finished in time."

"You can tell him yourself – come on." The two men each grabbed packages which evidently contained paintings. The other sighed loudly.

148

"I don't like this work, copying other artists. I can do original stuff, you know."

His companions ignored him and made their way outside. With a melodramatic sigh, the forger put down his brushes, slipped on his coat and followed them.

Dougie lifted his head to watch them go, careful to make no sudden movement that might attract attention. He motioned to Rebecca and Drew to remain still. He did not move for several minutes. At length, satisfied the men were not coming back, he got to his feet.

"Right, let's take a look around."

Inside the room, Rebecca and Drew confirmed their suspicions. A half-completed painting rested on the easel, at which the man had been working. On it was clipped a photograph of a picture which he was evidently copying.

"Wait, I recognise some of these."

Drew had found some other photos.

"These are at Rahsaig, the ones Becca painted – look."

The three of them huddled round as Drew leafed through them. Rebecca nodded.

"No doubt about it. This confirms their modus operandi, as Inspector Morse would say. Sibley visits each place and has a nose around, selecting the paintings. He photographs them, or his henchmen break in, photograph them and bring the photos back here to be copied. When the forgery is done, the thieves break in again and swap it with the original. That way, nobody realises a crime has been committed. Meanwhile, Sibley sends the real ones down to his London shop and sells them abroad for a fortune. They must mean to break in to Rahsaig again to steal these others. I *knew* Becca's paintings were valuable and this proves it!"

"There's something else we know," said Drew. "They are off to the cave, where the stuff is being stashed –"

"Okay, Sergeant Lewis," said Dougie, drily.

"As I was saying," continued Drew, with a glance of contempt at his brother,

"those men are away to the cave. We thought it was on Shadow Island or somewhere around Rahsaig ... they went *that* way, *up* the glen."

He pointed.

"The cave has to be on the Barradale side."

"Doesn't that mean the cave where the Princess is buried isn't where everyone thinks it is?" Rebecca looked sceptical.

"But nobody has ever really known where it is – it's always been guesswork. Great for the legend and the tourists. Those stones on the island could be anyone's grave. If we want to find out where it really is, we have to follow them. Come on!"

"Hold on!" said Dougie. "If you think we're all racing off in hot pursuit, think again.

I'll be much quicker on my own and a lot safer."

He held up his hands to stem the instant howls of protest.

"I promised Henry to keep you two out of trouble. All we need to do is locate this place and then leave it up to the police to sort out. We're not going in there like James Bond to fight the bad guys. It's only a few hours over the top to Barradale. You two will stay here – and I mean stay – I'll find out where they go and be back. Then we will all go back to Rahsaig and put this in the hands of the police. Agreed?"

Rebecca looked sullenly at Drew, whose face fell then quickly brightened again.

"You're right, bruv." Drew winked quickly at Rebecca, out of sight of Dougie. The elder Campbell looked sceptical, before his expression relaxed. He jumped to his feet.

"If I'm going to catch up, I'd better crack on." He gave his brother one last studied look.

"Take the tents. You can put them up, in case I'm not back

before dark. There's a good spot back up in the trees there, out of sight. By a ruined cottage – you'll see it."

Dougie looked at his watch.

"They've got fifteen minutes start."

"Nothing to a man of your physique," said Drew, smiling facetiously at his brother.

"Besides, they don't know this country like you."

Dougie hovered in the doorway while Drew and Rebecca both smiled at him. Then he was gone. Drew went to the door and watched him disappear up the glen.

"So – I saw that look on your face. What are we really going to do?" asked Rebecca.

"An old man in the village, known as Hamish the Haddock, on account of his quite unseasonal odour, once said there is a secret passage from the Old Ruin to the Barradale estate, used in days gone by to avoid capture. Old Hamish swore blind it was there. He said it leads into a labyrinth of caves and underground rivers under Ladhar Bheinn. There are lots of caves around here, so it could well be true. If we can find it and go quickly enough, we should catch them up. They've got to go over the mountain top by the path. They'll take hours while we will only have to go a fraction of the distance. But first we must find it."

"Right," said Rebecca. "You start out here in the sheds and I'll take the house."

Rebecca headed over the rough grass of what once was the lawn to the front door of the old house. This was now just a gap in the wall, framed by two stone columns. She entered, treading gingerly to avoid debris and fallen timbers. She found her way into the hall, from which various doorways led. The air held a dank, musty smell. Rebecca's eye fell on a door at the far end, noticeably lower than the rest. The door was still in position, sturdy and black with a heavy bolt at the bottom. Rebecca's first attempt to slide the bolt across was unsuccessful. It would not budge at all. She examined it as closely as the dim light would allow. It was badly rusted. Turning to seek something to help shift it, she found a pointed piece of rock. Gripping this as tightly as she could, she hit the end repeatedly until it moved and she was able to slide it the rest of the way across.

Rebecca had to put her shoulder against the door and shove as hard as she was able. It eventually gave, with a loud scraping noise, and she forced it open wide enough to squeeze through. She was at the top of a narrow staircase. The daylight coming through the roof above her guided her down the first few steps. The interior was dim and smelt of damp and decay. After about ten steps, she reached the bottom. Rebecca's eyes were not accustomed to the gloom and as she edged forwards, she stumbled over a low table, banging her knee. She let out a yell.

"Rebecca." A voice came from a few feet away. Rebecca jumped, startled.

The gentle face of a young woman appeared out of the gloom. Rebecca was struck by the strangeness of her clothing and pale complexion.

"Let me help you up." The woman held out her hand. "I am Siobhan."

Rebecca's mouth dropped open in utter astonishment. She reached down to steady herself, unsure whether to take the hand offered.

"Siobhan? … tell me, are you …?"

"I am companion to the Lady Rebecca McOwan. Don't be alarmed, I wish you no harm. Sit, please, there is much to talk about."

As she spoke, all around her the room came alive. The house suddenly seemed very much still in use, with furniture and ornaments. There was outside light from somewhere. A fire crackled in the corner.

Rebecca sat down suddenly, unable to take in what was happening.

Was she in the presence of a ... ghost? She felt herself becoming giddy.

"How ... I don't understand ..." her voice faltered and stopped. The woman rushed forward to stop her from falling and knelt beside her. Her face was very pale but her eyes were bright and reassuring.

"Of course," she said gently, taking Rebecca's hand. Her hands felt strangely cool.

"You do not understand. Let me explain. My mistress and I were imprisoned in this house by Lachlan McOwan, when he came to Rahsaig after the death of the Laird. Lachlan stole the family's most priceless treasures. At first, my lady tried to stop him. Lachlan was never welcome at Rahsaig and the Laird left him nothing. Lachlan was a bad lot, who gambled and wasted much of their father's money. Their father was weak and could never refuse him anything. But after his death, everything was left to Donald. He was not such a soft touch and would give his brother nothing. Lachlan secretly loved Mary, my mistress's mother, although she wanted nothing to do with him. Donald and Lachlan fell out. There was a swordfight, in which Lachlan received a bad wound to his neck. The Laird banished him that day and put him aboard a boat with orders never to darken his doors again. Lachlan swore bloody revenge.

He fell in with the evil McLeod on Rum and we heard little of him for a few years.

Then, one day, he came upon the Sanctuary, the burial place of the Princess Immelda of Norway – she who perished in the loch on her wedding day. Priceless treasures were buried with her. Lachlan stole everything he could find. He took the burial mask and the beast's collar. But he awoke the beast Hakon and his master, Knut, who vowed never to rest until these were returned. Lachlan brought all that he stole to the Manse. Most treacherous of all, though, he betrayed Robert to the English... he told them where to find Robert so that he could have Rahsaig for himself."

Siobhan paused, her eyes faraway.

"My mistress knew the whole story. The Warrior and the Wolf came to her. They demanded her help. After Lachlan's hand in poor Robert's death, she needed no second bidding. She came upon Lachlan one night, as he was returning from the Sanctuary and confronted him. He imprisoned her and me in this remote house, to keep us from telling anybody. He told everyone she had gone mad and must be kept locked away from the rest of the world. That was not so."

"I knew it!" Rebecca had recovered some of her composure.

"I knew she wasn't mad; I knew her paintings were not those of a mad woman."

"We lived here for some months but my mistress could not rest. She escaped on the night of a terrible storm, intending to take a boat and go to the Marquis of Morar, to seek his help. But her flight was discovered and Lachlan and his men gave chase."

She paused, biting her lip.

"Lachlan snatched her locket, in which was a picture of her mother. He pushed her off a cliff and killed her. The story was put about that she jumped, took her own life in her madness – but that is what his men were told to say. One confessed it to me."

"But ... how come you are here ... now? You died hundreds of years ago ... didn't you?"

"After my mistress's death, suspecting that whatever she had known, I would also know, Lachlan allowed me no food. I became weak, ill and my mortal life slipped away."

"... Are you a ghost?"

"Mortality is neither the beginning nor the end. I am gone

from the physical world but cannot enter the realm of the dead. My soul cannot find rest because my task is not finished."

"What task?"

"I must help my lady. We must do what Hakon and Knut bid us do."

Rebecca's expression was one of astonishment.

"Becca? ... she is with you here?"

Siobhan squeezed her hand in reassurance and smiled.

"She too is trapped until we can rid this world of Lachlan and return the treasures."

"Why have you chosen me? Why is Knut talking to me?" Rebecca's tone was imploring.

"You are a door into the mortal world because your mind is open. We can do nothing without the help of somebody from the physical realm. We inhabit the twilight, the blurred edges between the living and the dead – but belonging to neither. Yours is only one world; there are others but most mortals cannot see into them because they can only conceive of physical form."

"I don't understand," said Rebecca.

"Our humanity touches areas of the soul, the mind, of consciousness. You can see only if your mind is open to them."

"Can you ever be free?"

"Our souls are trapped and cannot find peace, nor Knut and Hakon, while the Sanctuary is disturbed. The collar and mask must be found. Thieves have stolen them again, just as Lachlan did. Only by returning them, sealing the Sanctuary and allowing the Princess and her guards to rest peacefully, can my mistress and I be allowed to go to our rest. Because you are my mistress's descendant, because you read her journal, we know you will understand."

"So ... the key, the journal left open at a particular page ... that was ..."

"My Lady. The key was a test. If you were inquisitive, you would make the connection. We knew you would read the journal. If you read it and believed it, we felt sure you would want to know more. Your heart is good. You knew that something was unexplained, that something important had been left unfinished. Just as the Warrior called to my mistress in our time, so he now calls to you in your time."

"So Becca is the lady in the crimson dress – of course!"

Rebecca stood up and took a few paces, trying to absorb everything and comprehend.

"Nobody is ever going to believe this," she shook her head. "I am speaking to a ghost!"

"Ghost is such a melodramatic word!"

Rebecca smiled for a moment before becoming serious again.

"So, Lachlan discovered the Sanctuary and stole the treasures. You must know then where the entrance is?"

"Beneath the mountain is an underground cave. One entrance is hidden among the rocks on an island on the causeway to Barradale Castle. The island is almost completely submerged when the tide comes in. Inside there is a narrow passage to a secret chamber in which the Princess was laid to rest. The caves fill with water at high tide, so you must take great care, else the waters will claim you. The secret chamber has not been entered for hundreds of years, since Lachlan discovered it."

Siobhan gripped Rebecca's hands.

"Rebecca, they must not be allowed to find the Princess."

"Becca! English person!" Drew's voice reached them from somewhere above. Rebecca turned to look back up the stairs.

"Down here, Drew!" She called. She turned back to Siobhan.

But she found herself all alone in a damp, dark, empty room.

CHAPTER 17

THE SANCTUARY

It took Dougie an hour to gain sufficient ground to bring the men within sight. Not only was he able to move much more quickly, since he was very fit and the artist, in particular, had seemed quite frail, but he had also used his knowledge of the country to cut off a good slice of the distance. The thieves were taking the Stalkers' path, a circuitous route to avoid the steep southern slopes of Ladhar Bheinn. Dougie could save two or three miles by making a direct ascent of Dead Man's Crag, from where he could scramble down the scree slopes on the Barradale side.

Dougie was breathing quite hard from his exertions and sweating. It had turned into a very warm day. As he stood at the top of the steep-sided ridge, he could see his quarry several hundred feet lower down, still on the Rahsaig side. Over this sort of ground, at the speed they were travelling, it would take them at least an hour to draw level with him. He would have plenty of time for a rest before he would need to move on.

He looked back down the Glen towards the Old Ruin, just visible in the distance, and wondered if Drew and Rebecca had heeded his warning to stay put. He frowned. His brother's swift acceptance of his order had made him suspicious, although the need to follow the thieves had forced him to take Drew at his word. He hoped that the rather less impetuous Rebecca, although younger, might be a calming influence.

A silly mistake could be dangerous.

Dougie set his watch alarm for half an hour and sat back against a rock to take in the magnificent view of the peaks and islands of the Western Highlands, laid out like a panorama before him in the beautiful summer sunshine.

***

"You've been talking to a spook?" Drew's face creased into a smile of disbelief.

"I knew you wouldn't believe me." Rebecca sat down on a wooden stump just inside the entrance to the Old Manse.

"I didn't say I didn't believe you but it is a bit unusual, forgive me!" said Drew.

"Siobhan the Ghost? Doubtless, some of the kooks round here will know of her.

Where did she go?"

"I don't know. When I heard you calling, I looked round and when I turned back, she had gone. It was weird. I was with her one moment and the room was real. Then, nothing. Why were you calling, anyway? Have you found something?"

Picking at a patch of moss in the wall, Drew shook his head and gave a wan smile.

"Nope. Not a dicky. I was hoping you had. Let's see where you found this Ghostie."

They retraced Rebecca's steps down into the cold chamber. Drew produced a torch from his pocket and swept the beam around the dripping walls. The room was better preserved than the rest of the house, having benefited, presumably, from being sealed off but was, nevertheless, in a severely dilapidated state. The chair and table had deteriorated in the damp and fungi were sprouting around the walls.

"Where's that draught coming from?" Rebecca held out her hand, feeling a faint but steady rush of air against her arm. She turned in the direction from which it seemed to originate. A small stone seat was cut into the wall. At one end of it, Rebecca noticed a section of the stone was missing. She knelt down and put her hand against the hole. Sure enough, she could feel a strong breeze.

"Wait a minute," Drew was on his knees next to her. "The seat comes off, I reckon. Here, give me a hand."

They each grasped an end of the seat and pulled upwards. It lifted easily. Drew shone his torch inside, revealing a narrow stone staircase leading downwards into the dark. A rush of cold air filled their nostrils. They leaned the lid of the seat against the wall.

"Haddock, you old devil you! It's a tunnel all right. The mad old fool wasn't making it up after all!"

"But here, in the very room where Siobhan spoke to me – funny she did not mention it."

"Maybe didn't know it was here. You said they were prisoners."

Drew looked up and smiled widely. "Ready to explore?"

Rebecca's eyes sparkled in the torchlight. She nodded eagerly. Not hesitating, Drew climbed over the edge of the seat. The steps stretched down into blackness.

"Here, I brought yours," he said, holding out a second torch to Rebecca. As he disappeared into the narrow aperture, Rebecca followed, over the sill and down.

After about thirty steps, they emerged into a natural corridor. Their torches lit up walls made up of layer upon layer of stone strata, a mass of colours. Water was dripping somewhere close by. Progress was slow, as the passageway frequently narrowed. In some places they could barely squeeze between the cold, slimy walls. The ceiling at times was very low, necessitating some uncomfortable squatting down and shuffling along.

Rebecca was glad she was not claustrophobic. As she played her torch beam along the jagged walls, she was awestruck to think that they were now somewhere deep inside mighty Ladhar

Bheinn, its one thousand metres towering over them, the weight of a mountain crushing down on them.

She shivered, imagining unseen eyes staring from the blackness, the spirits of people from long ago. Nobody would hear their cries down here.

"Not exactly giants in days gone by were they?" said Drew, a slight edge of exasperation creeping into his voice, as he scraped his knee for the third time in as many minutes.

"How did that tall fellow Hugo ever get through here?"

"Podgy Sibley would get stuck!" said Rebecca, grateful for the chance to break the silence. They noise of their laughter echoed. They rounded a sharp turn into a much larger chamber, where their torches picked out long stalactites hanging menacingly above their heads. Suddenly Drew halted abruptly, causing Rebecca to crash into him.

"Water." Drew's torch illuminated a small lake. The surface was black and glassy.

"I wonder how far it goes," said Rebecca, clambering to the edge of the lake and shining her torch ahead. The passage veered away from the water about twenty metres further along. At this point, they could see that the lake was much larger and stretched round into another, even bigger chamber.

"Are we about to find the Princess's grave?" asked Drew.

"Not according to Siobhan," said Rebecca. "She said the Sanctuary is on an island in Loch Hourn, halfway across the causeway."

"But Becca's journal said the entrance was between a grave and a sword, didn't it? How can that be in the middle of a causeway? It doesn't sound very likely."

Rebecca shrugged. "The journal hasn't been wrong so far," she said. "Come on – let's see where this passage comes out. How far do you think we've come?"

"I'd say the best part of a mile. According to the Haddock,

the passageway leads into a labyrinth of tunnels and underground rivers. They say that over the centuries men got lost down here and never came out."

"Oh great – now he tells me!" growled Rebecca.

"If you listen closely, you can probably hear the anguished cries of long-lost clansmen, begging to be freed from this living hell in the bowels of the earth!"

"Enough, Campbell! It's not funny if you've brought us down here and got us lost."

***

Dougie was watching the men from a vantage point high on Dead Man's Crag. Several hundred feet lower down, they were following a small burn down through the rocks and hillocks. Dougie could keep an eye on them and remain well hidden. Way below, the edge of the Barradale estate was marked by a forest, which would provide sufficient cover to remain unobserved to the shore of the loch.

The men struggled to carry the pictures. Although they were too far away to be heard, the artist did not seem to have stopped waving his arms about since they left the Old Ruin.

Barradale Castle stood on a barren, unwelcoming island, a few hundred metres from the shore. Its sheer grey walls were broken by narrow apertures, through which bowmen had once rained down arrows upon their foes. The castle was small and square, only fifteen rooms in total, but its history was long and colourful. Built in 1312, it had seen bloody confrontations and battles, as clans fought each other to possess it. It was completely cut off at high tide and could only be reached in safety for a few hours each day around low tide. After this, the causeway quickly submerged under dangerous currents sweeping up the loch. Many an enemy had floundered in the tides over the centuries

The glorious weather of the morning was now gone and Dougie felt a few spots of rain. He moved quickly. His path would bring him out near the causeway. There was no road, the causeway simply extending from a rough track by the shore as it had done since the days of horseback. The tide was on the ebb. If the men were bound for the castle, they must intend to spend the night. That meant he could return for Drew and Rebecca, camp by the shore and keep watch from the safety of the trees.

The men left the trees. Only a few days previously, Dougie had made the walk out to the Castle. He had been assisting McAllum, the estate manager at Barradale, checking the deer herds. The owner of the estate, the Honourable Anthony Gordon QC, was Member of Parliament for Skye and Knoydart and spent much time away in Edinburgh and the grand surroundings of Westminster. If Drew and Rebecca were right and his estate was being used as a staging point by the thieves, there was the possibility of a great scandal.

Dougie took out his binoculars and trained them on the men now starting out across the causeway. The forger was pointing ahead to a small island, halfway to the castle. When they reached it, one of them took the paintings and disappeared from view. A minute or so later, he was back, empty handed.

Dougie was startled. The man rejoined his companions and they continued on their way. Dougie scanned the rocks, searching for any sign of the paintings or an entrance of some sort but he was too far away to be able to make anything out properly.

"Is that the cave, then?" he breathed. He looked along the loch shore to gauge the tide. There was a marker which he knew to be the low water point, clearly visible on a small headland. This suggested an hour until the causeway would start to become submerged. He would have time to wait until the men had disappeared into the castle and then go and investigate. He sat back and closed his eyes for a few minutes.

Dougie had just stirred again and was about to put his binoculars back in his pack and get up, when a movement among the rocks on the little island caught his eye.

"Probably a seal," he muttered, training the glasses. A dark blob was moving about on the rock. Whatever it was then raised itself up. With a splutter of anger, Dougie recognised the unmistakeable figure of his younger brother.

"The little ... I knew I couldn't trust the wee blighter! He's going to get us all caught! ... How the hell did he get ahead of me?"

With a grim frown, he grabbed his pack and swung it onto his back. He set off at a run out of the trees towards the causeway, his eyes on the figure of Drew.

***

By keeping to what appeared to be an ancient pathway among the rocks, marked every so often with small piles of stones, Rebecca and Drew clambered through the labyrinth of caverns and pools in the heart of the mountain. The only light came from the beams of their torches, otherwise it was dark and spooky. Their footsteps made weird echoes. It was easy to imagine being lost down there forever.

They arrived in a large cavern, into which a little light seemed to penetrate, indicating the end of the tunnel was not far.

"Shh! Hold it a minute!" Rebecca grabbed Drew's arm and stood stock still at the edge of a deep pool.

"There! See that light moving about?"

From what seemed to be a passage leading away from the other side of the pool, they could make out a shaft of light, moving around. They both switched off their torches. The light flickered for a few moments, before it too disappeared.

"Wait here!" whispered Drew.

"Why should *I* wait?" Rebecca growled indignantly. "Stop playing the hero! Look, you go that side and I'll go this!"

They skirted around opposite sides of the pool, the dim light enabling Rebecca to keep an eye on Drew's progress as she went. A waft of salty air reached her. As it did so, she slipped on something wet and saw that she had trodden on seaweed. The sea must penetrate into this cavern. A surge of excitement ran through her as it dawned on her that this must be one of the caves of which Siobhan had spoken. She looked across to try and attract Drew's attention but he had already disappeared through the gap where they had seen the torch. Picking her way over the sharp rocks and flicking her torch back on, Rebecca rounded the end of the lake. She trod gingerly, for fear of slipping again. As she looked around, her torch lit up a narrow opening a few feet from the water's edge. Beside it, there was a sharp spike sticking straight up. On the far side was a regular oblong of rock which looked like a coffin.

"*you shall find it twixt the grave of your ancestor and the sword of burial*"

The sword and the grave? It was far too different from what was around it to be natural.

This must be the secret entrance to the Sanctuary! Drew was out of sight and she did not dare call out in case there was somebody else about. She would have to investigate alone.

Rebecca lowered herself into a narrow opening. From below, she could feel a rush of air. She pointed her torch down. The ceiling was so low that she had to shuffle along on her bottom until she emerged into another cavern. This one was smaller than the one from which she had just come but was illuminated by shafts of light. She looked down from a vantage point about seven metres up.

On a small lake rested a great Viking Longboat, glowing with strange, silvery light.

The Ghost Ship ....

Rebecca's mouth fell open. At the bow, proud and impassive, stood the Warrior, his sword grasped firmly in both hands with the point resting on the deck. And next to him, white eyes glowering and his mouth slightly open, Hakon the Wolf. As she watched, the beast threw back his head and howled. The sound reverberated around the cavern.

Rebecca was petrified, unable to move, even if she had wanted to.

"Come no further, mortal!" The force of the voice shook the whole chamber. Rebecca shrank backwards, quaking.

"This is a sacred place. Mortals shall not defile it. You know who I am and why I am here. You know what must be done. *Go!* Leave this place!"

The last words were delivered with such force that Rebecca stumbled and hit her head against the rock. She let out a cry, trying desperately to steady herself. The pain in her head was excruciating and she felt suddenly dizzy. She found a tissue and pressed it to the wound. It was bleeding. It took a few more moments to compose herself, before she could summon the courage to look back at the Viking.

But the Longboat had vanished and with it Knut and Hakon. For some reason, she was not surprised. Shafts of light reflected off the glassy surface of the water.

She was alone in the empty cavern.

CHAPTER 18

THE PRISONER IN THE TOWER

Dougie dropped his pack next to Rebecca and sat down on a rock. The rain had abated for the moment and the sun had broken through in the late afternoon, casting long shafts of yellow light across Loch Hourn to the mountains of Knoydart on the northern shore.

"How on earth did you get here ahead of me?" he asked.

"We found an underground passageway from the Ruin. It leads through the caves under the mountain and came out on this island. It seemed pretty easy."

Rebecca was dabbing at her head, which was throbbing. Dougie took a piece of cloth from his pack and moved closer to her.

"Probably more luck than judgement. Here – let me. You cannae see what you're doing." He wetted the cloth in a rock pool and dabbed it against the wound. Rebecca winced at the salt water.

"That stings!"

"It'll be the salt," said Dougie, drily. He studied her head. "No great damage – but you'll have one hell of a headache."

Rebecca looked up at him. It was a novelty to be nursed by the elder Campbell brother. Dougie was still scrutinising her head and did not notice her looking at him.

Cute, thought Rebecca, in a rugged, Scottish mountains sort of way.

"Do you have a girlfriend, Dougie?" she asked.

"Now why would you be asking me that, Rebecca

McOwan?" The question had not flustered him, as Rebecca had secretly hoped it might. Dougie looked at her through narrowed eyes. "You did not hit your head too badly, then. Your wit has not deserted you. Here, hold this against your head and keep wetting it. It will take the bruising down."

"I'll take that as a no then, shall I?"

Dougie stood up and looked towards the castle. "So where is that brother of mine?"

"You mean you haven't seen him?" Rebecca's voice registered alarm.

"I thought he was here. I saw him." Dougie looked down sharply at her, suddenly very serious. His tone became urgent. "Did you not say you came through the passage together?"

"Yes, but he went on ahead when we saw a torch in the cave."

"Aw jeez – what has the lummox done now? The thieves were right here. One of them disappeared for a moment – that must have been him that you saw in the cave. I didn't see Drew until a few minutes later. I lost sight of him while I came through the Forest. If he'd come towards the shore, I would have seen him."

Rebecca looked at the grey walls of Barradale Castle in the distance.

"He must have seen them and followed them to the castle. Why didn't he wait for me?"

Dougie gave a short, humourless laugh.

"Because he's Drew. That would have been the sensible thing to do. Unfortunately, Drew and common sense are not that well acquainted."

Dougie noticed a boat moored away down the loch that was starting to turn around on its anchor to face the open sea.

"Tide is on the turn. Pretty soon, nobody will be able to get across the causeway. Damn that young fool! Come on – you and I should get back to dry land and decide what to do."

Dougie held out his hand to help her up. Rebecca grasped it and was pulled quickly and effortlessly to her feet. She could not help smiling to herself. She looked at Dougie, trying to keep a straight face.

"Muscles like that, I can't believe the girls aren't queuing up."

Dougie gave her a disparaging look. Rebecca laughed mischievously. "Too … outdoors for me, though. Besides, you're nearly an old man."

Without waiting for a response, she got to her feet and walked on ahead, back towards the shore. She had not gone more than about ten paces before she realised that Dougie had not followed. She looked back. He was staring at the castle. She went back to join him.

"What is it?"

Dougie did not reply. Following his gaze, Rebecca could make out someone at the top of one of the towers. Dougie took out his binoculars and trained them on the figure.

"Drew?" she asked softly.

"Drew."

"Well, he's stuck there for the night now."

Dougie and Rebecca regained the safety of the forest and sat down a few yards into the trees to keep a watchful eye on the castle and decide on their next step.

"Do you think he's a prisoner?" Rebecca asked.

"I doubt we'd be that lucky. Besides, if he was, he wouldn't be out on the roof like that. And they would probably be out looking for us too."

Dougie picked up a stick and snapped it in half. His annoyance was obvious.

"Brilliant – all our stuff is back at the Ruin but we're going to have to stay here tonight so we are around when knuckle-head comes back tomorrow. It's about three hours till dark, which is more than enough for me to go back and get what we need."

"It's quicker through the tunnel –"

"You sure you could find the way? No disrespect but I think I'll be a lot quicker going over the top on my own. Now, can you be trusted to stay put this time?"

His tone was sharp.

"Yes, of course. I'm sorry we didn't do as you asked earlier." She felt quite chastened, suddenly aware of the seriousness of the situation.

"Aye well …" Dougie got to his feet and buttoned up his jacket against the breeze.

"No point in worrying now – it's done. Keep watch and even if they all come out and go off, *stay here* to tell me when I get back. I don't want two of you gallivanting off. Use that brain of yours to work out the crooks' next move while I'm gone."

Rebecca smiled glumly and watched him disappear into the Forest behind her, back towards Ladhar Bheinn and the Old Ruin. She picked up the binoculars and trained them on the castle, keeping her eyes peeled for a sign of Drew.

***

Drew had recognised the distant figures of his brother and Rebecca from his crouched position in the battlements of Barradale Castle. He guessed that Dougie had spotted him and knew he would be furious. However, he could see that the tide had now turned and was coming in fast. The water was rising against the causeway and, at some points, was already seeping across. In a few more minutes, crossing would be impossible.

"I guess I'm here for the night," he said to himself, cursing. "But he won't be so angry when he hears what I've discovered."

On leaving Rebecca in the cavern, Drew had spotted one of

the thieves concealing paintings among the rocks. Staying hidden until the man disappeared, Drew ventured out. There were about twenty bundles of various sizes, sealed into rubber, watertight bags. The thieves had certainly been hard at work. He wondered how many homes and castles had been burgled to amass this much.

Although he knew it was irresponsible, Drew decided to follow the men to the castle. He slipped out of the cave onto the island, keeping to the rocks for cover. At the gateway, he flattened himself against the wall so that anybody looking out would not see him.

Inside the gateway was a small, deserted courtyard. Voices were coming from behind a heavy door. This suddenly swung closed, the loud slam causing him to shrink back behind a pillar until he was certain nobody had come outside. Peering cautiously out, he crouched low and ran across the cobbles, until he was just below a window by the door.

He inched his way up until he could peek over the sill. Inside, some men were grouped around a table, poring over a map. None of them was looking in his direction. Drew recognised the three men they had been following. They were all silent, apparently listening to a man concealed from view behind the painter. His voice was muffled.

Drew knew he had to get inside somehow. He ducked down again and looked around. Close up, Barradale Castle was not very large.

The courtyard was barely twelve metres square and the walls not more than four storeys high. In the corner was a doorway. This would do. Gathering his courage, he crept over, undid the latch and slipped inside. It took a few seconds for his eyes to become accustomed to the sudden gloom of the interior. He had entered a small hallway, off which there were three doors. One of these was ajar, leading in the direction of the men he had heard. He knew that if he stopped to think, his nerve would fail him. He thrust the door open and stepped into a narrow passageway. His boots thudded on the floor, causing him to stop. Taking great care to tread softly, he edged slowly along the passage.

Halfway along, there was a tight, stone staircase. As he neared the door at the end, he could hear the men talking, their voices now much more clear. He stopped. The door was off the latch and open far enough to reveal a few inches of the room beyond. The high-pitched voice he could hear was that of the painter.

"… I just cannot do all you ask. Art is not a production line, it takes time. It must be authentic, so that nobody will suspect. And you stick me in a draughty, wet, ruined house in the middle of nowhere, where I am expected to reproduce the works of masters. I must have another week. I insist."

He was answered by a voice Drew did not recognise.

"Forget it – if you don't get the last one done in time for Sunday, we miss the shipment. You will just have to go as fast as you can – day and night – to get them finished."

The argument continued. Drew edged closer, hoping to be able to get a glimpse of the other men in the room. He could see the back of a tall man in a long coat with thick blond hair, evidently the one arguing with the painter. The man shifted his position and, for a second, Drew saw another man seated opposite.

The bushy moustache, chubby cheeks and shiny forehead were unmistakeable.

Mr Sibley of Holborn Passage, London now spoke.

"I think it prudent that we bring this issue to a conclusion, gentlemen. The shipment must leave on Sunday. It must be loaded before seven. There are collections to be made – one from Skye and then from our friends at Rahsaig. I am proceeding to

Skye in the morning, where I will be staying with Sir Angus McDonald, Lord of the Isles.

Balatte and Lemerre, you will follow me in the boat, arriving two nights hence at dusk, and take the prize piece, Balfour's 'Flora McDonald', from the great drawing room. You will replace it with the finished copy. Then you will come back here and take everything from the cave and put it in the boat, ready for transport south. McAllum…"

He looked directly ahead, at the tall blond man.

"Go back with Godfrey to the old manse and wait until he has finished the last McOwan. Take the painting and meet the boat at the far end of Loch Nevis on Friday. That night, I shall dine with the Laird at Rahsaig and you will swap the last painting. We will all rendezvous on Saturday, as planned."

"We had best be away – the tide has turned." It was McAllum who spoke.

"Come on, Godfrey. It's a fine evening for a walk."

Drew did not wait to hear Godfrey's complaints. Fearful of being discovered, he slipped quickly up the stairs, rounding the first turn and crouching down. He heard footsteps in the courtyard and the slam of the big door. Somebody came into the passageway where he had just been hiding. He heard Sibley's voice.

"And how is our guest?"

"No bother, sir," said a French accent.

"He enjoys the view from the tower, I think."

Drew heard the door being closed.

"You'd better check on him."

A surge of alarm seized Drew as he heard a heavy footfall on the bottom stair. He turned and crept quickly upstairs, looking for a suitable place to hide.

The footsteps were clomping towards the first turning. Drew dashed up another flight to the second floor, searching frantically. There were no doors, nor access to landings. The stairs seemed to lead only upwards.

He could hear the man behind him sighing heavily. There was no other option but to carry on up wherever the staircase led.

"Balatte!" Sibley's voice boomed from the bottom of the stairs. The footfall stopped abruptly. "Come back a moment – there is something I need to check with you."

Holding onto the handrail and panting with relief, Drew heard his pursuer retrace his footsteps downstairs. What should he do now? He could not go down for fear of being discovered. They might reappear at any second.

Perhaps the "guest" Sibley had mentioned was a prisoner, being held in this tower and Balatte was on his way up there.

Drew looked up and saw he was almost at the top. There were two doors. He tried the first one. It opened out onto the battlements. He stepped out onto a narrow walkway and looked back towards the shore.

In the distance, he recognised the familiar figure of his brother, standing on the beach. If only he could speak to him!

Drew slipped back inside. Next to the second door was a hook on which hung a black key. It had to be the key to the door. Drew went to grab it and open the lock but hesitated. He grasped the door handle and tried it. It was locked. He put the key into the lock and turned until he felt a solid clunk.

He pushed the door open and stood in the doorway. Over next to a narrow window, a man turned round to look at him.

Drew's jaw dropped in astonishment.

"Henry?" he gasped, uncomprehending. "How on earth did you get here?"

"I could ask you the same thing!" Henry McOwan leapt to his feet. "I watched you come over. How did you manage to find me?"

"I didn't know you were here. We didn't know they had taken you prisoner; we've been away since yesterday. I just followed the thieves across the causeway to snoop about." Drew related the events of the previous twenty-four hours as briefly as he could. Seeing Henry's face, he stopped.

"What's up?"

"Drew ..." Henry spoke very slowly. "... I haven't been at Rahsaig since I was taken prisoner ... the day we came back from Rum."

"*What?*!" Drew almost shouted, remembered their situation and stopped himself. He took a step closer to Henry and spoke in a hoarse whisper.

"You mean ... but you *were* at Rahsaig ... we had to get you to agree to this trip. If it wasn't you, then who was it? There is a guy at Rahsaig being you. You waved us off yesterday – gave me a right telling off about looking after Rebecca."

Henry smiled glumly.

"You have met Morgan ... my twin brother."

CHAPTER 19

MESSAGE IN A BOTTLE

Sunset over Knoydart was a dazzling blend of orange, purple and crimson. As the last shafts of sunlight finally sank across the loch, Rebecca felt an edge to the breeze almost at once. She rubbed her arms against the chill, hoping Dougie was well on his way. It was an hour since he had gone.

Barradale Castle was quiet and serene, out in the middle of the loch. The tide was creeping ever further up the shore, the causeway having long since disappeared. Rebecca watched a couple of noisy red-beaked oystercatchers at the water's edge, scavenging for food, until her attention was diverted by a movement just below the castle. A rowing boat was pushing off, one figure leaping aboard clutching a rope, while a second sat at the oars. They were silhouetted against the evening light, making identification impossible. The boat struck out for the shore. Rebecca realised it was heading straight towards her. She slipped back into the trees from where she could watch unobserved.

The men came ashore and started to head up the glen in the direction of Dead Man's Crag, which gave Rebecca immediate cause for concern. Dougie would be unaware that anyone was on the path behind him. She recognised the painter. The two men passed slowly by, in the sort of silence that exists when people have argued, the painter obviously annoyed and trailing a good ten yards back. The other taller, blond man glowered over his shoulder several times, to check he was still following.

Rebecca fidgeted nervously, wondering if she should go after them. The two men could not possibly catch up with Dougie but he might run into them. Dougie had been so very firm that she was to remain where she was no matter what happened, that she decided to stay put. There was little she could do in any case, since she would probably be slower than all of them. Her ankle was now feeling the effects of yesterday's walking. It would be better to wait and keep an eye out for Drew.

***

Drew's face was blank with astonishment. His mouth opened but no sound emerged. Henry explained.

"Morgan is in with Sibley. You have not met him before and the family does not speak of him – I hadn't seen him for twenty years. Rebecca will never have heard of him. We are identical apart from our hair colour, but that can easily be altered. Morgan ran away from home after a row with Father – we heard he had gone to South America. The row was over him stealing money from Father, a lot of money. It was to feed a gambling habit and pay off the loan sharks.

Well, when the boat from Rum arrived back in Arisaig and I went off to get the car, Morgan was sitting in the driving seat. I was astonished. He locked the doors so I couldn't get out. One of his henchmen tied me up, put me into a van and took me off to Morar, a couple of miles away then he came back to meet you – not me. I was driven to the beach, where they bundled me into a boat and brought me here."

"But he is so like you ... I'd never have guessed, nobody would. How can he do that? He knows everything about everyone, about Rahsaig ... it's incredible."

Henry smiled.

"That is because he has a little mole telling him everything he needs to know to pass himself off as me. I'm pretty sure I know who. They are using Lord Gordon's home while he is away because one of the men involved is McAllum, the head ranger. He's a hard case. They want me to sign some documents, turning over the rights on the estate to Morgan but I've refused. So by replacing me with Morgan, they can make it seem as if I did sign and get witnesses to the signature. Everyone will think it is me, just like you did." He paused and frowned.

"We've got to get out of here. One of them will be up with my supper in a few minutes. Then they won't come back until morning. If you hide on the roof until he has gone, you can come back to let me out. We can slip down, take a boat and be away and they won't find out for hours."

***

Of all the rangers in this remote corner of Scotland, when it came to speed over the ground, Dougie Campbell was acknowledged to be the fastest. As he had done on the way, Dougie took the most direct route back, straight over Dead Man's Crag. Supremely fit due to spending his life climbing up and down hills and mountains, a climb that would have taken an average person several hours, Dougie achieved in less than one. He paused at the top to catch his breath and looked back down the glen. Barradale Castle was now completely cut off, standing ghostly and grey in the fading light. Although the sun was still catching the very top of the mountain where he stood, Dougie knew he had only a limited amount of good light left. With a grunt, he set off at a run down the slope.

***

"Loch Hourn. How much longer do I have to stare at Loch

Hourn? Hourn means Hell, you know." Henry sighed in exasperation as he looked out of his tower prison.

"I'm sorry, Henry," said Drew, sitting with his head in his hands. "How was I to know that numpty Sibley likes 'to take the evening air on the battlements'?"

"It's not your fault," said Henry.

"But it does leave us with rather a predicament, now that we are both 'guests' here. I hope our podgy friend believed your tale about coming to deliver a message for McAllum from Dougie. All he has to do is ring Rahsaig and speak to Morgan to find out the others came with you. Then they will be on the look out for Rebecca and Dougie as well. We have to get out of here and find them first."

***

The snap of a twig somewhere close by caused Dougie to look up sharply. Having retrieved his rucksack and enough food for the night, he had just arrived at the place where his return route crossed the stalkers' path from Barradale.

He heard voices, one raised in whining protest. He ducked behind a large rock not a moment too soon, for somebody emerged from a small copse into a clearing nearby. Dougie recognised the painter and, with a sharp intake of breath, McAllum of Barradale.

"So ... Mac is in this thing too," he whispered under his breath.

"That explains why he wasn't around much when we were counting the Barradale deer."

"...You must start as soon as we get there," the tall McAllum was saying. "You heard the boss. Everything has to be ready by Saturday. You have to have the painting done in two days. I'm away in the morning to see our friendly Laird at

Rahsaig and I'll be back on Friday to pick it up. Then you can get back to your French loft."

"It's a Parisian attic studio, actually," said the painter, with a haughty sniff. "Not that I would expect a fellow like you to have any understanding about how an artist lives or draws his inspiration."

The men passed on down the hillside towards the manse. When he was certain they were out of sight and earshot, Dougie re-emerged, crossed the path and continued the same direct ascent he had taken earlier.

***

"So our friends won't be back tonight, then?" asked Rebecca, watching as Dougie took off his boots, sighed in pleasure and wiggled his toes. She rolled her eyes and pretended to faint from the fumes.

"Okay, okay," smiled Dougie. "No, they won't. And we should get some rest now so we can be up and about early if wee lummox decides to put in an appearance."

"I've been thinking about that," said Rebecca. "Drew's situation has changed while you've been away. He is now inside the castle, in the tower. I saw him through the binoculars. He has either got himself caught or found somewhere to hide for the night."

Dougie gave a hollow laugh. "He'll have got himself caught, don't you worry. Well that's blown it, sure enough. Was this before or after those guys came ashore?"

"After."

"Good. It's likely that they won't know. I overheard McAllum say he is headed for Rahsaig in the morning to see Henry. At least he hasn't been warned off. What's this thinking you've been doing?"

Rebecca smiled wryly.

"Well – I don't think your pal McAllum will be seeing Henry tomorrow… since he is in the tower as well."

"What?!" Dougie sat bolt upright and stared at her incredulously.

"I saw them both at the window."

"What's Henry doing there? Is he a prisoner too?"

"I've no idea. My plan is to take that boat" – she pointed to the rowing boat the men had come ashore in earlier – "and go and find out. If necessary we'll carry out a little rescue under the cover of darkness. McAllum and his pals have a free hand to steal whatever they want from Rahsaig, if Henry is locked up in the tower."

Moments later, Dougie and Rebecca had loaded their gear into the boat and pushed out from the shore. The water was black and still. The first stars were showing in the sky.

Dougie took the oars and rowed strongly and as soundlessly as he could. Rebecca sat facing him, one eye on his muscular arms, the other on the castle.

"There's only one place on the island we can land, so we'll just have to pray they've all turned in for the night," said Dougie, grimly. "If we're spotted, we've had it."

The silence of Loch Hourn was almost deafening, its stillness enhanced by the dark. Rebecca felt sure even the splash of an oar and the wash of the boat through the water would be heard. They were rounding the edge of the island, when they were startled by a noise in the water next to the boat.

"What the – what was that?" Dougie hissed, turning his head sharply.

"I've no idea," whispered Rebecca. "Wait a minute!"

She pointed up at the tower. In a lighted window at the top, the tousled head of Drew could be seen, waving frantically and pointing down at them.

"What's he on about?" growled Dougie.

"That!" said Rebecca, pointing to something floating in the water a few yards from them. Dougie took one of the oars from its rowlock and managed to drag it alongside.

"It's a plastic bottle."

Rebecca grabbed the bottle from the water and opened it. There was a piece of paper stuffed into the neck. She took out her torch.

"Oh no – message in a bottle!" sang Dougie, sarcastically.

"It's quite ingenious, actually," said Rebecca. "Listen to this.

'QUIET!!!! Don't try rescue – too dangerous! Sibley's men below. Henry and I held in top of Tower. Sibley going to Skye tomorrow to steal a painting from Lord Mac and taking us for cover. Tell Lennie to arrest Laird at Rahsaig.'

"Arrest the Laird at Rahsaig? What is he on about – the Laird is up in the tower and going to Skye tomorrow. He's lost it." Dougie made a helpless gesture up at Drew. Henry appeared at the window and threw another object out. It landed beside the boat.

"How many bottles have they got?" muttered Dougie, grabbing it from the water and almost tearing the cap off. Rebecca shone her torch on it. Inside was another, hastily penned note, this time in Henry's handwriting.

Bogus Laird at Rahsaig – do not be fooled. Tell Lennie that Morgan is back – he'll understand. Act as if nothing has happened – tell them you know nothing of our whereabouts and Drew has gone to Barradale on an errand for you. Sibley is planning getaway on Saturday with all paintings. Coming to Rahsaig with gang on Friday, so watch out!

Rebecca scratched her head in bemusement. "What does he mean, 'bogus laird' at Rahsaig? And who is Morgan?"

She stared up, uncomprehending. Unseeing in the darkness, Henry merely made a gesture urging them to depart.

"We'd best get going," said Dougie. "To Rahsaig, I suppose, but I'm blowed if I know what's going on now … or what on earth we are going to do."

He manoeuvred the boat around and began to row away from the castle and down the Loch. Rebecca sat in the stern, looking at each note in turn and then back at the fast-disappearing figures at the window. After a few more strokes, they had been swallowed up in the gloom. She shrugged her shoulders.

"How far is it back to Rahsaig?" she asked.

"Well, we'll have to go all the way round the coast. Seven kilometres, maybe more. It would be quicker on foot over the top but it's dark and I doubt you'd make it fast enough."

Rebecca grudgingly conceded he was probably right. Even without a sore ankle, she would have had no hope of matching Dougie's pace over the mountains.

"Should we not put in and phone? You said there was a Mountain Rescue post here."

Dougie looked up sharply and smiled.

"Of course! Rebecca McOwan – were you not the boss's niece and but a slip of a lass, I would kiss you for that!"

"Don't worry on my account," said Rebecca under her breath, smiling.

"We can call our friendly neighbourhood cop and then Willie to come and pick us up."

"Where is the Mountain Rescue post?"

"Half mile down there towards the sea – as long as we don't get lost in the dark. There's a small beach just along the shoreline. Look out for rocks below the water. Don't want to go holing ourselves."

They rounded a headland and Dougie steered into a tiny bay. A small stream flowed into the loch from a narrow glen, cascading steeply down from the slopes of Ladhar Bheinn.

Where the river left the trees, was a small, wooden hut, no bigger than a garden shed.

"That's it?" said Rebecca in disbelief. "You call that tatty little shed a Mountain Rescue post? Where are the rescuers?"

"It's not quite the AA, I'll grant you but then that's not the point. It's a place to rest up and communicate with the outside world. It's deceptively big inside, you'll see."

"Oh, amaze me!" said Rebecca, sarcastically. "A bijou pied-a-terre, here in the middle of the wilderness, with every home comfort!"

She followed Dougie through the door. Once he had found some matches and lighted a large hurricane lamp, she could make out a rather basic room with chairs and table.

"There's a stove, coal, first aid kit, kettle – which I suggest is put on – and tea, sugar, tinned food, maps, blankets, bedding and even a few camp beds. Everything you would need if you got stuck here in bad weather. You're impressed, I can tell."

Rebecca was looking around, still sceptical. Dougie laughed and handed her the kettle.

"And over here is the radio, which I am going to use."

Rebecca looked down at the kettle and back at Dougie, mock affront on her face.

"No running water, I'm afraid. But you'll find plenty of water in the river. Don't fill it from the loch – that's sea water."

He turned to the radio and started to rummage through a pile of papers. Rebecca made a face at the back of his head and went outside. She bent to fill the kettle from the river. Then she sat down on a rock to think.

"Has that kettle got a hole in it?" Dougie yelled from the doorway of the hut.

"No. Just enjoying the peace of your Highlands, Mr Campbell."

"Aye, well you'll enjoy it better with a cup of something. I'll see what I can rustle up to eat as well. I've lit the stove."

With a warm mug of soup clutched between her hands, Rebecca ventured back outside. She climbed the point and sat down in the heather. Above her, the sky was a mass of stars, twinkling brightly. She could even see the swathe of the Milky Way. The only noise was the river and the gentle lapping of the water on the beach. The shadowy outline of the castle was now almost a mile away. She thought of Drew and Henry, in their tower. She would have to pretend she knew nothing and hope the bogus laird, whoever he might be, did not become suspicious. But if the thieves were going to Rahsaig, did that not mean she would become a prisoner too?

"Dougie!" Rebecca ran back inside. Dougie was on the phone and held up his hand.

"…okay …that's what he said, constable, Morgan… Do you know who Morgan is? … So what should we do when we get back to Rahsaig? …I don't like the idea of that …okay, I hear what you say …yup …yup, goodbye, constable."

Dougie replaced the receiver with a frown and ran a hand through his hair.

"… Well?" said Rebecca, impatiently. "What did he say?"

"They won't arrest this bogus laird until they hear it from Henry. I told him what we suspect and what we know but he wants evidence."

"Doesn't he believe it?"

"Don't think so. Says he wants to speak to him personally. So I have persuaded him to go to Skye and call in on Lord McDonald on some pretext. He can get to Henry then."

"And what about this Morgan?"

"He just said 'Oh'. The way he said it sounded like he thought the guy was bad news."

"So what do we do now?"

"The constable doesn't want us going back to Rahsaig in case it's dangerous. But he doesn't believe us enough to arrest the Laird. So we need to find out what's going on. If the thieves are going there, they must be pretty confident they will be safe, which probably guarantees we wouldn't be."

"We have two options then. One, you help me over the mountain and we camp out above Rahsaig and keep an eye out. There's nothing we can do to help Drew and Uncle Henry yet. Sibley is going to Rahsaig on Friday with, we presume, both of them. We need to be around then to find out what they know and make a plan."

"And the other option?"

"We go to Skye and try to see them there. And we must try to stop the thieves stealing from Lord MacDonald. Now we know how they operate, we might be able to switch paintings on them again, like Drew and I did before. We can meet the constable, tell him everything and hope he believes it this time, if he hears it from Henry and us."

Dougie was lost in thought for a few moments. He looked at his watch.

"There's a lighthouse on the Sandaig Islands at the mouth of Loch Hourn. I can get Willie to meet us there and then take us over to Skye before dawn. Lord Mac's place is not far. We should get a chance to talk to Henry and wee lummox. I'd feel a lot better if we all knew what we were doing, rather than running over the hills in the dark ... metaphorical as well as the no light kind."

CHAPTER 20

THE LIGHTHOUSE

Under the brilliant starlit sky, Dougie and Rebecca pushed the small rowing boat out onto the black waters of Loch Hourn. The great dark amphitheatre formed by the loch and hills was silent. Their destination was the lighthouse on the Sandaig Islands, whose beam could just be seen flashing at regular intervals, several miles away beyond the mouth of the loch, into the open sea.

Dougie had managed to get through to Willie McHarg, who would set out from Mallaig to meet them in a few hours' time. Rebecca looked at her watch. It was already midnight.

"What is the lighthouse keeper going to think when we turn up there in a rowing boat in the middle of the night?" asked Rebecca, as Dougie settled into his rowing.

"And isn't a lighthouse supposed to warn people off dangerous places boats shouldn't go? … Like our boat?"

"The last keeper left about ten years ago. It's all operated remotely by the coastguard at Mallaig these days. And don't worry – I know my way. Besides, the islands are usually covered in seals basking on the rocks when you go by."

"We aren't likely to run into Sibley's boat, are we?" Rebecca peered anxiously ahead, noticing a red light bobbing up and down some way in the distance.

Dougie looked straight ahead, unconcerned. "It was still tied up at Barradale when we left. They'll not leave till morning. Only an idiot would be out on these waters after dark, particularly near the Sandaig rocks."

Rebecca gave him a disconcerted look. "Thanks … that is really comforting."

***

Two hours later, a weary Dougie was guiding the boat carefully alongside a small jetty below the lighthouse. Already moored there was the motor cruiser *Duke of Argyll*, which Rebecca recognised from Rahsaig. Willie McHarg called out a greeting. A rope landed on Dougie's knees.

"Dougie. Miss McOwan. It's a fine night," he said, pulling them alongside.

Rebecca smiled to herself. Willie's manner suggested he found nothing out of the ordinary in this situation. His face was as straight as a statue in a museum. It was the first time she had really observed him close up. She could see vague traces of his sister, but his expression was altogether more open. She guessed his age as older than her uncle but could not be certain.

There was an indefinable quality to him.

"Rebecca, please. Nobody calls me Miss McOwan."

Willie McHarg raised his eyebrows almost imperceptibly. "You'll be wanting me to take you on to Skye now then?"

"First light will be fine, Willie," answered Dougie, breathing hard and shipping the oars thankfully. "Unless you reckon you can hit Isleornsay in the dark. We've got to pay a call on Lord Mac in the morning. The Laird and Drew will be along later. Besides, I think we'd probably like a wee rest before we go anywhere."

"Funny," said Willie. "The laird didn't mention anything to me when I dropped him off this evening."

Rebecca uttered an involuntary "Oh!" and looked at Dougie. Dougie's eyes narrowed.

"You saw the laird this evening?"

"Aye. He was in Mallaig."

Rebecca and Dougie exchanged puzzled looks but neither pursued this any further until Willie disappeared back inside his boat to the cabin for a moment.

"I don't understand," whispered Rebecca. "Henry is a prisoner. How can he possibly have been in Mallaig this evening? Unless he wasn't and Willie is lying. You don't think Willie is in with the crooks, do you?"

"Not a chance," responded Dougie, swiftly. "Perhaps there really is a bogus laird and he convinced Willie that he's the real one. I've known Willie for years and he's as straight as they come. If he says he saw Henry, he believes it. I was intending to tell him everything."

This last part was said with a questioning look, as if seeking Rebecca's agreement.

"If you trust him, that's good enough for me."

They were interrupted by the reappearance of Willie, clutching three mugs. They jumped aboard and stowed their packs below.

"We'd best grab some sleep," said Dougie.

"A dram first, lad," said Willie to Dougie. "You've had a long day. And you'd better tell me what is going on, seeing as you've got me out here in the middle of the night."

"Fair enough," said Dougie and sat down. Willie produced a bottle from his pocket, lined up two mugs and poured a splash into each. He saw Rebecca eyeing the bottle.

"Uisge Beatha … in Gaelic, the water of life … Whisky! Not for you, I think." He smiled and produced a bottle of lemonade out of his other pocket and held it out.

"Your uncle would fire the pair of us if we plied you with whisky."

Rebecca took the proffered bottle and leaned forward to sniff the contents of the mugs. Instantly, she recoiled, making a face.

"Poo-wee! You can keep that!"

Dougie and Willie laughed.

As Dougie began to tell Willie the events of the last couple of days, Rebecca slipped ashore and climbed up the path to the lighthouse. They were five kilometres from the dark mass of the mainland away to the south. Ahead of them the southern tip of the mystic Isle of Skye was bathed in silvery moonlight. Although the weather tonight was warm and clear, Rebecca could imagine the small collection of rocks comprising the Sandaig Islands could be a wild, unforgiving place in bad weather. It would have been a lonely existence for a lighthouse keeper. She found it difficult to imagine what would possess anyone to want to live in a twelve-metre steel tube in the middle of the cold, stormy sea.

Back towards Loch Hourn, Barradale was no longer visible in the dark of the night.

Rebecca noticed a glow on the water, some distance away. She narrowed her eyes to try and make it out. Gradually, it became bigger and Rebecca realised it was moving. She sensed it was travelling slowly in the direction of the lighthouse.

A sudden rush of cold air swept up the rocks at her and began to swirl around. She could now discern a low mist, preceding the light across the water. It quickly enveloped the lighthouse and reduced visibility to a few yards. But there was something else too… an atmosphere.

Rebecca's feet were rooted to the spot.

Slowly, the thick fog swirling around the rocky island parted slightly. The luminous glow shone from within, now much closer and brighter.

Through the waves emerged a figure in a black hooded cloak.

It seemed to walk straight out of the water.

"Who are you?" Rebecca heard herself cry out.

The figure did not reply. It seemed to glide slowly up the rocks towards her.

Rebecca shrank back, frightened.

"What do you want?" She pleaded.

It came inexorably on. A yard from her, it finally stopped. She could see nothing in the hood other than blackness.

Silence.

Rebecca was about to call out in fear when, slowly, a hand rose to the hood and pulled it back, revealing tresses of long dark hair and a pale but beautiful face that Rebecca realised instantly she knew.

"Becca?" Rebecca's voice faltered slightly.

The woman made no reply.

"I have read your journal... I... I've seen you, that dress, your paintings in the castle ... Siobhan has told me about what Lachlan did."

Two dark eyes looked at her expressionlessly.

When, at last, the woman spoke, it was in a strange, echoing voice that seemed to come from all around and inside Rebecca's own head.

"I come to warn you of Lachlan. He is here. He means you harm."

"Lachlan is here? What do you mean? Where? Why does he mean me harm?" Rebecca looked around anxiously, almost expecting Lachlan himself to emerge from the mist. She felt as if she knew this woman, and yet she now felt more frightened than in any of her encounters with the Wolf and the Warrior. There was no trace of the gentle soul whose life she had read about, who had been spoken of with such love by Siobhan. The tone of Becca's voice was chilling.

"You would try to stop him. If you return the treasure to its rightful place, he will be lost to eternity. But be warned, he will stop at nothing. You must be on your guard."

"But how will I know him?"

"You will know him. He is the man you do not know but yet you do know. I cannot stay here, I must go back."

Becca swept the hood back over her head and began to slip back down towards the sea. Rebecca stood up.

"Wait!" she cried.

Becca stopped. The hooded head turned.

"You will help. You must help. Only you can help. Help us!"

With that, she turned again.

"Don't go, please!"

But Rebecca's pleas went unheeded. The hooded figure slipped back into the waves.

The mist evaporated and, just as soon as it had changed, everything was as before.

Rebecca wrung her hands. This encounter had shaken her.

There was so much she had wanted to say to Becca, so many questions to ask.

Yet Becca had spoken in riddles. Rebecca did not understand what she had meant about Lachlan being here and meaning to do her harm.

For the first time since she had come to the Highlands, she was really frightened.

CHAPTER 21

OVER THE SEA TO SKYE

Down on the shore below Barradale Castle, a small group of birds were searching for food, as the tide slowly receded, their shrill calls the only noise disturbing the peace. To the north and the south, the glens, corries and ridges of the mountains of Knoydart looked on, majestic and timeless.

"I wish we knew what was going on at Rahsaig," said Drew, gazing out from the castle tower. "You don't think we'll get back to find the place robbed?"

"No," said Henry McOwan definitely, stretching out on a lumpy mattress.

"My guess is they want a few very specific things – all of which are worth a great deal of money on the black market. What time is it?"

"Just before seven. I wonder where Rebecca and our Doug are now?"

"Back at Rahsaig, if they rowed through the night. I hope they take heed of what we told them. They must be careful around Morgan. He'll latch on in an instant if he thinks they're acting strangely."

"He had everyone fooled after we got back from Rum. None of us had an inkling it wasn't you. Although, that might explain why you – I mean 'he' – agreed to us going on our little trip so easily. Took very little persuading. A good deal less than you might have needed, boss – I s'pose he wanted us out of the way."

Henry gave a wan smile. He was not really concentrating on what Drew was saying.

"I'm worried they are going to get away with it. We cannot let them. I wonder if people even realise they have been robbed. Dougie *has* to get the police to arrest Morgan. And we have to warn Lord Mac. It won't be easy as Sibley won't let us out of his sight. They'll try the switch at some stage – probably after dark. That painting on Skye is part of our heritage, it must not be lost. And it's worth a fortune."

"Why would anyone pay lots of money for a painting they can never sell?" Drew rested his chin on his hands as he looked out of the window. "If it's been stolen, and people know it's been stolen, nobody would buy it, surely?"

"Collectors are a strange breed. Some of them want things just to have them, not to show off or profit from. Possessing something of great beauty is enough for them."

"Seems daft to me," said Drew, dismissively.

The metallic rasp of the key in the lock caused both of them to turn. The door opened to reveal the portly frame and bristling moustache of Simon Sibley.

"Good morning, Gentlemen. I trust you slept well. Please join me downstairs for breakfast. I see no reason why, even in the current circumstances, we cannot still be civilised. We shall be departing for the Isle of Skye after breakfast – that is Mr McOwan and I will be. You –" he addressed Drew "– will remain as our guest at least until we are long gone from this country. And as insurance, my dear Mr McOwan, that you do not try anything, shall we say, unwise. "

In a flourish, moustache and upturned nose revolved one hundred and eighty degrees and disappeared back down the staircase. One of the Frenchmen leaned around the door and gestured that they should follow.

"Great!" muttered Drew. "Looks like I'll be enjoying the view a while longer then." He followed Henry through the door, giving the grinning Frenchman a glare.

***

"Beyond misery, despair, hatred, treachery,
Beyond guilt and defilement;
Watchful, heroic, the Cuillin is seen
Rising on the other side of sorrow."

Willie McHarg stood at the wheel of the *Duke of Argyll*, as they approached the Isle of Skye, gazing at the distant jagged peaks which formed the famous Cuillins. Dougie and Rebecca turned to look at him.

"Very lyrical, Willie," said Dougie, smiling.

"Is that Shakespeare?" asked Rebecca.

"Sorley MacLean, Gaelic poet of modern times. I don't spend all my time on boats and heaving seaweed, you know." Willie's face creased into a smile.

"The Cuillins inspire many things. Mystery, music, poetry – somebody even tried to sell them a while back. Then he realised they were not his to sell."

A police car was parked on the pier at the small harbour of Isleornsay on the south end of Skye. Willie moored the boat alongside. As Dougie and Rebecca jumped ashore onto the jetty, Constable Lennie's tall, angular frame extracted itself from the passenger side of the car and strode purposefully towards them.

"The long arm – and legs – of the law," murmured Rebecca, just loud for Dougie to hear.

"Mr Campbell." Lennie nodded briskly in greeting.

"I'm trusting this is serious, since I've come all the way to Skye and disturbed the Sergeant in Portree before his breakfast, in order to meet you."

"It's straight from the Laird, Constable, I promise you, and it concerns major art theft," replied Dougie. As he began to recount the full tale of the past few days, the Constable listened, his face betraying nothing.

"And you say this Sibley will be visiting Lord Mac today, and Henry with him?"

"That's right," said Rebecca. "They're coming from Barradale this morning. We must get to talk to Henry and –"

"A moment there, lass, before we get to deciding what we will be doing." A tone of reproof was introduced by the Sergeant, who had been listening in silence but now saw fit to exercise the authority of rank.

"These are serious matters. One thing is for certain and that is that you two must stay out of sight. If this Sibley sees you, the element of surprise will be lost."

"But we must talk with Uncle Henry –" Rebecca began but the Sergeant held his hand up, as if directing traffic on the Skye Bridge, thought Rebecca uncharitably.

"You will please leave the talking to the constable and myself," he said, a little frostily. Rebecca ground her teeth. Why would these policemen listen patiently to Dougie but not take her seriously? The Sergeant continued.

"Now, Mr Campbell. What is this demand that we arrest a 'bogus Laird' at Rahsaig? Would you mind telling me who this bogus person is and what they have done? Without evidence there is no crime and without a crime, there will be no arrest."

The Sergeant looked challengingly at Dougie. Rebecca decided he perhaps required a sound reason why he had missed his breakfast that morning.

"That is why we have to talk to Uncle Henry," interjected Rebecca, determined that this man would not block their purpose today and that he would listen to her.

"Only he knows why. His message said to arrest the Laird at Rahsaig."

"Ah yes. This would be the message he threw out of the castle in – what was it – an empty cola bottle?"

Rebecca took the message from her pocket and handed it to the Sergeant.

"Here it is, if you don't believe us."

The Sergeant took the crumpled scrap of paper and made a show of spreading it out so that he might be able to decipher it. Lennie looked over his shoulder.

"And this is the evidence with which you want us to arrest a man? You would have us believe that the Laird of Rahsaig instructs us to arrest the Laird of Rahsaig … by cola bottle." The Sergeant's tone was becoming ever more superior.

"It does look like his writing, Sarge," said Constable Lennie. The Sergeant turned a withering glare on him, causing PC Lennie to look at his boots. Dougie now spoke.

"Look, he also mentions this guy Morgan. He said you'd understand, constable?"

"Aye, I do." Lennie paused and pursed his lips. There was a pause while everyone looked at him.

"Well?" demanded the Sergeant. "If you know something, Lennie, tell us."

"Morgan McOwan … the Laird's twin brother …"

There was a gasp from Dougie and Rebecca.

"… he was a bad lad. He was sent away to boarding school but got heavily into drugs. He stole money from his father and one day he vanished. Nobody has heard a word from him in twenty years."

"Uncle Henry and my father have another brother?" said Rebecca, incredulous.

"I don't believe it. They would have said."

"It's true, Miss Rebecca." Willie McHarg stepped forward from the bows of his boat.

"Alexander and I grew up with them. Alexander is right.

Morgan was no good. Your Grandfather saw to it that the family disowned him entirely after he had left. He would not hear people round here even mention the boy's name. Your grandmother went to her grave with an aching heart. She would have forgiven him as only a mother would forgive her child but to your grandfather, he no longer existed. If Morgan is back, then I'm willing to bet he's after something."

"Well," said the Sergeant, with an air of finality.

"Be all this as it may, we cannot arrest somebody on the unsubstantiated whim of another, however well thought of the 'other' might be."

***

From the window of the tower, Drew watched the boat carrying Henry and Sibley depart for Skye. He banged his fist on the sill in frustration, wondering how much longer he would be a prisoner. He was certainly regretting his impetuous decision to follow the thieves. He had not considered the consequences. The root of his annoyance was that Dougie and Rebecca were somewhere on their trail. The perilous aspect of the situation had never really occurred to Drew. His mother had always referred to him as the eternal optimist. He was quite certain the thieves would be caught and that no harm would come to either himself or the others.

A small brown mouse scuttled along the floor beside the open fireplace and disappeared behind a chest of drawers. Drew frowned. He got down onto his knees and peered under the chest, to see whether he was sharing his accommodation with any more. Unable to see properly, he grasped the chest and dragged it to one side. There was a recess, just big enough for a man to squat down inside. An idea occurred.

A while later, the Frenchman arrived outside the door

with a drink for the room's occupant and placed his key in the lock.

"English Indian tea, Scottish boy!" he called, entering the room. It was empty.

"*Merde!*" He looked around in a flash of anger and rushed over to the window. A look of consternation crossed his face when he could see no trace of Drew. He tossed the cup onto the table, spilling its contents and rushed out of the door and downstairs.

There was a scraping sound as the chest started to move forward. Drew poked his head out and squeezed through a gap between the chest and the wall. He paused at the window to check the coast was clear. He saw the Frenchman dash out of the castle gates and look frantically around, searching for any sign of his captive. The causeway was now passable and, after a moment's indecision, the Frenchman set off, at a run, towards the shore.

There was no time to lose.

"You could have been more careful with my tea, Frenchie," sighed Drew, draining the dreg that remained. He shoved the chest back to conceal his hiding place, should fate transpire that he needed to use it again. The castle was empty and quiet, confirming his suspicions that he and his jailer had been the only two left. He slipped quickly down the stairs and into the courtyard. Stopping at the gatehouse, he spied the Frenchman on the far beach. He would head for the tunnel entrance, he decided, and go back to the Manse.

"Damn!" he muttered, remembering that McAllum had stolen his torch. He could not navigate the tunnel without it. Perhaps it was in the castle somewhere.

He felt inside his pocket and his fingers closed around his penknife. Another thought occurred. He went over to a grey wall-box, concealed behind the gatehouse, which contained the telephone connections. Opening the blade, he cut the wires he could see.

"That'll stop him warning anyone," he smiled to himself.

Drew noticed his jailer was on his way back. He breathed hard, trying to decide his next move. He needed to buy enough time to get away and be sure the gang could not be alerted. McAllum and Godfrey were at the Old Manse without the means of communicating with anyone, other than by a further day's walk to Rahsaig. Hopefully, the Frenchman would not know about the Mountain Rescue post.

The man was too big for him to think of trying anything brave.

He smiled to himself as a solution occurred. He would resort to good old Highland guile. It had already worked once, so why not again?

***

Lord MacDonald of Skye, the authentic Lord of the Isles and Laird of the biggest clan in Scotland, greeted Henry McOwan with the warmth of an old friend long parted.

"My dear, dear Henry!" Lord Angus MacDonald, known fondly by the locals as Lord Mac and to a certain privileged few as Gussie, embraced Henry warmly.

"It's been too long! I am not so young I can afford to lose a good friend and I truly miss your father – as fine a golfer as ever I knew!"

"Thank you Gussie, that's kind of you. There's been an awful lot to do at home since he passed, just to get things straight."

"Ah well, it's not so easy is it, this being stinking rich?!" His Lordship threw back his head and guffawed. Finally breaking their handshake, Gussie turned to Sibley.

"Mr Sibley? You are most welcome. We've not much here to interest you I think, as the dastardly McOwans thankfully didn't manage to get their hands on this place! But the portrait of the fiendish Lachlan is in the study for you to have a look at."

Lord MacDonald spoke merrily and heartily. Sibley was at his most simpering.

"Most gracious, your Lordship! Although there is one other treasure I would like to see as well, if I might be permitted to impose. I understand you have the original Flora McDonald by the great Balfour?"

"Indeed we do, though that is not for sale at any price! I think the clan would drum me out, were I to sell our most famous ancestor! Shall we go through? It's early for a dram … perhaps you would take some coffee?"

"Sir." A young man in the black suit of a butler appeared at the door and stood patiently. Lord MacDonald raised his eyebrows, questioningly.

"More gentlemen to see you, sir. I've shown them into the drawing room."

"I'll be right there. My apologies, gentlemen. Why don't you go into the study and I'll join you? My man will show you."

As Lord MacDonald departed, the butler showed Henry and Sibley into a beautiful wood-panelled room, with a large bay window overlooking the sea and mountains. Sibley went over immediately to a magnificent oil painting on one of the walls.

"The Balfour!" he sighed. He half turned towards Henry, who was staring out of the window. The sigh turned to a hiss.

"Remember that while you are useful to me for a while longer to introduce me to your wealthy friends, you should not get so carried away in this touching reunion that you forget your friend at Barradale. His welfare should be your primary concern."

"You put it so well," muttered Henry, contemptuously.

The door opened behind them. Lord MacDonald's head appeared.

"Henry! The police are here warning about some salmon poaching in the area. They were going to see you later but since you're here, they'd appreciate a word now. Mr Sibley and I can enjoy the Balfour and start our tour. You can join us later."

Sibley turned quickly round at the mention of policemen. His eyes flashed dangerously at Henry, out of sight of Lord MacDonald. Henry read the message only too clearly. As he made for the door, Gussie gave him an almost imperceptible wink. Henry followed his butler out of the room and down the ornate corridor, into a sumptuously furnished Drawing Room. Alexander Lennie stood up as he entered.

"Alex! Boy, am I glad to see you!" Henry rushed over and clasped the tall Constable's hand. Lennie indicated his companion.

"Sergeant Gillespie from Portree here on the island."

The Sergeant stood up.

"Duncan Gillespie, Mr McOwan."

Henry sat, taking a nervous look over his shoulder, lest Sibley should somehow contrive a reason to follow him.

"How did you know I was here?"

"Dougie Campbell phoned me last night and suggested we would find you here. We need to know what this business is about. I don't doubt young Dougie for a moment but we'd rather hear it from you."

"We need full details, Mr McOwan. You'll understand that we cannot go about arresting anybody until we have firm reason for doing so. Your young friend Campbell and Miss McOwan outside said you could provide that."

"Rebecca and Dougie are outside? I'd like to see them."

"We thought it best to keep them out of sight for the time being, you understand. So, we need the facts, sir."

The Sergeant nodded at the Constable, who produced a notebook and pen.

"Well, Sergeant. Until this morning, I was being held against my will in Barradale Castle. The captor is here, Simon Sibley, antiques dealer from London. He has a team of accomplices, who have been carrying out thefts of valuable art from a number of great clan houses in the Highlands. I have reason to believe they have stolen already from my own house, that they will do so again and that they intend to steal from here tonight. Some men came across with us and they have disappeared."

"Odd that we should not have had reports of these thefts, sir. Do not these paintings leave rather large gaps on the wall?" The Sergeant was rather proud of this joke. Henry looked at him for a just a fraction of a second longer than was necessary.

"They have a man producing forgeries. They replace the genuine painting with a forgery, so nobody suspects anything and they keep the real one."

Henry explained everything he knew, making particular mention of the arrival of his twin brother at Rahsaig and the precarious situation of Drew. The policemen listened, posing the occasional question, PC Lennie dutifully writing everything down. Eventually, the Sergeant spoke. His manner had now changed considerably.

"I will have to consult with CID in Inverness, since this matter is of the utmost severity." He uttered the name CID with great gravity.

"We must decide what to do. The gang is too spread out just now to consider arresting anybody without that affecting our ability to catch the others. If we can catch the thieves and the looted art together, then that is obviously the best solution. I will use the phone here right away. Please wait with the Constable."

He disappeared through the door. Henry turned to Alexander Lennie, who spoke first.

"So, Morgan is back. That must have been a wee surprise."

"You can say that again! But my god, Alex … he's not the lad we knew twenty years ago. He's so … cold. He's the brains behind all this. His years away seem to have turned him into a real hard case. He says it's his revenge on father, that he's taking his rightful share of the family fortune. Look, can I have a word with Rebecca and Dougie? Where are they?"

"I don't know Henry. They're in the car out back but if the sarge finds out, he'll have my guts for garters."

***

The Frenchman was hot and bothered. He kicked angrily at a stone as he came into the Barradale Castle courtyard and scowled. Grunting, he disappeared inside and climbed the staircase to the top of the tower. He crossed the room to the window, glowering at the loch outside.

"Where are you, you little…?" He growled through clenched teeth.

"Behind you!" Drew's voice rang out merrily from the doorway. With a snarl of rage, the Frenchman swung round. Drew was leaning casually against the door frame, dangling the key in front of him.

"You forgot the key!" he said, shaking his head. In a trice, he whipped the door closed and turned the key, just before the Frenchman could cross the room to stop him. His former jailer was furious and beat his fists against the door.

"Open, Scots boy – I kill you!"

"Then I don't think I'll be opening it, if that's all the same to you," Drew called, as he twirled the key on his finger, wondering whether to fling it into the loch below. Thinking better of it, he slipped it into his pocket and went quickly downstairs.

Having retrieved his torch, Drew left the confines of the castle and headed along the causeway. The Frenchman was bellowing at him from the window of the tower. He looked back and waved cheekily.

"Rahsaig, here I come," he said to himself.

As the castle and the raucous oaths of his jailer receded behind him, Drew decided he would be in no great hurry to return to Barradale.

***

Rebecca looked out of the window of the police car and breathed long and hard. Laird's Leap was another magnificently appointed Scottish Castle, nestling in a forest of Scots Pine, its grey towers and turrets looking out over a panoramic view of the Sound of Sleat, the strip of water dividing Skye from the mainland.

'Slate', Dougie had corrected her.

Rebecca was not used to such opulent surroundings and was surprised her father had never mentioned his grand ancestral origins. Their home was a normal semi in a normal street. It was a far cry from Rahsaig and the circles in which her uncle moved.

She looked across at Dougie, seated next to her, his eyes closed in apparent sleep.

"Dougie!" she nudged him but he simply grunted and turned sideways, facing away from her. His strenuous hours at the oars seemed to have caught up with him. Rebecca was frustrated. How could he sleep at a time like this? She was determined to get to see her Uncle somehow. The policemen had been very firm that they were to remain in the car but she was restless. She felt as if she ought to be doing something.

Her patience finally snapped. She wound down the window and took a cautious look out. Everything seemed quiet. She opened the door and slipped out onto the gravel. Clicking it shut as noiselessly as she could, she tiptoed round the side of the great house. She had just reached the corner when she heard the scraping of metal, as if somebody was forcing a bolt. She darted behind a tall bush and peered out from between some leaves. She heard low voices. Two men were on hands and knees, on the path at the side of the house. From where she was, she could not see their faces.

There was more metallic scraping as one of them raised a trapdoor. He gave a quick look around before swinging his legs over the edge and jumping. Rebecca heard a thud and then his voice, urging his companion to follow. The other man lifted a large, flat package from near the wall and passed it down through the opening.

In that split second, she recognised the sharp-featured man who had appeared at the window that night at Rahsaig. He too disappeared and the trapdoor banged shut.

"What on earth are you up to?" said a loud whisper. Rebecca nearly fell over.

At the window behind her stood Henry.

"Uncle H.! Oh thank goodness, I thought I was in trouble!"

Henry gave her a look as if to suggest that this was not yet out of the question.

"Wait there – don't move an inch!" he said and disappeared. He emerged from a French window a little further along and came quickly over. He put his finger to his lips, grabbed her arm and propelled her round the corner.

"Safer here. We won't be overheard. Where's Dougie?"

With Henry's help, they roused Dougie and the three of them slipped into the trees so they could talk, unobserved. They brought each other up to date.

"I still cannot believe it about Morgan," said Rebecca, shaking her head. "Or that I didn't understand he wasn't you."

"We are going to have to play it very carefully from here. The Sergeant is talking to CID on the phone just now. With Drew still being a prisoner, I have to do what Sibley says. I'd best get back. Sibley will be getting twitchy, wondering where I've got to."

"But I have to tell you something else," said Rebecca, urgently.

"Just now I was watching some men round the back of the house. They had what looked like a painting and went through a trapdoor."

"Into the house?" said Dougie, puzzled. "Not out of it?"

"Yes, definitely into it. If they are up to their usual trick, I think they must have been taking the forged painting inside, ready to swap it later. What should we do?"

Henry was about to speak when they heard the crunch of footsteps running along the gravel path. They ducked back into some bushes as two men came hurrying round the corner. They passed the police car without stopping and headed off down the drive. Somewhere, an engine started up and then a vehicle careered off at high speed.

"There they go!" said Rebecca, a gleam in her eye.

"I was right. They must have hidden the painting inside, ready to come back later – tonight, I'll bet. I have an idea to stop them getting the real one."

"This way," said Henry and led the way quickly across the gravel and into the house. They went into the drawing room, where the Sergeant had just returned and was on the point of taking Constable Lennie to task. He turned, his eyebrows rising immediately as he saw Dougie and Rebecca with Henry.

"I gave strict instructions that you –" he began but was interrupted by Henry.

"Sergeant, we can stand here listening to you or we can deal with something serious that Rebecca has just witnessed. I would suggest we do not have any time to waste. Therefore, please listen, as she has a plan – a very sensible and ingenious idea." The Sergeant closed his mouth in surprise. Rebecca could not restrain a smile.

"But I haven't told you my idea," she whispered to her Uncle. Henry smiled.

"Gentlemen, I must return before I give cause for suspicion, please excuse me." As he turned to leave he spoke softly to Rebecca, out of earshot of the others.

"You're going to suggest they swap the paintings over now, aren't you?"

"How did you know?"

"Great minds." His eyes twinkled as he left the room to rejoin Lord MacDonald and Simon Sibley.

Rebecca smiled to herself. She noticed everyone else looking at her, expectantly. Looking straight at the Sergeant, she spoke.

"We can prevent the theft of the Flora McDonald painting. The thieves have just broken into the cellar and concealed what I suspect is a forgery. They must intend to return tonight when everyone is asleep and swap this for the genuine painting. I suggest that we find the forgery and swap it now, so that when the thieves return, they in fact put the genuine one back onto the wall – thereby preventing a theft but making them believe everything is proceeding to plan. Drew and I did the same thing at Rahsaig. You could put some of that indelible powder stuff on it to be able to identify them. Uncle Henry can then go with Mr Sibley to Rahsaig and you can catch the whole gang and recover the other stolen property at the same time."

The Sergeant bristled and adjusted his collar. Rebecca suspected she had gone too far suggesting invisible powder, but was enjoying the look on the Sergeant's face.

"I will have to speak again with CID." He left the room, tightening his tie as he went.

"Makes sense to me," murmured PC Lennie to Dougie.

***

Rebecca took advantage of the absence of the Sergeant to slip into the study, once she was sure that the coast was clear of Sibley. She asked the butler where to find the painting of Lachlan and he had shown her in with a conspiratorial nod.

The face in the painting stopped Rebecca in her tracks. It was like looking at a photo of Henry and, by definition, presumably also of Morgan. She had not expected such a likeness.

Lachlan McOwan stood proud and haughty, hand on hip, a sneer on his face. At his feet lay two fierce dogs. Rebecca noticed a long, livid scar on his neck. Perhaps a memento of his fight with his brother Donald, Becca's father? So this was the scourge of her family, the black sheep.

"So you mean me harm, do you?" she whispered, more bravely than she felt.

"We'll see about that."

***

"It's going to be a novel experience, standing back and allowing thieves to steal from the house tonight. I hope these Inverness CID fellows know what they are up to," Angus MacDonald whispered into Henry McOwan's ear, out of the earshot of Simon Sibley, as they prepared to depart.

"Thank you for your kind hospitality, your Lordship," said Sibley, coming forward to grip his hand. He cast a sideways glance at Henry as he did so. "We're off to Dunvegan Castle now at the other side of the island. One more visit today."

The goodbyes completed, Sibley and Henry departed. Angus watched the car disappear down the driveway, a thoughtful expression on his face.

"There's no danger, your Lordship," said Sergeant Gillespie, emerging from an adjoining doorway where he had been concealed. "Everything will be captured on video by CID and thanks to our plan, the original painting will be left. Shall we go into the drawing room and run over the details?"

Rebecca, who had emerged behind the Sergeant opened her mouth to protest at this blatant theft of her idea but closed it again under his glare as he passed by. Dougie put a comforting hand on her shoulder.

"Let him have his moment. You have to work out how to keep Morgan sweet until the cops can get to Rahsaig. You're going to have to go back now. Once Sibley gets back there tonight, he'll tell Morgan about finding Drew at Barradale, they'll put two and two together and realise we know something. You'll have to find out what Morgan's been up to and phone Alex Lennie to tell him how many thieves are there."

"But once he knows about Drew, what is he going to do with me?"

Dougie was silent. He shook his head.

"He won't be hanging around once he's got what he wants."

"But how do they intend to get away?" asked Rebecca, frowning.

"They're bringing everything to Rahsaig, or so we believe, because they think it's safe. It's secluded, away from prying eyes. They've taken care of Henry and they must be planning to take care of you, me and Drew as well. And if that artist sees the Flight of the Bonnie Prince, he will know it's his painting."

"And?" said Dougie, sensing she was still hiding something.

Rebecca looked out across the gardens to the sea beyond, a faraway look in her eyes.

"Morgan. I've got a horrible feeling about who he might really be."

CHAPTER 22

THE BOGUS LAIRD

In the Great Hall of Rahsaig Castle, Rebecca McOwan gritted her teeth and hugged the man she now knew to be masquerading as her Uncle Henry. "Rebecca. Why thank you – what an unexpectedly warm greeting."

Rebecca felt him recoil. She was thankful to relax her grip. She stood back and looked at Morgan McOwan. For the first time she noticed how unnaturally cold and empty his eyes were. So this was the black sheep of her family, the criminal mastermind. She could not believe that she had not seen the difference in this man to her Uncle Henry.

"How long have you been back from your trip with Mr Sibley?" she asked, trying to appear as normal as possible. She clenched her fists into tight balls behind her back, to stop her hands from shaking and steady her nerves. She must not give anything away.

"I should be asking you that question," he replied, with a laugh that seemed entirely forced. He took off his coat.

"I have just been out walking the dogs. Did you enjoy your little adventure in the wilds?

I trust the Campbells took good care of you."

He turned away momentarily to put his coat back on its hook. As he stretched, Rebecca noticed a livid purple scar on his neck as it appeared from under his shirt collar.

She stepped back, startled.

"Well?" He had turned back and stood, smiling expectantly.

"I er, yes, yes, great fun," she said hurriedly. At that moment, Miss McHarg appeared behind her and requested his attention. Rebecca excused herself, for once grateful for McHarg. She hurried up to her room, shut the door and sat down, her mind racing.

A new fear gripped her. Henry had warned her that Morgan was shrewd and canny.

But the scar unnerved her for another reason. The painting of Lachlan at Lord MacDonald's had borne a remarkable likeness to Henry and to Morgan. The scar she had just seen on Morgan's neck was identical to that in the portrait of Lachlan. What had the ghostly figure in the cloak said to her at the lighthouse?

I come to warn you of Lachlan. He is here. He means you harm.

Unnerving thoughts and ideas were racing through her mind.

Something was glinting on the window seat. Rebecca went over. It was a gold locket and chain, lying on top of one of the cushions. She unclipped the fastening and opened it. Inside was an old-fashioned portrait painting of a dark-haired woman. There was an inscription:

For My Darling Becca from Mother

Becca's locket! Surely this was the locket stolen from her by Lachlan before he threw her to her death! Another sign from Siobhan?

What else had the ghostly Becca said?

He is the man you do not know but yet you do know.

She had believed Morgan to be Henry, knowing one but not the other.

Siobhan had warned her.

As she gazed at the locket, the idea that had seemed too far-fetched suddenly seemed entirely plausible. Morgan and Lachlan must somehow be one and the same.

Drew crested a rise in the foothills behind Rahsaig and looked down at the castle. The dusk was gathering quickly. He had retraced his steps through the tunnel and emerged back at the Old Manse. The tunnel entrance seemed to have remained undiscovered. Using all his strength, Drew returned the stone slab to its position. Careful to avoid discovery by McAllum and the artist Godfrey, whom he had overheard talking outside, he slipped out of a hole in the wall, skirted the outbuildings and headed up into the hills away from the main path. He knew an old stalkers' path below Ladhar Bheinn, which wound its way several kilometres through the hills to the edge of the estate. The route was little known and quite perilous in places and he had had only a herd of deer for company. He could make the journey much faster than by the route which they had taken on their journey from Rahsaig a few days before.

A boat was chugging slowly down the loch. It seemed to be heading for Rahsaig but was still some distance off. Drew decided to go down to the castle, keeping well out of sight. He wondered if Dougie and Rebecca were back, although he had no way of knowing about recent events on Skye. He would hide, see who was about and decide what to do.

He descended warily through the forest to the gardens. The place seemed deserted.

When he approached the shed where they had discovered the stolen paintings, he crept up to the door. The damage had been repaired and it was closed and padlocked.

Drew passed on, keeping to the bushes.

Looking towards the landing stage, he saw that the boat had now arrived alongside the small jetty. He could make out four figures.

One was securing the boat. Another followed ashore,

leading a taller man by the arm. The other man, smaller and squatter, was the last to leave. Drew narrowed his eyes and then smiled. Even at this distance, the rounded silhouette and upturned nose of Simon Sibley was unmistakeable.

The figure being led must be Henry. Drew watched as he was taken up to the castle by Sibley, disappearing around the back. The others jumped back aboard the boat. They turned inland, perhaps to rendezvous with McAllum and Godfrey up the loch.

So, the thieves were now back, having presumably completed their business on Skye.

Drew had to find Rebecca and Dougie. He retraced his steps through the bushes to the greenhouses in the walled garden behind the castle. He looked up at Rebecca's window, wondering if she was in her room. No light was showing. He would try to get inside and, if she was not there, hide in her room until she returned.

Drew passed the door to the passage outside the kitchen. As was usual, it was open. Ducking, he scrambled over to the kitchen window and pressed himself against the wall below. He stopped, listening for any sound from within. Hearing nothing, he crept inside the doorway. There was a staircase opposite the kitchen door from where he could find his way to Rebecca's room.

He was about to go upstairs when a door opened, throwing light into the corridor and he heard the unmistakeable tones of McHarg. She was evidently in high dudgeon about something. Drew leapt up the stairs and crouched down on the first landing to listen.

"…Nothing was said to me about these people coming. That brother of mine will be here shortly and what if he notices anything? Everybody around here will know. I will be ruined …"

"Then we'll just have to make sure your brother doesn't see anything," said a man's voice, which Drew did not recognise.

The kitchen door closed behind McHarg and her unseen companion. Taking his chance, Drew went up to the first floor passageway and headed towards the East wing.

There was no answer to his gentle tap on Rebecca's door, so he undid the latch and tip-toed inside. The room was empty. He went over to the window seat and sat down.

A while later, the door opened and Rebecca came in. She did not notice him at first and switched on the light on her bedside table and sat down on the bed.

"Hi!" said Drew in a hoarse whisper.

Rebecca shrieked and leapt to her feet.

"Oh it's you – you idiot, you nearly gave me a heart attack! I thought you were a prisoner at Barradale."

"Sorry to disappoint! Sibley thinks I'm still locked up in the tower."

"And why aren't you?" asked Rebecca acidly, still recovering from the shock.

"Anyway, Sibley is on Skye, stealing another painting."

"No, he's here. I saw the boat come back. Henry was with him."

"I'd have seen them downstairs – are you sure?"

Drew nodded vigourously.

"Aye. Certain. Anyway, what's been going on? Where's Dougie?"

Rebecca sat down opposite him.

"He's round here somewhere. There is so much to tell you. Dougie and I didn't come back to Rahsaig after we saw you in the Tower. We telephoned Constable Lennie and went to Skye to meet him. There was this awful little Sergeant too but I'll tell you about him later. Anyway, the plan is to catch them all at the same time back here – the police are coming from Inverness –

the CID. Sibley and Morgan don't suspect anything and think everything is going to plan. The police were waiting on *Skye* to watch the crooks break in to steal the famous painting there. Only we had swapped it already, not that they were going to arrest them anyway… thanks to my plan."

"Eh?" Drew was completely bemused.

"It doesn't matter – the point is all the gang are due here tomorrow and that's when the police plan to get them."

"What if something happens between now and then to make them change their minds? All the stuff is in the cave at Barradale."

"Yes but you heard Sibley tell the Frenchmen to load it all onto a boat."

They were cut short by the sound of somebody in the passageway outside. Rebecca leaped to her feet and opened a large oak wardrobe. She urged Drew inside and quickly closed the door behind him. Then she sat down again in the window seat and waited nervously.

There was a rattling at the door and the noise of the key being turned in the lock from the outside. The footsteps receded. Rebecca jumped to her feet and ran over to the door. She tried to open it but it was locked.

"Well of all the …" Furious, she banged on the door and shouted. She heard muffled tones from inside the wardrobe and went back to let Drew out.

"They've locked me in! How dare they?"

"Us, Rebecca, although they didn't know I was here."

"Why lock me in, though? What has happened? They must know something, perhaps they found out about you escaping." Rebecca looked at Drew. He was lost in thought.

"Damn," he said quietly. "This really blows it. How are we going to get out and warn anybody now? We have to let the cops know, somehow."

They sat down in the window again, at a loss for a moment.

Suddenly, Rebecca let out another startled yell and pointed over Drew's shoulder. He turned quickly.

There was a face at the glass outside, staring in at them.

"Let me in!" Dougie's muffled voice called at the instant that Drew recognised his brother. He undid the window latch and helped him inside.

Rebecca closed her eyes, disbelieving.

"Flamin' Campbells! What is it with you two, scaring the wits out of me this evening? And how in heaven's name did you climb up here?"

"Evening all," said Dougie, softly. "I used the fire escape. It's hidden in all the creeper just here."

"Great!" said Drew. "Then we can all get out of here."

"Why don't we just go out through the door?" asked Dougie.

"Because they've locked us up. Well, Rebecca that is, they didn't know I was here too ... but I am ... as you see."

Dougie looked at his brother in bemusement.

"Yeah – we'll get to the issue of you going AWOL at the castle later."

"Nice to see you too, bruv," smiled Drew, sweetly.

"Boys, boys! Let me fill you in." Rebecca rapidly brought Dougie up to date.

"I think I can guess who your jailer is," said Dougie. "I had to duck to avoid being seen through the window just now. McHarg was in the corridor."

"I bet she's the mole in the camp Uncle Henry was talking about," said Rebecca, her eyes glaring with contempt. "Traitor! I always thought there was something about her."

Drew interrupted her.

"That would explain what I overheard downstairs. She was worried about something being discovered that would ruin her reputation."

"Right – we need a plan," said Rebecca, sitting down again in the window seat.

"We have to get back to the cave and find the stolen mask and collar – the police mustn't find them. I have to put them back in the Sanctuary. And we have to make sure nothing happens that disrupts the thieves from meeting up here tomorrow. And, last but not least, somebody has to get to Uncle Henry and telephone the police. It's important that everybody knows what's going to happen when."

"Right," said Dougie, getting to his feet. "You and Drew will have to go to the cave – only you know the way in. I'll get to Henry. He isn't going to be too pleased I've let you go off into the night but let me worry about that one. You have about an hour of light left. Rebecca has to be here in this room when they unlock it tomorrow, which means you won't have time to hang about out there. They don't know where Drew and I are, so we don't matter so much."

"Then there's no time to waste," said Rebecca, opening the window and beckoning Drew through it, with an exaggerated bow.

CHAPTER 23

MOONLIGHT RUN

Dougie was the last to leave Rebecca's room. As he swung through the window and onto the balustrade outside, grasping the iron ladder concealed in the creeper, he was careful to leave the window slightly open to permit their return.

He watched Drew and Rebecca run swiftly across the lawn, losing sight of them as they disappeared into the rhododendron bushes and the woods. Now he had to locate Henry, somewhere inside the castle, and contact PC Lennie without being discovered. Not for the first time in his life, Dougie thought how much easier it would be if mobile phones worked in the Highlands. Using the phone in the Great Hall might prove a little tricky. If Rebecca had been locked in, the likelihood was that Henry was also.

He decided to start his search in Henry's upstairs rooms.

***

In a high, darkened window in one of the turrets, somebody else had been observing the departure of Rebecca and Drew.

Through narrowed eyes, Morgan McOwan watched them go into the trees. His lips creased into a thin, humourless line.

It would have been stretching a point to call it a smile. "So, my little plan worked. Now let's see where they go."

Grabbing a long, black coat, he swept out into the night.

Rebecca and Drew went back along the old stalkers' path, neither speaking much. They were moving as quickly as they could and the physical effort absorbed all of their concentration and breath. Rebecca looked up at the towering bulk of Ladhar Bheinn, its slopes softened into velvet shadows in the pale moonlight. She was grateful that the moon was out tonight. At least it provided some light to guide them over the rough ground. The batteries in the torches they were both carrying were low and needed to be saved for the tunnel. The mountain had a strange, reassuring presence in the half-light.

The pace Drew was setting was very fast.

"Say if you can't keep up," he had laughed, annoyingly, over his shoulder. Rebecca had glared at him.

"Just say when you want to stop dawdling," she had countered.

Finally, the path rounded a small summit and they found themselves at the top of the ridge at one side of Glen an dubh Lochan, high above the Old Ruin.

"There," said Drew, pointing down to where the darkened roof and walls of the ruin were lit up by a pool of moonlight at the foot of the glen.

"We've made good time. And, careful. Remember McAllum and the painter are around, somewhere. We don't want to run into them now."

They began a careful descent of the slope towards the ruin. Although they were some way away, the silence seemed more deafening in the darkness and Rebecca felt as if each crack of a twig was as loud as a gunshot.

When they were within a hundred yards of the ruin, they stopped and crouched down in a small wooded copse. Bathed in the glow of moonlight, the glen seemed somehow closer and smaller. From the outhouse where they had seen the painter working, a light was shining, casting a long yellow beam through the doorway and across the grass. McAllum and Godfrey must still be up and about.

"Make like mice," whispered Drew and started forward again. The small copse of trees gave them cover right up to the bank at the rear of the outhouses. From here, they slipped round the back of the ruin and clambered over a pile of broken bricks and inside. The damp, musty smell greeted them again.

Rebecca took a cautious look out of a window across to the studio. Through the half-open doorway, she could just make out the back of one of the men, presumably Godfrey, standing at the easel.

They did not appear to have been seen. Tentatively, she clicked her torch on.

"Quickly," she whispered, indicating the far end of the ruined house with the beam. Together, they made their way along to the black door. Rebecca bent to grasp the rusty bolt, gritting her teeth in case it made too loud a noise. It was still open from their previous visit, so she need not have worried. They both applied all their strength to the door and it slid open with a screech. They stopped instantly, hearts beating faster, listening out for a sign that somebody was coming to investigate.

To their relief, it remained quiet.

Eager to proceed, the two passed through the door and down the narrow staircase into the small room where Rebecca had encountered Siobhan. For a few moments, Rebecca wondered whether they would find her there again but the room was deserted. They put down their torches and grasped the slab over the opening to the tunnel.

Sliding it to one side, a rush of cold, dank air hit them. Without hesitating, Drew hopped over the edge and began to climb down the steps into the tunnel. Rebecca followed.

"You let them go off gallivanting about in the middle of the night? Where are they going and why?" Henry McOwan was, as Dougie had feared, incredulous.

"They said it was important, to do with the cave, or something but they wouldn't tell me why." Dougie hated lying to Henry but felt it he best option in the circumstances. "I had to let them go, since one of us had to come and find you. Sorry, Henry."

"Well it's done now. I just hope they don't come to any harm – for your sake!" said Henry grimly.

Now was not the time to attempt to explain to him about the legend and Rebecca's encounters in the mist. Dougie was far from sure that Henry would believe the story anyway. Indeed, he was not even sure he did himself.

"Sorry, boss. They were gone before I could think properly. They'll be okay, I'm sure. Our Drew may be a bit daft at times, but he's a good kid and he does know what he's about out there. And Rebecca has brains enough for the two of them. Look, we have to get to the phone somehow and get hold of Alex Lennie."

Henry sighed and shook his head.

"We'll just have to hope you're right – okay, okay. There's a phone in the observatory at the top of the north turret. We'll have to climb out the way you came in and over the roof. The outside door's never locked. I can't believe they've even found it, let alone bothered to lock it."

With Henry leading, they went back out onto the balcony. Henry pulled himself up onto a tiny ledge below the battlements. It was just wide enough for his feet and from here he was able to squeeze between two battlements and onto the roof. He sank back against a parapet, panting, unused to the exertion. Seconds later, Dougie's head appeared through the same gap and he landed on the sloping slate roof alongside Henry.

"Up there," breathed Henry, pointing up to a small turret at the end of the wall. They followed a narrow walkway around the edge of the roof, just inside the battlements.

The observatory was open as Henry had anticipated. Once inside, Dougie skirted a large telescope and went quickly over to the door to the main passageway. He opened it as quietly as he could and peered outside. The castle seemed to be asleep.

"Quiet as the grave."

Henry immediately grabbed the receiver of the phone from the table next to the telescope and began to dial a number.

"Is this the same line as downstairs?" asked Dougie. Henry shook his head.

"No fear … Alex? Henry. Listen, there's no time to lose. What is CID planning for tomorrow? …Alex? Oh … Yes, hello Chief Inspector…" Henry turned and raised his eyebrows at Dougie, who smiled.

Henry listened in silence for some time.

"I see … I understand … Yes, we are all fine. I have been locked in my bedroom on the first floor and my niece is also in her room…" He looked knowingly at Dougie as he said this.

"… I see … the Campbell brothers are both able to move about freely. Dougie is with me now. We are pretty sure the thieves are unaware they are here. We saw their boat go up the loch earlier this evening. We think this is to pick up the artist and another man, together with the final forgeries intended for Rahsaig. They'll have to go back to Barradale to pick up the rest of the stolen property …. Yes … right … as you say, Chief Inspector. Goodbye."

Henry replaced the receiver and turned to Dougie, who was now pointing the telescope up the loch and attempting to spot the boat.

"Are they still there?" Henry asked.

"Can't see a lot. The boat's some way up the loch. What did the 'Chief Inspector' say?"

"He wants us to do nothing at all, basically, other than keep Morgan and Sibley sweet until the rest of the loot arrives tomorrow. They will post policemen in position around the castle from before dawn to keep an eye out and then make a move later on. There will be speedboats just round the corner in case the gang try to get away by sea and even a helicopter standing by at Mallaig."

"That'll frighten the sheep," murmured Dougie.

"When the whole gang is together, they'll move in. This is really big. They've even got a man from Interpol here to advise them. Apparently, the French police have been on the trail of this for some time. The French mime artists are a little bit more than actors: wanted by most of Europe's police forces in connection with art fraud and theft."

"And they've all come to our wee corner of the world. I bet Sergeant Gillespie is in heaven," said Dougie wryly.

"Yes, but they reckoned without my niece Sherlock McOwan and that eedjit brother of yours," smiled Henry.

"Talking of whom … you'll notice I didn't give them – or you – away. I just hope they'll be back like you say. If not, the whole plan will be blown."

***

Unaware of Henry's misgivings, Drew and Rebecca were following the path through the labyrinth of caves under Ladhar Bheinn by torchlight.

"Is the tide on its way in or out?" asked Rebecca, looking at Drew. "I don't want to get to the end and drown."

"It should be on its way out," he replied. "High water was

at seven this evening. If you feel water on your feet, though, stop." Rebecca jabbed him in the darkness.

"What was that?!" This time she grabbed his arm suddenly. They quickly switched off the lights and hunched down, listening intently.

"What did you hear?" whispered Drew hoarsely.

"It sounded like a cough."

"Let me see if I can get a look," whispered Drew and clambered up onto a ledge. He disappeared completely.

"Drew!" It was too late for Rebecca to stop him. She grimaced. Why did he always go jumping in without thinking? It was pitch-black, just what did he expect to see?

Rebecca stayed exactly where she was for several minutes, hearing nothing. Her immediate fears subsiding, she rose slowly to her feet and gripped the end of her torch, hesitating whether to turn it on. In the end she decided to risk it.

She shone the beam in front of her, straight into the unblinking face of Morgan.

***

Rahsaig Castle was in near darkness. A shaft of light from under the door to the study cast a dim glow into the Great Hall. Inside, Simon Sibley sat in Henry's high-backed leather armchair, reading some documents. There was a gentle tap at the door.

"I'll be away now, then, sir." The pale countenance of Miss McHarg appeared, her outside coat buttoned up to the neck, despite the fact that it was the middle of summer. Her hair was pulled back into its habitual harsh bun, her expression as frosty as ever.

"Thank you, Miss McHarg. Is everyone turned in?"

"The Laird and Miss Rebecca are locked in their rooms as you ordered and Mister Morgan was upstairs quite early, once the other gentlemen had departed. I have not seen him for a couple of hours, so he has probably turned in."

"Well tomorrow is going to be a busy day. Not long now, and we'll be out of your hair."

"To London is it, you will be going?"

"Best you don't know, just in case." Sibley attempted a conspiratorial wink, fingers twiddling the ends of the moustache as was his habit. McHarg appeared to find the result somewhat alarming. "You'll of course be paid tomorrow. We thank you for your assistance."

"You are certain the Laird will not know of my involvement?" McHarg's severe features betrayed evident concern.

"It will be as if we were never here. The only people aware of your help to us are Morgan and myself. And when Henry asks people to believe his story after we have gone, nobody will, since he was, de facto, here all the time. To which you will attest."

McHarg pursed her lips, inclined her head and departed.

***

"Well I couldn't find diddly-squat," said Drew, arriving back at the spot where he had left Rebecca. He stopped and swung his torch around the underground chamber.

A rush of ice-cold air blew his hair across his face.

He suddenly felt he was being watched.

He shivered. His hands began to shake and he clenched his fists tightly.

"Rebecca? Rebecca? Where are you? Don't mess about. It's creepy enough down here without an English woman hiding in the darkness as well."

But the only reply in the dark was the echo of his voice.

CHAPTER 24

THE OUBLIETTE

Rebecca came to in total darkness. She was not aware she had passed out but, since the shock of turning around and finding Morgan, she had no memory of anything.

The coolness of the air and the silence suggested she must still be underground. As she tried to move her feet, she felt a sharp pain and discovered she was restrained by cold iron manacles, locked around her wrists and ankles. She was hunched into a sitting position and felt hard rock against her back and legs. She was chained to the wall, and wondered how long she had been there.

Shuffling her feet beneath her, she tried to stand. She would have succeeded except that as she started to straighten up, her head made abrupt contact with more rock. She uttered a sharp cry of pain.

A distant, muffled sound reached her ear. A low rumble, some way off, seemed to rise and then fall away again in a rushing sound. Listening keenly, she realised it was the sound of waves echoing through the caverns. She must be near the entrance.

A sudden noise much closer to hand caused her to stiffen. Footsteps were ringing on the stony floor. They were coming her way.

A light was shone unexpectedly in her face. She winced, closing her eyes.

"So you are awake then, Rebecca?" Morgan's chilly tones.

"Good. I want you to be aware of what will happen to you.

It is always important to let people know what plans you have for them, I think. You are sitting in what is called the oubliette, from the French *oublier*, to forget. It is a very simple concept. I put you inside, roll the stone over the entrance, and you are forgotten."

Rebecca gasped.

"It was a favourite device in olden times to dispense with unwanted enemies and criminals. They had a talent for these things then. Such a shame that their artistry is now neglected. Nowadays, we are much too, shall we say, civilised. You have probably already heard the sea outside. In a few more hours, the tide will rush into this chamber and fill it. And then, you will drown."

"Why?" shouted Rebecca. She was surprised at her own reaction. She was not scared so much as angry.

"Why not just tie me up until you have got away with your paintings?"

"Ha! These little paintings of Sibley's aren't important. If I was merely worried about being caught, I wouldn't go to all this trouble with you, now would I? No, this is about much more than that. But then ... you know that, don't you?"

There was a long pause.

As she looked into his eyes again, a vivid image of Becca flashed into her mind, pleading desperately in her last moments on the cliff-top all those years ago.

She felt a very odd sensation.

"You're Lachlan!" screamed Rebecca. "You are Lachlan McOwan ... aren't you?!"

He did not answer. The torch snapped off. Rebecca heard the rock grating into place and then the sound of laughter. She beat the soles of her feet against the rock with all her might but it would not budge. She could get her hand into a gap between it and the wall of the cavern but to no avail. The chains prevented her bringing any strength to bear. For a moment she allowed herself to imagine the water was starting to sweep into the cavern.

Somebody will come, she told herself. The alternative was too dreadful to contemplate.

Half in fear, half in anger, she yelled for help as loud and long as she could.

***

Drew was in a quandary. Rebecca seemed to have disappeared into thin air.

He had walked right to the end of the cave, poked his head outside into the moonlight but had not found a trace of her.

Barradale Castle and the causeway were bathed in silvery moonlight. The night sky was lit up by a myriad of stars. Barely a ripple disturbed the tranquillity of Loch Hourn. It would have been completely still but for the turning of the waves at the edge of the shore.

No lights showed from the castle. Drew wondered whether his French jailer was still locked in the tower. He was not about to go and find out.

Where could Rebecca have gone? She was not the sort to play tricks.

Drew was concerned. He sat down on a rock. He could retrace their steps through the tunnel to the Ruin to see if she had gone back. She could have fallen and injured herself but surely he would have heard her or stumbled upon her? He had not heard a sound.

It was too far to Rahsaig to seek the help of Henry and Dougie. By the time he arrived, Sibley and his cronies would be awake and discover Rebecca was not there.

Somehow he had to warn the others. He could go to the

Mountain Rescue station and raise the alarm with the police. Ringing the castle was too dangerous, for Sibley might answer. He knew Henry had a private line but did not know the number.

On balance, the police seemed his only option.

***

Rebecca could hear the sounds of somebody moving in the cave. She beat her feet against the rock again and cried out.

"Help! Help me, please! Drew? Is that you? Please, help me!"

The sound came closer. She could hear a man's voice, calling. He seemed to be pleading. The voice was getting closer and becoming more frantic. In a few more seconds she sensed whoever it was to be the other side of the rock blocking her in. She was about to cry out again when she heard something infinitely more frightening.

A sudden, ferocious snarling echoed off the walls all around the cavern. The pleas turned to screams of terror and then of pain. Rebecca shrank back, pressing herself as far away as possible. Somebody was clearly being attacked by what sounded like a wild beast.

And in a trice, it was ended.

A deafening silence followed, almost more terrifying than the noise of the attack.

Manacled to the wall of the oubliette, Rebecca could only wait for what was to come, the blood pounding furiously in her temples. She held her breath, afraid to make a sound.

Inexorably, there came the sound of something scraping and pushing at the other side of the huge stone. It started to roll slowly back. Rebecca was paralysed with fear.

She let go a small, strangled cry.

A thin glow of light seeped through the widening gap until the stone had rolled away completely.

Standing in front of her, panting, was the wolf.

Rebecca trembled, uncontrollably.

Seeing him this close, she was awestruck by the size and power of the beast.

Had she been standing, his great head would be at the same level as her own. The pale glow seemed to radiate from his silver coat. She stared into his white eyes, transfixed, unable to look away. At his feet lay the prone, crumpled form of Morgan.

In the dim light surrounding the wolf, she could see the marks of the beast's jaws and claws upon the body and dark patches of blood oozing from his head and chest. She shuddered, presuming him dead.

The wolf's unblinking eyes looked down at Morgan. Then they stared into Rebecca's.

Hakon raised his nose, as he had that time by the loch, taking in her scent.

Then he took a step forward and licked the tips of her fingers.

Rebecca was taken completely by surprise at this docile gesture. It was almost affectionate, something to expect from a friendly dog.

The wolf grabbed the chains around one of her wrists between his powerful jaws and snapped them, effortlessly. The manacle fell away. He did the same to the one around her other hand and then to her feet.

The force sent her staggering across the rocky floor, out of the oubliette. Rebecca rubbed her wrists but remained on the ground, startled and still not certain if she should feel safe. The wolf flicked his eyes away from her. His bloody jaws seized the body of Morgan and flung it against the dungeon wall.

Drawn by a strange, unseen compulsion, Rebecca reached

out and took hold of the wolf's powerful neck and swung herself onto his back.

Instantly, as if he had been waiting for this, Hakon leaped off down the tunnel into the blackness. Rebecca could not see an inch in front of her face but felt strangely safe. In the rush of air across her face, she could smell the fresh salty smack of the loch outside. The wolf was gliding effortlessly through the cavern towards the opening to the causeway.

They soon arrived in the larger chamber where Drew had discovered the stolen paintings. Hakon stopped at the water's edge and sat down. Rebecca slid from his back.

There was just enough light to be able to make out the shapes of the various rubber bags, hidden among the rocks by the thieves. Rebecca's gaze fell upon two smaller bags. She grabbed them and undid the zip fastenings. She was not surprised to find that they contained the Princess's burial mask and the wolf's studded collar. She stood up and turned to Hakon, raising them into the air in excitement.

But the wolf was no longer there.

Rebecca gripped the mask and collar in her hands. Now, at last, she could return these treasures to their rightful place and release Becca and Siobhan from their torment.

She threw the two empty rubber bags high onto the rocks, clambered carefully back around the cavern to the second chamber and looked for the sword which marked the entrance to the Sanctuary. Stuffing the mask and collar inside her jacket to keep her hands free, she squeezed down into the narrow opening as she had before and pushed herself along the low passage. She emerged into the wider chamber and stood up.

Long shafts of silver light shone down from high in the cavern, casting eerie pools of light on the glassy lake. Rebecca made her way down the side of the rocky cave wall.

As she reached the water's edge, a few yards in front of her, shimmering in a pale glow, the mighty Viking Ghost Ship materialised out of the darkness. Its oars were poised at right angles above the water, motionless. Hakon's white eyes now stared down at her from the bow, beside him the mighty figure of Knut the Strong.

"Why do you return to the Sanctuary?" boomed the angry voice of Knut.

Rebecca took a step forward, holding out the mask and the collar.

"Hakon brought me here. I have what you seek. I have the collar and the mask. Look!"

On the edge of the lake a few feet further along, the figures of Becca and Siobhan also emerged from the shadows and came to stand in front of Rebecca.

Becca pulled back her hood and smiled at her. Her face seemed changed, no longer empty as when they had met on the island at the Lighthouse. Rebecca was struck by how beautiful she was.

Becca held out her hands and took the mask and collar. She ran her fingers over the burnished gold of the mask as if she were barely able to believe she held it. She handed them both to Knut. They all watched as he fastened the collar around the powerful neck of the great wolf.

Becca turned back to Rebecca and gripped her hands in her own.

"You have risked much to come here, Rebecca and much on our account these past days. We owe you a great debt of thanks."

"What will happen now?" asked Rebecca.

At that moment, a pale slim figure in a white robe stepped forward from behind the Warrior and the Wolf. She had long, auburn hair and a gentle face. Rebecca guessed that she could not have been much older than herself. She took the mask into small, delicate hands and studied Rebecca. After a moment, Rebecca heard a soft voice inside her head. The lips did not move.

"I am Princess Immelda, daughter of Karl of Norway. I have been a prisoner of these labyrinths for centuries, left for dead by the Machoiann."

The Princess held the mask in front of her and studied it.

"This mask of my ancestors was for the eternal rest I have never had. On the day I married the Machoiann, the Scots chained me to the rocks down here and pretended to my father that I had been lost in a storm. Lachlan stole the mask for its gold. Hakon has finally avenged his foul deed and you have restored what is mine. There is but one more thing which must be done and that rests with Knut and Hakon.

Then, at last, we shall set sail to eternity."

As her words faded, the Longboat turned slowly and its oars pulled it away across the lake where it was swallowed into the darkness. Rebecca could no longer make out the far side of the chamber.

She turned back to Becca.

"What is the one more thing which remains?"

Becca put a hand lightly on her shoulder.

"You must leave this place. It is no longer safe here."

"But what of you? What of Lachlan?"

"There is nothing more to fear, child. Our duty is now fulfilled, thanks to you. Go home to Rahsaig and worry for us no more." She tightened her grip on Rebecca's arm.

"With all my heart, thank you. I will never forget you and what you have done."

With that, Becca and Siobhan turned and vanished into the darkness.

Rebecca felt a surge of happiness as complete as anything she had known in her young life. Remembering Becca's warning, she decided to leave without delay. Pausing for one last look around the Sanctuary, she turned and hurried back through the passage.

CHAPTER 25

THE RECKONING

When she reached the outside, Rebecca was filled with a sense of fulfilment and happiness that Becca and Siobhan would at last be freed from their misery.

She was proud that she had helped to bring this about, although was not sure that she would ever fully understand what had happened, or be able to find an explanation for it. Her friends back home would never believe a word about the Ghost Ship, Hakon, Knut and the Princess.

Sitting on a rock in the middle of the peaceful loch, with the stars overhead, Rebecca was aware she had grown very fond of this mystic, magical place. She now understood what her uncle had meant when he spoke of the Highlands getting under one's skin and calling one back. It was the first time she had ever felt empathy for a place, a sense of belonging.

But she was still troubled. Rebecca harboured uneasy thoughts about Lachlan and was disturbed about his connection with Morgan. The young princess had called her Machoiann husband the "ancestor of Lachlan". Was there some sort of evil connection in her family, handed down through the generations?

She began to question what she had actually seen in the tunnel. When she had looked into Morgan's eyes, she had been convinced she was looking at Lachlan. The man, who had been killed in the tunnel, had appeared to be Morgan. However, she was far from certain that she would not return to Rahsaig to find him there. She wondered fleetingly about re-entering the tunnel and going to check if he was still lying there, but decided against it.

The picture of Morgan lying bleeding at the feet of the wolf was still all too clear in her mind. She would need time to come to terms with this jumble of emotions.

"There you are, Rebecca McOwan! I've been searching high and low for you!"

"Campbell! Well for once I am really glad to see you." Before she was aware of what she was doing, Rebecca jumped to her feet and threw her arms around Drew, hugging him. This took them both completely by surprise. She relaxed her arms and stepped back, not quite sure what to say. He too let go, gazing at her, for once silenced.

"Blimey," said Rebecca, the first to recover herself. She jumped down from the rock and onto the causeway. An impish grin broke out on her face. "For a second there, I thought you were going to kiss me."

Drew looked perplexed.

"Aye, I know. Frightening. For a second there, so did I."

Rebecca permitted herself a small smile. She turned back and looked up at him.

"Well don't worry about it too much. Others have tried too, you know."

"Did they succeed?" Drew lowered himself back onto the causeway and they began to walk back towards the shore.

Rebecca smiled again.

"Depends how you define success."

"Oh," said Drew. He frowned, not altogether understanding this answer. Rebecca did not give him time to dwell on it, however.

"So where were you when I needed you?"

"I was away to ring for help at the Mountain Rescue when I looked back here and saw you come outside. What happened to you? I looked everywhere but you had just vanished."

Taking a deep breath, not sure how much she believed in

what she was about to say, Rebecca recounted the events in the cave. Drew was incredulous.

"You really know how to have a good time! Ghosties, ghouls, wild savage beasties and underground dungeons! ... Are you telling me Morgan is ... dead? In there?"

He pointed to the entrance of the cave. Rebecca gave him a look that was all the answer he required. He shivered.

"I can't believe it," he said, more slowly.

They were both silent for a long time.

"We've got to get back," said Rebecca eventually, stopping and looking towards Dead Man's Crag away up the glen.

"Should we go back through the tunnel or overland?"

Drew looked up at the moon and then out towards the sea, where some thick clouds were gathering ominously. He nodded towards them.

"If that lot is coming our way, looks like the tunnel will be better ... if you really want to go back in there. I'm not sure I do. Hold on a moment! Listen!"

He grabbed her arm and they both fell silent for a few seconds.

Rebecca heard it too, the unmistakeable rumble of a boat's engine. Moments later, she saw a light on the water, further down the loch. It was coming towards them.

"Our friends coming to collect their stash, do you think?"

Drew nodded, chewing his lip.

"Aye. Well, we can't go by the tunnel now. There'll be people here in a few minutes. And they'll be back to Rahsaig by morning. You'll need to be safely in your room by then. Mind you, they'll find out I'm not where I'm s'posed to be."

"Well somebody there doesn't trust me either, seeing as they locked me in my room."

They crouched down in the darkness on the beach and watched as the boat drew level with Barradale and chugged gently along the edge of the causeway. It stopped just short of the island and somebody leaped into the water with a splash. A man appeared in the bow and dropped an anchor over the side. He then followed the first man into the black waters. They waded ashore. One headed off towards Barradale Castle, the other disappearing into the entrance to the cave.

Drew identified his former jailor appearing out of the darkness from the direction of the Castle, to greet the first man. After a brief exchange, the jailor leapt aboard the boat.

"I hope you've tidied up that teacup, Frenchie," said Drew.

"Eh?" Rebecca looked at him blankly.

"You had to be there."

Rebecca and Drew watched as the men came and went from the cave, carrying the black rubber bundles containing the stolen paintings. The wind had stiffened. Rebecca felt a drop of rain on her cheek. In seconds, it was raining quite hard. Drew tapped her on the shoulder and indicated the trees behind them.

In the time it took to reach shelter, several mighty cracks of thunder shattered the peace of the loch. The water was swelling up and the boat in which the men had arrived was now being tossed around by bigger and bigger waves. The men could be seen, fighting to get their cargo below deck and keep the boat righted.

A storm was on the way.

"Where did this come from?" asked Rebecca, looking around open-mouthed and having to shout to be heard above the roar of the wind.

"Search me!" shouted Drew, his eyes full of wonder at the suddenness and power. Thunder rumbled, lighting flashed across the sky and lit up the whole glen. Fierce wind and torrential rain swept in, causing streams to sprout up all around.

But the most dramatic part of all had been waiting until now. From the end of the loch by the sea came a low roar, which gradually swelled and became stronger. Rebecca yelled something incomprehensible and gesticulated in the direction of the sea, her eyes fired with a mixture of fear and excitement.

Further down the loch, a mighty bank of water, at least ten metres in height, was welling up. It stretched from one shore across to the other. From where they stood, it appeared to be a gigantic wave.

As they watched, mouths open in astonishment, it surged up the loch, swamping the banks of the normal shoreline and sending other waves crashing up the sides of the loch.

It was rushing headlong towards Barradale and the causeway.

"Run!" shouted Drew. "Get higher or it will take us with it! Come on!"

They turned and fled up the hill, scrambling on their hands and feet, stopping only when they had climbed a good distance. They turned and looked back, gasping for breath.

Rebecca gripped Drew's hand. The scene was almost unreal. The mighty wave was now level with where they had been standing watching the boat. It seemed as if it might break at any second and pound into oblivion whatever lay in its path. Had they stayed where they were, they would have been swept away for certain.

The wave reached Barradale and erupted in a huge white froth of spray against the walls of the castle. The water was flung far above the tower itself. Barradale Island, the causeway and the smaller island were totally submerged. In the melee of spray and surf, Rebecca could no longer see the boat.

The beach had now disappeared under water.

And in the midst of all this, the mournful howl of the wolf. Three times it rose above the roar of the waters, long and tremulous.

As the wave crashed down, the silvery shimmer of the Ghost Ship materialised.

Rebecca could see Hakon at the bow, his great nose raised into the wind. The Ship seemed to hang in the air, before it vanished beneath the spray.

Rebecca turned to Drew, her eyes shining.

"Did you see? Did you hear Hakon?"

Drew was silent, unable to tear his eyes away. He slowly nodded his head.

Above their heads, the thunder and lightning ceased abruptly. The clouds began to roll away. On the slope below them, the waters gradually started to recede. Trees had been uprooted and the water had torn a searing gash through the beach where previously there had been just a small stream in the smooth sand down to the loch. Little by little, the causeway re-emerged.

"If I had not seen that with my own eyes …" Drew's voice tailed off.

"I now understand what that word awesome really means."

"The wave stopped when it reached the castle. Why?" said Rebecca, shaking her head in mystification.

"Look – the boat!" She pointed to where the boat had reappeared at the edge of the loch below them. There was no sign of the men who had been on board.

"Come on."

Before Drew could protest, she led the way back down through the battered, soaking trees to the water's edge, through pools and streams that had been formed by the wave. They crossed the sodden beach, knee deep now in water and waded out towards the boat. It appeared to be deserted. They slipped quietly over the side to take a look around.

"The stuff is all here," said Rebecca, looking into the cabin.

"No sign of them though."

She looked perplexedly at Drew. He shrugged his shoulders.

"So where did they go? Washed overboard?"

"I don't know. I didn't see anybody in the water." They scanned the waters and shoreline for signs of the men, to no avail. Rebecca sat down on the edge of the boat.

"So, what do you reckon we should do now?"

Drew went into the cabin where the wheel and instrumentation were. The key was still in the engine. He shrugged and tried it. The engine fired up first time. Rebecca appeared at his shoulder.

"Back to Rahsaig?" she asked.

"Don't see why not," he said. "Don't think there's anybody left to come after us now."

CHAPTER 26

TRUE SELVES

The first glimmers of a bright yellow sunrise were catching the tops of the hills of Morar, as Rebecca and Drew rounded the high cliffs at the mouth of Loch Nevis and pointed the boat towards Rahsaig. Out on the loch it was cool and still, a light mist hanging just above the surface of the water, parting silently around the boat.

"Atmospheric," murmured Rebecca, to nobody in particular.

She looked up at the steep, forbidding cliffs, from which Becca had been thrown to her death by Lachlan, and shivered. How tranquil it now seemed.

The chugging of the engine seemed loud and intrusive in the early morning. Aware they would be conspicuous, Rebecca slowed the boat right down and looked cautiously ahead.

Tucked into an inlet about half a mile before the castle, she spied identical blue and white boats, moored side by side.

"Cops," said Drew, anticipating the question formulating in her mind.

"I guess we'd better stop and say hello."

Rebecca killed the engine as they approached. Their arrival provoked considerable activity. They were waved alongside the first launch by a large constable with a ruddy face. Other officers appeared next to him and quickly secured the boat with ropes.

"Is that Drew?" Rebecca and Drew recognised the tall angular frame of PC Lennie.

"It's okay, Sir, I know these two. This is Henry McOwan's

niece, Rebecca; and Drew Campbell, one of the Rahsaig rangers. The Laird told the Superintendent all about them."

"The redoubtable Rebecca," said a smiling officer in plain clothes.

"I understand you'll be after my job if I'm not careful. Lord MacDonald, no less, suggested we have a lot to thank you for."

Rebecca did not know quite how to react and offered an uncertain smile in response. On the other boat, she noticed Sergeant Gillespie looking stony-faced. Probably bemoaning another breakfast missed, she thought mischievously.

The senior officer came aboard.

"I'm Chief Inspector Craig. Are you both okay?"

They nodded. He continued.

"We thought you were here in the castle, Miss. Where have you been?"

Rebecca and Drew exchanged nervous looks. Rebecca swallowed, aware that she might be about to tell a lie to a policeman.

"They locked us in the room – er, both of us. We escaped out of the window. We went over to Barradale to see if we could spot the thieves removing the stolen goods. I guess it was a silly thing to do, really. Quite how we could have stopped them, I don't know …"

Rebecca crossed her fingers behind her back, hoping that the Inspector would be willing to believe in a youthful prank. He favoured them with a superior, indulgent look.

"Quite … and pretty much as I expected. Lucky you came to no harm. Right now, it's important that we get you back into your room in the castle as soon as possible. But from here, everything is done our way, understood? No more heroics." He looked searchingly at both of them. Rebecca and Drew offered no protest.

"Right – you'll go the rest of the way back on foot. I'll put some officers aboard this boat. We are coordinating an operation to catch all of them together."

"Isn't there a question you should be asking us?" said Rebecca. Inspector Craig looked at her, puzzled, a slightly affronted twitch playing around the corners of his mouth.

"I mean, how come we are aboard the thieves' boat with all the paintings?"

The Inspector's mouth fell open in shock. Rebecca quite enjoyed the effect of her revelation, given his evident disdain a few moments before.

"This is *their* boat?" He turned angrily to his assembled officers. "Why did nobody tell me this is the boat we've been looking for? Lennie, McIntosh! Get on here and get the art expert to check this lot out – now!"

He turned back to Rebecca and Drew, attempting a half-hearted smile.

"All right. So just how come you are aboard their boat?"

"We found it adrift at Barradale, with no sign of anyone. So we thought we'd take it. There was a – er, storm. The men may have fallen overboard."

The Inspector looked sceptical.

"A storm, you say? We have had no storm here. When was this?"

"A few hours ago," said Drew. "It was fairly localized," he added, hurriedly, sensing it would not help their cause to mention the tidal wave and the Ghost Ship.

It was obvious that the Inspector was far from convinced. "We only arrived an hour ago, so I suppose it might be possible …hmm." He turned to one of the other launches.

"Gillespie! Take your boat and search the waters and shore around Barradale for these missing men, possibly swept overboard in a storm. Stay in radio contact."

"But that will take some time, sir. Surely I will be needed

here…" The Sergeant began to protest but a dismissive hand from the Chief Inspector indicated that the conversation was over. Smiles forming on the faces of Rebecca and Drew at Gillespie's plight were immediately wiped away as the Chief Inspector turned his attention back to them.

"You and I will talk later. I'll pass the word to my men that you're coming through the woods. Some of my men can pose as the thieves on the boat. Wait here a moment."

A man in plain clothes on the next boat had caught his eye. The Inspector stepped carefully back aboard the police cruiser and went to talk to him. Every so often, one or both of them would look across at Drew and Rebecca. Eventually, the other man disappeared into the cabin and the Inspector returned.

"We need to change our plans slightly, in view of the missing men and this being their boat. We think it's necessary to arrest Sibley, Morgan and the rest here without delay."

"Oh, but…" Drew was stopped by a sharp dig in the ribs from Rebecca, who feared he was about to divulge the real whereabouts of Morgan.

"What?" asked the Inspector. Rebecca leaped in before Drew could open his mouth.

"Oh, you should wait for the boat from Mallaig. It brings the housekeeper across every morning and she is in on it too. It will be here very soon. You need her too if you want all of them. She will be the one to unlock the Laird and me."

"How do you know that she is part of it?"

"Uncle Henry worked it out. He said Morgan had to have an accomplice at the castle."

She looked for affirmation from Drew, who latched on immediately and nodded vigourously. The Inspector nodded more slowly.

"Very well. We'll take her in for questioning. Warn Henry

that we'll be starting our operation fifteen minutes after her boat gets in. Exactly fifteen minutes."

He looked at their tired faces for a moment. His expression softened.

"You pair look done in. But I'm afraid it's going to be a while longer before you can rest – away to the castle now and keep out of sight."

***

"Is Morgan up yet?" asked Simon Sibley, tucking a napkin into his shirt and surveying the breakfast Miss McHarg had just placed before him. The clock in the Great Hall began to chime the hour.

"I have not seen him – would you like me to check on him?"

"Indeed. And while you are at it, please unlock our other guests, the Laird and Miss Rebecca. Have them join me down here." McHarg looked alarmed. "If I unlock the Laird's door, he will know I am involved."

"Not if you simply tell him I have ordered you to open the door and you knew nothing of it until you arrived here this morning. You must of course feign ignorance of Mr Morgan, if your performance is to be convincing."

Sibley sniffed disdainfully and took a large bite of sausage. A twirl of his fork indicated to Miss McHarg that she was dismissed.

***

Henry McOwan noticed some movement in the bushes near the boathouse as he stood on his balcony. Retrieving a pair of binoculars, he trained them on the exact spot. He made out what he thought was the shoulder of a man.

A tap at his door brought him hurrying back inside. The key turned and the door opened, to reveal the pallid countenance of McHarg. She stepped forward uncertainly.

"Good morning, sir. This is all most dreadful. I had no idea … Mr Sibley told me to come and unlock your door … you a prisoner in your own home – what is going on?"

"What do you think is going on?"

"I, I, I, well of course I don't know. I…" Henry's measured tones had unnerved her.

"We think you know perfectly well." Rebecca stepped out from behind the door through to Henry's bathroom. McHarg was startled.

"Miss Rebecca, why, how did you get in here?"

"After you locked me in my room, you mean? And don't deny it."

McHarg opened her mouth but no sound came. Henry put his binoculars on the table.

"It's no good, Miss McHarg, we know everything. Morgan had to have had some help here, to tell him all about the house and everyone at Rahsaig. I became aware it had to be you when I recalled how little things had started to go missing recently. Papers, bits of clothing, photo albums, things only you would know where to find."

McHarg was crestfallen. She sat down heavily on a chair, taking out a handkerchief and pressing it to her nose.

"Oh sir, oh sir! I am sorry – please forgive me, I needed some money, I don't know what possessed me …I have slipped from the path of righteousness …"

"We can worry about all that later, when uncle decides if you are sacked or not. What we need to know is where Sibley and Morgan are?" Rebecca scowled at McHarg, enjoying her evident discomfort. McHarg could not look either of them in the eye.

"Er, Mr Sibley is downstairs, at breakfast. He asked me to fetch you both to join him. And I was just on my way to wake Mr Morgan. He has not been down yet. Oh sir, you'll be wanting to dismiss me, I am sure. I will leave this very minute."

"Just hold on a moment," said Henry, sitting down opposite her and putting a hand on her shoulder.

"I haven't decided what to do about your job yet but there is something you are going to do right now. You are going back downstairs with Rebecca and you will tell Mr Sibley that I am unwell and remaining in my bed and that you have locked my door and given the key to Morgan. You will say that Morgan will be down in a moment. When I appear, you will act as if I am Morgan, do you understand?"

The housekeeper looked confused for a moment.

"But what happens when the real Mr Morgan appears?"

"Do you understand?" Henry repeated his question. She nodded and sniffed. "Good. Go now then." He turned to Rebecca. "And send Drew in on your way out."

Rebecca nodded and the door closed behind them.

Henry crossed to the mirror on his dressing table and stared at his reflection. If Morgan had been able to pass himself off as his identical twin, Henry, so that nobody suspected, then the reverse should also be possible. Henry was more worried about acting and reacting in the way that would be expected of his brother. If Rebecca was correct, and Morgan and the others were not coming back, that would leave Sibley, McAllum and Godfrey. He checked his watch. The police would be making their move in a few minutes' time. He trained his binoculars back on the boathouse. He had a shrewd idea that the figure he had seen in the bushes was a policeman.

***

Chief Inspector Craig stood in the middle of the Great Hall at Rahsaig Castle, hands on hips, evidently very unhappy. Around him, his officers were standing nervously, anxious to avoid doing anything to become the object of his wrath.

"Gone?" He looked angrily at the Constable standing in front of him.

"Gone where?"

"I don't know, sir. We've searched the whole castle and there is nobody here."

The constable looked down, not daring to make eye contact with the furious Inspector.

"Well search it again! This place is full of nooks and crannies and hiding places. Find them all! Go on the rest of you – stop standing about like a bunch of bananas!"

The officers dispersed hastily, leaving the Chief Inspector fuming in the middle of the Hall. He crossed to a window and looked out over the lawn to the landing stage, where other policemen stood aboard the thieves' boat.

"At least that hasn't 'disappeared'," he muttered, darkly.

"Sir! We've found the housekeeper!" The Chief Inspector turned swiftly to where a constable was escorting a frightened-looking McHarg from the kitchen.

"Locked in the pantry, sir."

"You are Miss McHarg, the housekeeper?"

McHarg nodded.

"So where have they all gone?"

"I have no idea, sir," McHarg's voice was frail and distressed. "It was awful! Horrid! The Laird held prisoner in his own home…"

"You can cut the act, Miss McHarg," the Chief Inspector interrupted her sharply.

"We know all about your part in this little affair. Aiding and abetting a crime is what the law calls it. Now, without adding wasting police time to the list, tell me what you know about where they went."

"It's the truth, sir! I really have no idea. They locked me in the pantry, that man with the long hair from Barradale."

"McAllum?"

"Terribly rough, he was. He shoved me onto the floor."

If McHarg had expected sympathy, she was disappointed. The Inspector frowned at her.

"So, they up and vanish into thin air, taking Henry, Rebecca and young Campbell with them and nobody knows anything about it."

"Mr Sibley did see some police officers through the window at breakfast, sir. Perhaps that's why they left?"

The Inspector, who had turned away, now rounded on her again.

"What? I told you lot to keep well hidden! Which officers? I'll break their batons!"

"Sir? The suspects' boat is leaving." A constable was looking out of the window.

The Inspector's face registered renewed anger.

"What is going on? Who gave orders for that? Right – come on!"

The policemen dashed outside. The thieves' boat was now heading away from the landing stage, in the direction of Mallaig and the open sea.

"Radio them and find out what the hell is going on!" shouted the Chief Inspector.

"And get our launches to intercept that boat. They must be on it! Heaven only knows how but it has to be them."

The Constable spoke quickly into his radio and waited for the crackle of a response.

"No reply, sir. Was there anyone left on our boats?"

The Chief Inspector closed his eyes in disbelief.

"This is not happening – tell me, somebody, that this is not happening. Come on, back to the boats. Leave a couple of officers here with her…"

He pointed angrily at McHarg.

"Lose her and you'll spend the rest of your life handing out parking tickets in the Outer Hebrides – everyone else with me – now!"

***

From his position at the bow of the escaping boat, Henry McOwan scanned the police launches for signs of movement. He had been counting on the police following and intercepting them. Their powerful launches would be too fast for the little motor cruiser. When he could see no sign of life aboard any of them, he became worried. He took a quick glance over his shoulder to where Sibley was speaking in low tones with McAllum, who held the wheel. McAllum and Godfrey were dressed in police uniforms.

Henry must be careful not to let his concerns show.

"Where are the cops?" whispered Rebecca urgently, standing beside him and trying not to appear as if she was speaking. "Shouldn't somebody be on those boats?"

"Yes they flamin' well should!" muttered Henry through clenched teeth. "What are we going to do now?"

"We'll just have to play along until we find out what they are up to."

"Yes but they'll expect *me* to know what they are up to." Henry's hoarse whisper held a note of desperation.

"I think we should put our guests below, Morgan, with their police friends." Sibley's tones reached them from the wheelhouse. The policemen the Inspector had posted on board the boat had been taken unawares, stripped of their uniforms and locked in the cabin by McAllum, holding a shotgun on them.

Rebecca and Drew, standing at the bow alongside Henry, exchanged nervous glances. Henry turned, trying to appear calm. He smiled at Sibley and tried to introduce some of Morgan's coldness into his voice.

"No need, is there? All going according to plan. I'd rather have them where I can see them. We can always push them overboard if we need to."

Sibley snorted, as if Henry had been making a bad joke.

"All going swimmingly, apart from being surprised by the police and this sudden need to make a run for it without half our men. I want to know how the police knew where we were and where the others are."

"Maybe the police caught them and that is why they were on our boat," said the artist.

"So what now? Do we still go to the truck?"

For once, Henry was grateful to hide behind Sibley's natural pomposity, which now led him to reply on their behalf.

"Yes we do – but it still doesn't explain how the police came to know anything in the first place. Unless it's down to them." Sibley pointed at Rebecca and Drew, a venomous edge entering his voice.

"Poking and snooping about. You escaped somehow from Barradale, young laddie, so perhaps you can tell me what happened to the men there?"

Sibley put his face up close to Drew and glared at him. Drew caught a blast of his sour breath and turned his head away. "Your French jailer was easy to trick." He looked back, defiantly, at Sibley. "And your breath stinks!"

"We can't leave without the others," said Henry quickly and

loudly, seizing on a possible opportunity to force a delay and trying to distract Sibley's attention, as the latter made as if to strike Drew.

"They all know the plan. If the police have caught them, who's to say they won't tell them everything and we'll find PC Plod waiting in our truck?"

Sibley had clearly not considered this. He diverted his scowl from Drew and looked studiedly at Henry.

"My thoughts entirely, Morgan. So, what do you recommend?"

A flash of inspiration occurred to Henry.

"To Barradale to look for them, of course. They are most probably hiding out there."

Sibley was momentarily nonplussed.

"But … if the police have apprehended them, and one would have to deduce that is a considerable likelihood given the appearance of our young friend, our window of opportunity to escape is closing fast."

"So what do you suggest?" Henry winced as he said this. He sensed Sibley was becoming suspicious. Sibley spoke slowly in response, as if weighing something up in his mind.

"We go to the truck now, load up and head south as we had always planned."

"Mr Sibley!" The rasping tones of McAllum barked from the wheelhouse. They all turned. He was pointing the shotgun straight ahead, to where a boat had appeared.

"Police?" said Sibley, making his way back to join McAllum. Henry followed him.

"I don't think so."

Drew had been watching the approaching boat and now quickly turned to Rebecca.

"It's the *Duke*, with Dougie and Willie on board, I'll bet. This could be our chance. We need to stop this boat and get that gun away from McAllum somehow."

Rebecca put a restraining hand on Drew's arm.

"Campbell! You're not the SAS. That gun fires real bullets and I don't think he'd think twice about using it."

"He can't shoot straight. I've seen him miss a stag at ten metres."

"Poor stag!" said Rebecca, horrified. She looked at Drew accusingly. "What were you doing shooting deer? Anyway, I doubt he would miss all three of us at one metre."

The *Duke of Argyll* was drawing closer. Rebecca could now see Willie at the wheel. He appeared to be heading straight at them. A glance at the wheelhouse told Rebecca that she was not the only one to suspect this.

"He's going to try to force us onto the rocks at Shadow Island!" whispered Drew to Rebecca, with a tremor of excitement. They withdrew to the side of the boat alongside the wheelhouse, where Henry had taken up position.

"Suggest to him that he alters course, McAllum," said Sibley, taking the wheel for a moment and slowing the engine down. McAllum stepped onto the deck and pointed the shotgun towards the other boat. He fired, emptying both barrels into the air just above it.

"Quick!" Drew dug Henry in the ribs. "Before he reloads!"

Together, they rushed at McAllum, catching him unawares full-square in the back and knocking him over the side. He landed in the water with a big splash, the gun flying across the deck. Henry retrieved it. At the wheel, Sibley watched in astonishment.

"Morgan? What on earth..." he began. Henry smiled. Drew wrenched the wheel away from Sibley, which was not as difficult as he had imagined, since the portly man put up very little resistance. He killed the boat's engine.

"Not Morgan, I'm afraid ... Henry. Rebecca, unlock the cabin and let the policemen out. Here's the key." He pointed the gun at Godfrey, who immediately flung his arms in the air, not registering that it was no longer loaded.

"Get that uniform off and get in the cabin," he ordered. He turned back to Sibley.

"Your little game is over, Mr Sibley."

"But your gun is not loaded, Mr McOwan," sneered Sibley, his lip curling viciously under his moustache.

"This one is though!" Dougie Campbell leapt aboard as Willie McHarg steered the *Duke of Argyll* alongside.

"Sure it's only a flare gun but it'll make a pretty big hole!"

He pointed a pistol at Sibley, who raised his hands apprehensively. The policemen had now re-emerged sheepishly from the cabin, clad only in their underwear. Rebecca could not hold back a giggle.

"Once you've dressed, officers, you might like to arrest these men."

Smiling impishly, she pointed at Sibley and Godfrey, and at McAllum flailing in the water some distance behind the boat.

"We can still cuff 'em, boxer shorts or no boxer shorts," said one constable gruffly, as his companion seized the wailing Godfrey and retrieved his uniform. He produced some handcuffs and in moments both Godfrey and Sibley were secured inside the cabin.

"Quite the cavalry, aren't we?" said Rebecca, turning to the elder Campbell, who was still brandishing his flare gun.

"A poncho and you'd pass for Clint. Would you really have shot him?"

"God no! It's empty, too." Dougie waved it merrily. "But he wasn't to know."

"Perhaps we should retire graciously now and leave things to the pros," said Henry. He pointed towards the police launches, now heading towards them at high speed.

"Willie, Dougie, thanks for showing up when you did. We were running out of ideas."

"I don't know," said Rebecca. "You make a pretty convincing crook, threatening to throw your own niece overboard. I don't know what my parents will say about that."

"To say nothing of the poor, oppressed workers," added Drew.

"Aye, well, now your brother is back from helping out at Barradale, I need to find some way to cut my costs," said Henry.

CHAPTER 27

ONE LAST QUESTION

Rebecca's stay in the Scottish Highlands was almost at an end. She would soon be catching the train back to London. Her parents had phoned the previous evening. Her mother was alarmed to hear of her daughter's adventures and it had taken all Henry's powers of persuasion to calm her and stop her jumping on the first train to Scotland.

As she opened her curtains and surveyed the familiar view over the waters of Loch Nevis to the hills beyond, Rebecca reflected on how, on her arrival, she had been dreading the weeks to come. That seemed a long time ago.

She decided on an early morning walk. Restless after the excitement of recent days, she had woken before six and now headed along the shore of Loch Nevis. Birds and an otter, foraging among the seaweed, were her only companions.

As she rounded a rocky point near the head of the loch, she saw the *Duke of Argyll* anchored just off shore. Sure enough, Willie was on a sandy beach, tying long lengths of dark brown seaweed into bundles and packing them into sacks. He raised his head at Rebecca's cry of greeting and nodded. She made her way down to join him.

"So the Campbells weren't lying. You *are* a seaweed farmer!"

"Aye, among other things. A man needs a few strings to his bow in these parts.

The kelps just here are good. Not the most lucrative living but there's a market, as the suits would say."

He tied up the bag he had been filling and threw it onto the sand a few yards away. Stopping for a moment to stretch, he studied Rebecca.

"You're up early this morning. Do you like our little corner of the world?"

"It's stunning. I never realised there were places like this in our country. It's so big it makes you feel really insignificant."

"Most of us are," said Willie.

"So what happened with your sister?" Rebecca asked tentatively. "I saw her being taken away to be questioned by the police."

Willie carried on tying up his bundles. "Oh, they released her after the Laird spoke with them. She's away to the Orkney Islands to cook kippers," he said quietly.

Rebecca smiled, taken aback.

"A distant relative needs some help running a guest house. So she took the last train to Fort William yesterday – after dark, so nobody would see. They'd only whisper in the pews at the kirk, so it's the best thing. Young Tom Gordon will be a pound a week lighter on the collection plate, though. And your uncle will be needing somebody to keep house but sure he'll have no problem finding takers for *that* job. They're queuing halfway down the street at the hairdressers already, so Mrs Campbell says."

Rebecca could not help grinning. Willie seemed entirely unconcerned about his sister's fall from grace. Indeed, he seemed to find a great deal to smile at.

"So ... will she be back?"

"Well now that would need to be carefully considered. Orkney is a fearful long way and I've a tenant for her bungalow."

"Already?" Rebecca grinned again. Unable to stop herself, she ventured another question.

"Is the story about rugby true – that you played a game on a Sunday and she wouldn't speak to you for twenty years because it was ungodly?"

"The Sabbath is not to be trifled with according to some in these parts," he said, lightly.

"Why a good Lord who created all this beauty would want us to wear uncomfortable clothes, not smile and be miserable all day might be a mystery to others, though."

"Are these to go onto your boat?" Rebecca indicated the sacks of kelp on the sand.

"Aye," answered Willie. "If you give me a hand getting them aboard, I'll give you a lift back to the castle for breakfast, how's that?"

"Deal!" Rebecca began to take off her shoes and socks immediately.

They waded out, loaded the sacks onto the boat and climbed aboard. Willie started the engine and began to reverse out into the loch.

"So, do you think we've heard the last of the wolf?" he asked. Rebecca was taken by surprise. She had imagined Willie would be a sceptic.

"You believe in the legend?"

"There's those as believe and those as don't. We all have our tales to tell in these parts. I'd not like to think you've seen him off forever. Kind of comforting to know he's around, somewhere."

***

Rebecca was thoughtful as she and Henry sat beside a crackling fire in the study later.

"So they haven't found the men or any bodies?"

"None, so far," answered Henry. "And nothing in the tunnel or the oubliette."

For the first time, she had related the entire tale of her adventures to him, including the parts she had not previously dared divulge, concerning the mists, Becca, Knut and Hakon and the encounter with Morgan. Henry had sat throughout in silence, listening intently.

"Do you believe me? That it all happened, Uncle H.?" Rebecca's face was serious.

"Do you?" smiled Henry. He put down the cup of tea he had been drinking.

"It's important to me." Rebecca did not smile. Henry rose to his feet and looked up at the picture of the Bonnie Prince above the mantelpiece.

"I'm going to tell you something I've never told a soul – if you promise to keep it secret."

Rebecca nodded eagerly, sitting forward.

"Many strange things have happened here over the years. I've been thinking about it a lot lately. When we were young, Morgan used to go off exploring. One day, he said he'd found something really important. He tried to tell me about it but he used to tell so many tales that I didn't believe him. But he had found something this time… That."

Henry pointed at the locket which Rebecca held in her hands.

"A year after Morgan left home, I found the entrance to the cave at Barradale. I didn't find the sanctuary, but I found the oubliette. There were bones, chained to the wall, just as you were. I knew it was a man by his clothes. Around the neck was that locket.

I took it and have kept it ever since. I recognised the picture of Becca's mother from a portrait in the castle. So, with the inscription, I knew whose locket it was."

Henry paused. Rebecca looked up and saw tears in his eyes.

"I never told a soul about what I found in the oubliette. I guess I just didn't want to have to face up to it, in case it had been my brother there in those chains. Nobody else was ever reported missing. When he came back here, for the first time I really believed it could not have been him, that it must have been somebody else.

As for those bones, I don't know who that was or how the locket got there."

Rebecca was silent. Henry wiped his eyes and smiled at her.

"I've always thought it was tied up with the legend somehow. Morgan was a bad lot, there's no denying it. But he was my twin brother, too and it seems that he is now dead. I can still remember him as a young boy, playing just like any other normal kids with your dad and me. He wasn't always bad."

Rebecca spoke slowly.

"The Princess said the McOwan who chained her in the cave was Lachlan's ancestor. Have you seen that picture of Lachlan at Lord Mac's on Skye? There is such a likeness between it and ... well, you and Morgan."

"You think there's some sort of link?"

"I don't know what to think. It's probably just coincidence. But it's odd. I looked into Morgan's eyes and I swear I saw Lachlan. But how could I know?"

Henry remained thoughtful for a long time. Eventually he spoke.

"I want you to have the locket now. I think Becca would want that too. You're a true McOwan, Rebecca."

Rebecca felt tears welling. She blinked and smiled and put it around her neck.

"Beautiful," smiled Henry. "Like its new owner."

***

Later that morning, Rebecca and Henry were seated in the Dining Room, enjoying a brunch. Outside, it was now a glorious Highland day, the sun shining on the hills, the purple heather and on the sparkling waters of Loch Nevis. Rahsaig had resumed its customary tranquillity and gentle pace of life.

"Did you hear the news, Uncle H.?" asked Rebecca, reaching for another piece of toast. She took her plate across the to the window seat and installed herself on the cushions, tucking her legs underneath her.

"We've become quite famous."

"I know. I think we're quite popular in Mallaig just now. Apparently, the place is crawling with reporters, all trying to get out here and paying small fortunes to the boatmen. The locals have been living on free whisky, telling tall tales in the Tavern."

"I haven't seen any reporters here. I suppose we should be pleased but it seems strange."

Henry smiled.

"I think our Willie and Dougie have been enjoying a little fun at the expense of the city types. They have got the local fishermen to offer trips out to what they promise is the actual hideout, owned by the famous MP, where the crooks operated their forgery ring. They take them round to Barradale and drop them off, warn them about the tide and say they'll be back to pick them up later! And because none of their mobile phones work up here, they're all like lost sheep! One guy spent a night in the pouring rain, since the Honourable Mr Gordon had returned, put the portcullis down and refused to let him in!"

"I don't know where you get these slanderous stories from, Boss," said Dougie, coming into the dining room, a mischievous smile playing about the corners of his mouth.

"Willie McHarg is a fine, upstanding citizen who would never stoop to childish games."

"Aye," said Henry slowly, favouring Dougie with a sceptical smile.

"Willie might be."

"There's something you need to read here, Rebecca." Dougie opened the newspaper he was carrying and handed it to Rebecca tapping a headline which read "Mystery Deaths of Divers". Rebecca dropped her toast and grabbed the paper from his hand. She read aloud.

'The bodies of three divers were found yesterday, washed up on the shores of the Isle of Rum in the Inner Hebrides. It is not yet known where the men had come from, or who they are. Nobody has been reported missing and no boat has been found. Coastguard estimates suggest the men could have been carried by the currents and drifted for many miles. They had been dead for at least a day when they were found by local landowner Hamish Balloch –'

"I might have known the Ballochs would get a mention somehow... "

'There is no suggestion at this stage that this event is in any way connected with the recent art thefts from some of the great houses in the Highlands, including that of Anthony Gordon, MP for Knoydart and Morar –'

"If there is no suggestion, then why mention it?"

'The police remain perplexed about the deaths. The Coroner's Report suggested that cause of death was not due to drowning. Each man is said to have had mysterious gash marks on their body, which could have come from an attack of some sort and are being attributed as the cause of death. And how did the bodies manage to drift together without becoming separated? Were they dumped there on purpose? The police are not yet prepared to say whether they are treating this as a murder inquiry and are continuing their investigations.'

"Old Haddock was in the Tavern last night, telling anybody who'd listen how he had seen Vikings attacking a frogman down by the Sound," said Dougie.

"Nobody paid him any mind."

Rebecca caught her breath. What had the Princess said?

'There is but one more thing that must be done and that rests with Knut and Hakon'.

"Post!" said Drew, following his brother into the dining room. He held out a single envelope to Henry, before pinching a sausage from his plate.

"Missed my breakfast this morning."

"Mr McOwan? There is a gentleman to see you." An attractive young woman with long auburn hair stood in the doorway, her eyes on Henry.

Drew nudged Rebecca, a smile playing about the corners of his mouth.

"Who is that?" he whispered.

Rebecca looked up.

"Katriona," she said, simply. "New housekeeping. Close your mouth."

"Bit of an improvement on McHarg!" he grinned.

"Well done Henry!"

At that moment, Inspector Craig entered the room. Henry rose to greet him.

"Inspector, good morning."

"Don't get up, please, I'll not disturb you from your breakfast. I just thought you might want to hear the latest."

"Of course – look, help yourself to coffee and anything else."

The Inspector took a cup offered by Katriona and sat down opposite Rebecca.

"Well. We have had positive identification on two of the bodies found on Rum – they are a couple of French actors, a Serge Balatte and Auguste Lemerre ..."

"... they were with the Camden Players on Rum," interrupted Rebecca.

"Balatte was the ghost and I'm sure he was the man I saw looking in through the window that night in the castle."

"And Lemerre was my jailer at Barradale," said Drew.

"The other one?" asked Henry, cautiously. "Morgan?"

"No – and no real ideas yet. But the really good news is we have recovered everything that has been reported missing and – you will enjoy this, Miss Rebecca – Mr Simon Sibley is behind bars in Glasgow, singing like a sparrow and formally charged with masterminding the whole business. We'll not be seeing him around for a while, I think."

"About twenty-five years, with any luck," said Dougie.

"Sounds much like what you people call 'a result', Inspector," said Henry, smiling.

"Indeed. Oh! And the other thing I heard is that the Honourable Mr Gordon MP will be announcing later today that he has resigned from the government."

"Was he involved, then?" asked Dougie from the window.

"No suggestion of that. But allowing his house to be used as the base for a bunch of criminals was publicity his political masters probably thought they could do without."

The Inspector drained the cup of coffee and stood up.

"Well, I'd best be on my way. Before I go though I wanted to pass on our sincere thanks to you all, particularly to you ..." he had turned to face Rebecca.

"I'm not sure I gave you the credit you deserve, Miss Rebecca. You had things pretty much figured out. You'll have to reveal your source one day."

Nobody seemed to notice Drew splutter into his coffee.

CHAPTER 28

THE UNFINISHED JOURNAL

On her last afternoon at Rahsaig, Rebecca was sitting reading in the library. Rain was lashing down outside and she was glad to be inside in the dry, a warm fire burning in the hearth. She was so comfortable and cosy that she gently dozed off.

She came to with a sudden start, a cold draught around her legs. The fire had gone out.

Rebecca frowned. She did not think she could have been asleep that long.

An odd sensation took hold of her, as if somebody had just been there in the room with her and left suddenly. She went over to the window and looked outside.

As she turned away, she noticed something on the edge of the desk. She picked it up.

Becca's journal!

Rebecca was baffled.

"I don't understand" she muttered. " … How did this get here? It's … I left it upstairs."

She flicked over the pages. All of a sudden, she stopped, her mouth open.

"This is new!"

Rebecca sat down beside the fire and read aloud.

To a friend,
Never forget that time is ever-lasting.
The people we are and the things we do echo beyond our mortal lives.

We are the people we have always been and always will be.
I live on through you and you have lived through me.
May time know us always, you and me.
Becca McOwan

Rebecca looked up and out of the window. She was certain she had seen a flash of something crimson pass by.

CHAPTER 29

COMING HOME

Henry McOwan was not able to take Rebecca to the station to see her off, owing to an unavoidable appointment on Skye. He said his goodbyes at Rahsaig, with a bear hug.

"Back to dear old London, then? It won't be the same around here without you, lass. You sure liven things up, although I think we could probably do with a little bit less excitement for a while! You will take the journal? It's right it should be yours."

"Thank you, Uncle. I'm very pleased to have it but it should stay here – it belongs at Rahsaig, Becca's home – the home of all the McOwans. I can read it whenever I visit."

"I've been thinking on Morgan and the oubliette," said Henry, quietly.

"Maybe it really was him that died in there all those years ago... Puts things to rest. That man who came here was no brother of mine."

"I hope we are rid of Lachlan," said Rebecca.

"I'll never forget that look in his eyes..." Her voice tailed off.

As they passed through the Great Hall on their way out, Rebecca lagged behind to stop by the painting of Knut and Hakon. For a few moments she stood gazing up at it, as she had done on that first afternoon at Rahsaig.

"Time has stood still in yesterday's shroud ..." She smiled. Her eyes dwelt on Knut and the white, haunting stare of the Wolf.

"Goodbye, old friends," she whispered.

"Keep a watch over everybody for me."

Catching up with Henry, she fell into step with him as they crossed the lawn.

Henry grasped her hand for a moment as they stood on the landing stage and smiled.

"Come back and see us again soon, won't you?"

"Aye, I will."

He smiled at her put-on Scottish accent.

Rebecca suddenly felt quite sad as she waved him off. She would miss her uncle.

In her experience an adult who listened to what she said, did not patronise her and allowed her to live by her own decisions, was unusual. He had shown her one could always look at things in a different way. She would be back.

Around her neck she was wearing Becca's locket, which she fingered thoughtfully as Henry's boat disappeared down the loch towards Skye.

***

Drew and Dougie both arrived with the boat to take her to Mallaig, even though she knew they were supposed to be working. Rebecca was pleased by the unspoken compliment. As they all stood together on the station platform, she knew she would miss her new friends. For once, none of them knew what to say.

Eventually, Dougie broke the silence.

"Well, you have a safe trip and mind you come back here and see us one day not too far away. I must go and see Willie, so you'll forgive me if I don't hang about. Not much of a one for goodbyes, anyway."

He bent down and kissed her quickly on the cheek.

"Thanks for everything, older Campbell brother," smiled Rebecca.

"And get yourself a girlfriend or I'll send some try-ons up from London," she added as he began to walk away. Dougie laughed and waved his arm in the air, without turning.

At the end of the platform, she saw Willie sitting in a van waiting. She caught his eye for a moment and waved. McHarg simply nodded in his calm, imperturbable way.

Rebecca smiled. She might be leaving but life would go on up here the same as normal.

The Fort William train was now pulling in to the station and Rebecca bent to pick up her shoulder bag. She looked up at Drew, who was fidgeting nervously. He caught her gaze and looked quickly down at his feet. Rebecca could not help giggling.

"What?"

"Nothing," he said. "Erm… look, I just wanted to say … We'll miss you."

He still looked unsettled.

"Never thought I'd say that to the English."

Rebecca smiled again.

"Well, seeing as mobiles don't work round here and I can't teach you the modern art of texting, you'd better write to me, hadn't you?"

Drew's countenance brightened up immediately.

"Aye, letters, that's good. Old fashioned. I do email too, you know."

He leaned down, picked up her bags and swung them into the luggage rack inside the train. He came back out onto the platform. Rebecca stepped up into the doorway and took a last look around, across the sea and the loch to the islands and mountains that she had come to know so well in the last few weeks, basking peacefully in the sunshine.

"It always leaves you like this," said Drew.

"Rain when you arrive, sunshine when you leave to call you back again."

"Bleak," she said, shaking her head.

"Beautiful," said Drew. They both laughed.

Drew regarded her for a second or so, as the guard blew his whistle.

"Well?

"Well what?"

"I know we're all backward in these parts but it is customary to kiss a friend goodbye.

Anything less would be inhospitable."

Rebecca's brown eyes flashed.

"Get on with it then!"

Layout: Stephen M.L. Young
                 touv@mac.com

Font: Adobe Garamond (11pt)

Copies of this book can be ordered via the Internet:

www.librario.com

or from:

Librario Publishing Ltd
Brough House
Milton Brodie
Kinloss
Moray IV36 2UA
Tel /Fax No 01343 850 617